A VISTA OF

THE PLAYER

AND THE

PopStar

CAIT ELISE

The Player and the Pop Star
Copyright © 2025 by Cait Elise

Published by Honey Rock Press.

This book is a work of fiction. The characters and events in this book are fictitious. Any similarity to real persons, living or dead, is purely coincidental and not intended by the author.

Cover Illustration by Sonia Garrigoux
Typography by Carla Aceves
Editor: Katherine Messina with Prose Perfect Editing

ISBN: 979-8-9919693-1-4 (ebook), 979-8-9919693-0-7 (paperback)

First Edition: 2025

10 9 8 7 6 5 4 3 2 1

For Brandon
I'd let you steal my sour gummy worms any day.
I love you.

PLAYLIST

Scan in Spotify to access the playlist for
The Player and the Pop Star

CHAPTER ONE

LENA

ALL I CAN THINK about is the craft services table. The cold cut sandwiches, the cute little bottles of sparkling water, and my favorite sour—

"Lena?"

I stare through my three-hours-of-sleep haze at the man with the slicked-back hair, the garish teeth refracting the myriad of stage lights. The one with the forced laugh after all my mediocre jokes. "Yes, Billy?"

Billy Lanza wags his finger at me from behind his microphone, which is just some antiquated thing on his desk for show. "Are you daydreaming about Callum Porter again?"

I shift in the unyielding hot seat, the couch stiff under my purple beaded skirt. "Have you heard half my songs? I'm always daydreaming."

A few whistles and sporadic giggles trill from beyond the incandescent lights, followed by a chorus of *"We love you Lena!"* rippling through the audience.

Two cameramen in black baseball caps pan from the stage to the seats, capturing the crowd the blinding lights won't let me see. I blow kisses to them all, anyway. After a sleepless night and this commotion, my throbbing head will need a dark room and some ibuprofen to recover.

Billy smiles. Raises his brows. "The overwhelming consensus is that your songs are inspired by your breakups and the men you've loved."

I lean closer, lowering my voice. "Or at least the men who've loved me, right?"

He lets out a whooping laugh, and the crowd follows suit like a good little audience. Leaning back from his desk, he perfectly centers himself under the *Late Night with Lanza* sign emblazoned on the back wall of his set. "True, true. I suppose that could be the case."

It takes everything in me not to roll my eyes.

"Now that you're in the happiest—and dare I say *longest*—relationship of your twenty-five years, how will that affect your inspiration? Aren't you afraid your fans who have built their love for you and your music through your shared... romantic *traumas*, for lack of a better term, will move on to the next sad girl?"

Sad girl. I've heard the words mumbled through tabloids and comment sections I never finish reading, but to have that stupid label thrown straight into my face siphons all the air from my lungs. Even more so than the tactless mention of my age.

I pray he can't see my nostrils flare as I steady my voice. "I only hope that they can all find something—*someone*—as genuine and loving as I've finally found in Callum."

2

There's a hushed, collective swoon from the audience.

I take it as my cue and hoist my favorite guitar from where it's propped next to me, carefully threading my head through the strap without disturbing my waist-length, clip-in hair extensions. I'm one step closer to crawling out from under Billy Lanza's microscope and my post-show snacks.

"That reminds me," I begin, strumming the first chord to the song I still love despite how much I've changed since I wrote it, the one that hurtled me into the spotlight at sixteen. "Genuine love can be—" another strum and the cheers pick up— *"Pretty Hard to Find."*

At the mention of the name of my first single, everyone roars, effectively drowning out any more too-personal questions or insults from the prying host. I find my way to center stage, and the lights in the house dim as a single buttery spotlight finds me. For a split second, it's just me and my acoustic guitar. I'm back in my element, where I began, *why* I began. Then the band picks up for the second verse. The tempo rises as the floodlights brighten, and I toss my guitar to a stagehand as I rip my mic from the stand. My record label says I need to give the people something to dance to if I want to stay at the top of the charts. So I do.

I perform my new choreography immaculately, and I know I'll be met with praise from my team when I finally finish my set. As I strike the ending pose of my last song, the crowd explodes, standing and cheering. My heart pounds as I catch my breath. For a split second, as I stare out at their smiling faces, I remember why I started singing in the first place. Billy Lanza jogs on stage, sidling up to me and throwing an arm over my sweaty shoulder as he announces the rest of his lineup for the night: everyone's favorite rom-com actress, Ada Lane, and some football player from this year's reigning Super Bowl champs, the Vista City Kings. I clap along with the audience as though I'll stick around to meet either of them. As the cameramen pull off their earphones and step back from their cameras, I bid my goodbyes to both Billy and the enthusiastic audience and dart offstage.

Someone hands me a towel and a bottle of spring water as soon as I disappear behind the curtain. I dab my hairline and chug the water, my mind locked in on one thing. My post-show tradition. The one my dad unintentionally started after my first public performance over a decade ago. The one steady thing I can count on despite whatever chaotic work crap I may be facing. It's not just a bowl of sour gummy worms. It's the equivalent of Dad's smiling face meeting me backstage, no matter how long it's been since I've seen him or how certain I am that I'll crumble where I stand. It's the pick-me-up this "sad girl" needs after last night's red-eye flight and another pushy interview.

"Your elbows were bent. You need to fully extend."

I spin to face the voice, the one that's been critiquing me since I fell out of her womb. My manager. "Thanks, Mom."

"The audience went nuts for it, though, didn't they?" Antonia, my publicist, beams. Her dark curls bounce as she hums and scrolls on her tablet before jotting down some notes with a stylus. "There's not a doubt in my mind the choreography for So Demure will be going viral within

4

hours of this airing. People will be mimicking it for *months*."

I smile wide, hoping I look as excited as she expects.

My mother butts in, smoothing a hand over her dark bun that shines like an oil slick even in the dim backstage light. "Our flight's in four hours. Your dressing room is currently being packed up, and I need you to change into something else so we can prep your garments for dry cleaning."

That's right. We land in another city tonight. I wilt, wanting to ask my mom when we get to go home, when we get to see Dad again, but her phone rings and she excuses herself. Antonia tracks her, making a call of her own. I breathe a sigh of relief as I watch them disappear and toss my towel to one of Billy's crew members before beelining toward the craft services table.

I always request the same three things: ice-cold peach seltzer water, deviled eggs, and a heaping pile of sour gummy worms. My craft services order is a far cry from what it once was, but I soon realized a growling belly does nothing to help my sanity or my show quality. I need to fuel my body, and I like the way my curves fill out my costumes. The eggs are half gone when I arrive, but I lift one from the glass dish and slip it into my mouth before my mom can remind me I need to remove my costume first. Sipping on a peach water, I move down the line to the desserts, waiting my turn behind a couple of guys I can hardly see around. When they peel off and I'm face to face with what I've been dreaming about, it's like I've been sucker-punched in the gut. The bowl that had been brimming with individual packs of my beloved sour gummies

5

before my interview now sits almost completely vacant, save for a couple of empty worm baggies and flavored dust sullying the dish.

A booming laugh pulls my attention to a behemoth of a man. One that dangles a sour gummy worm into his mouth as he yucks it up with some other meathead. The guy from the line. I narrow in on him, moving before I think of my next move.

"Hey!" I say, closing in on my target.

He keeps talking and laughing like it's ever okay to be the person who empties a dish. Didn't his mom teach him anything? Never take the last slice of pizza, never swipe the last bottled drink, and *never* be the one who empties the candy bowl. It's common courtesy.

When he drops the rest of the worms into his mouth, it's like it's happening in slow motion. And then I watch as his perfectly square jaw crushes them, his Adam's apple bobbing as he finishes them off. His buddy backs away, and when I stop moving, I'm standing under the behemoth. His green eyes sparkle with residual laughter, and for a moment, they're all I can focus on. And then he wipes his sour-dusted hands on the sides of his pants like it's nothing. My pulse spikes, and I feel my face compiling all the stressors of my day—gummies included—into one twisted expression.

He stares down at me, his dark brows knitting, and then recognition passes over his face. "Lena Lux? I loved your set. Hadn't heard much of your new stuff 'til tonight, but that first one—"

"You ate my candy," I say.

"Your candy?" He eyes me, then the table, his gaze

6

landing on the desserts. He smirks. "The candy that was put out for everyone by craft services?"

"The candy I specifically requested that I'm not so sure the crew is supposed to be eating." I cross my arms. "Does Billy always let you guys snack on the guests' food?"

He runs a hand through his dark waves, and I watch as the pomade in his hair gives up. "Aren't you high and mighty?"

I scoff. "No, just hungry."

"So eat something else."

"I want my worms."

"*Sour* worms." He grimaces. "So send out your *help* to get you some. You act like everyone isn't at your beck and call or something."

"They aren't."

He pinches his stubbly mouth into a tight line. "Sure. You tell your little Lena Lover mob that. You know, they can be pretty brutal online."

A woman wearing an earpiece approaches with a clipboard in hand. She smiles at me before turning to the worm stealer. "Decker, hair and makeup wanted to powder you one more time before filming."

He nods and gives her an irritating grin before she disappears.

So he isn't crew. He's a guest. From his size—and arrogance—I'm assuming he's the Vista Kings player. Charming.

He turns back to me. "I've never seen someone get so worked up about candy. I don't know if you know this, but there are way bigger problems out there to worry about." He shakes his head and backs away. "I gotta run."

7

"Yeah, go get *powdered*," I say, rolling my eyes.

"I will." He heads toward the makeup station, but turns back one more time. "And by the way, you have something right here." He taps his chin before retreating again.

I scowl and lift my fingers to my face, swiping at my chin. They graze something wet, and when I look down, a glob of deviled egg filling is smeared across my fingers. I wipe it against the dumb costume my mom picked out and head off to find her.

CHAPTER TWO

DECKER

I WATCH in the makeup mirror as she stomps back to the table of food, the fringe of her purple skirt glittering with every step. Lena Lux. I know she's in high demand these days, but I didn't expect her to act like such a brat. If she'd been nicer, maybe I'd have offered to make things right—gotten her number, at least—so I could try. To be honest, even with food on her face, I don't know if I've ever seen anyone more attractive. Not in person, at least.

Leaning back into my chair, I close my eyes as last night's activities start taking their toll. Thirty is too old for thinking I can survive on four hours of sleep. It may have worked in college, but after eight extra years of football and last year's knee injury, I'm not sure how much longer my body can take it. I swallow a deep breath, a useless attempt to steady my spiraling thoughts. Athletes have a shelf life, I'm aware enough to know that, no matter how much I hate it. Football is all I have. It pays the bills. It offers a cushy lifestyle, but some day it'll all end, and when I have lofty aspirations that require ongoing investment, I need other options. At least when those ambitions have anything to do with starting a nonprofit. It says it right in the name. I won't be profiting. Maybe my manager's right. Maybe appearing on this show tonight could garner a brand deal offer or two since I refuse to "brand myself" on social media, despite his insistence.

Desperate for a distraction, I sit up straighter, pulling out my phone and scrolling through messages. A disappointed groan resounds somewhere behind me, and I can't stop myself from glancing up at the mirror again. Lena's still visible in its reflection. Her full bottom lip pushes out in a fat pout as she scrounges around for something to satisfy her craving. I almost feel bad about emptying the candy bowl. Almost.

The makeup artist returns with her kit and stands in front of me, loading a brush with powder before pummeling me in the face with it. I find myself leaning around her, my eyes still locked in on Lena as she swats her long, dark hair out of her face and grabs a glazed donut. She checks her surroundings before biting into it and darting off out of my line of sight.

"Face forward, please." The makeup artist stops, craning her neck in the same direction I'm looking. "Who are you looking for? Can I get something for you?"

I clear my throat, shaking my head. "No, no. I just thought I saw my manager."

She resumes powdering my forehead and pomading my hair, and I pull out my phone. Three missed calls from my mom and two from my brother. Glad to see my absence back home is noted. I shoot off a text to our family group chat.

ME

Can't a guy get interviewed for a late night show without his mom and brother interrupting every second?

IAN

Don't flatter yourself. Just wanted you to know Princess misses you. The only woman who could ever truly love you.

MOM

I love Decker! And you, Ian! Love you both!

My brother sends another text, this time only a picture. Princess, my pitbull mix, sits looking out a window, presumably for me. I can't wait until I'm back with her

ME

Give her kisses and some beef jerky. I'll update you guys soon.

My phone buzzes again. An incoming text from an unknown sender. I open it and remember that last night, after three old-fashioneds, I gave out my number to some girl at a bar who promised to show me some restaurant with "the best old-fashioneds in town."

I took the bait, handed over my number, and promptly forgot. When she texts and asks me to meet her tonight, I don't hesitate. I have nothing planned after filming wraps, and my flight back to California isn't until tomorrow.

The makeup artist excuses herself again to grab a fresh can of hairspray, so I save Ian's picture of Princess to my photos and scroll through the rest of the album looking for more of her. I'm happy Ian takes such great care of her while I'm gone, but I hate leaving her behind.

"Decker?"

I drop my phone in my lap and look up to find a pretty blonde with brown eyes smiling down at me.

She extends her hand. "Hi, I'm Ada."

My eyes drop to her cherry red lips and the cute little space between her front teeth before meeting her gaze again. I take her hand and try not to squeeze it too hard as I shake it. Which, I have to admit, feels entirely too formal. "Hi, Ada, I'm Decker."

"I know. I've been wanting to meet you." She releases me and reaches into the pocket of her dress, brandishing a slip of paper. She waves it in the air before folding it into my palm. "I don't know what your plans are later, but I have reservations for a new restaurant down the block and my friend just bailed on me."

I unfold the paper to find her number written on the inside. When I look up, she stares down at me expectantly. "Are you asking me on a date?"

"Kind of. I guess. Is that weird?"

I shake my head.

"Too forward?" she asks.

I chuckle. "No. It's fine."

"Ada! You're on in five!" Someone with a clipboard butts in.

Ada smiles sweetly at them and nods.

The makeup artist returns and asks me to close my eyes as she shakes up her can of hairspray.

"I'll text you," I tell Ada as she starts heading toward the set. "And it was great meeting you."

"You too." She smiles widely as she turns around and is ushered onstage by a crew member.

"Just one second," I tell the makeup artist.

She continues to shake the can of hairspray as I send off a text to the girl from last night, telling her I need to reschedule. I hear the crowd screaming for Ada as her interview begins, and I squeeze my eyes shut as the makeup artist sets my hair. Come to think of it, I am pretty hungry. I don't know what Little Miss Lux was so worked up about. Sour gummies don't do much to fill you up.

CHAPTER THREE

LENA

Six Months Later

HE SMOOTHS his patchy mustache over his lip. "It says here your last name's Lukowski."

I snatch back my I.D., shielding my eyes from the flashing blue lights atop the patrol car.

"Lux is my stage name."

When is Antonia going to get here? I knew I should never have ditched my team, but three—or five?—tall gin and sodas later, here I am. Alone in the dark with—I check the name on the front of his uniform—Officer Everett.

He clears his throat, a gust of sour coffee breath knocking me back a step. "And where did you say you were coming from?"

"I was just out for a walk."

"You had nothing to do with the commotion at Allister King's Music Hall?" His eyes dip to the ground before he flattens his mustache again, a thick chuckle exploding from his lips. "They must've meant *all* boots when they said they're made for walkin'."

My stomach sinks into the stupid Swarovski crystal-encrusted thigh-high boots I should have never agreed to wear. If they didn't look so good on camera, maybe I would have told someone they cut off circulation to my toes. I push back a fresh blonde chunk of my hair, still annoyed by the recent change. The pale shade is a jarring contrast to the chocolate of the rest, and I kind of hate it. Yet another thing in my life that's completely out of my hands.

"I'm in the city to record my new album and just needed some fresh air." I smile, wondering what Antonia might coach me to say. Should I have a lawyer present? Was I *incriminating* myself?

"Recording?" His eyes glint. "Anything you can share?"

"Just that this is going to be the most *epic* album yet." I paste on my ever popular I-don't-want-to-be-here-but-thanks-for-having-me smile, the one I've had to utilize more and more recently.

He nods enthusiastically and jots something in a notepad before flipping to a new page. "You know, my daughter loves you."

I perk up at the sight of a car turning off the brightly lit main drag and down our desolate side street.

"Aw, cute," I manage to say as the vehicle closes in, and much to my dismay, passes us. Still not Antonia.

"What's that one song you have? The cheaters one?"

Because I'm still not sure what this man has witnessed, I decide it's in my best interest to play along. I think through everything I've ever written, and for a girl who's only been cheated on once out of however many relationships she's ever been in, there's quite a few involving the implication of unfaithfulness. However, I have a feeling he's referencing my newest single. The one I wrote to help me process the passing of my most recent relationship. One my agent and record label coerced me to release to "stay relevant." My tears had barely dried by the time it was hitting the charts.

"You Did This? Killing Yesterday? What You Asked For?" I jog my memory for more titles, though my set list is never far from mind. Reluctantly, I drop the name of my newest one. *"Cheater Eater?"*

"Cheater Eater! That's the one. I can't tell you how many times I've had to endure it." He nods his head, humming the melody before diving into the lyrics. *"I'm a cheater eater. You couldn't leave her, tried my best, but couldn't beat her. Told me you didn't need—"*

"Loved writing that one," I fib.

"I heard that song's about that Callum boy. The singer. Is that true?"

Callum Porter. The guy who ripped my heart out and crushed it into impossibly tiny pieces under his Italian leather shoe. The one I was certain was going to take me back tonight but didn't. My smile falters, and I hope Officer Everett doesn't notice. Why is everyone always so invested in my love life?

"Isn't he in town for a show tonight?"

I shrug.

He eyes me suspiciously. "I thought I'd seen his name on the board at King's."

"You know, it's just a song, but you can tell your daughter—what's her name?"

"Riley."

"Beautiful name," I fawn, hoping to win him over a bit. "You can tell Riley that sometimes the best way to get over something is to write through it."

"Something or *someone?*"

Does he honestly think I'm going to dump every shattered fragment of my heart out to him here on the side of the road? I was being generous with the "write through it" advice.

He shoves the notepad and pen into my hands. "Can you sign this for her, please? She'll never believe who I saw tonight." He shakes his head. *"The* Lanna Lux."

"It's *Lee*-na," I correct, but before I take them from him, we're being spotlighted by headlights.

I freeze as the familiar black SUV screeches to a halt beside us and my publicist hurdles out.

"Don't answer any questions!" Antonia yells as Gustav, my main security detail, joins her on the curb. "Were any arrests made?"

The officer looks at her, his brow furrowing in confusion. "No, I was just asking about the King's Music—"

"Incident," she completes. "We heard about it and were worried sick. We stopped production when she texted us that she was just down the street from it and needed a ride." She wraps her arms around me, her dark curls tickling my face as she squeezes me unnecessarily tight. "Poor thing was scared to death. Are you okay, Lena?"

I remove her hand from where it cups my cheek.

"Yeah, but I wish I hadn't chosen to take my nightly walk so close to... all of that."

A fire engine sounds, and there's not a doubt in my mind it's on its way to King's.

"I know you love these little walks. I just wish you would have let us know you were taking your recording break," she says pointedly.

"You forgot your jacket." Gustav's bald head gleams under the streetlights as he wraps my bare shoulders in the ratty sweatshirt I've seen him wear several times already this week.

"Thanks," I sigh.

"We better get you back to set," Antonia says, ushering me away with Gustav on our heels.

"Wait." Shaking free of Antonia's grip, I bolt back to Officer Everett.

It's hard to see much under the dim streetlights, but I grab the notepad and scribble *Riley rocks!* followed by my signature heart and *Lena Lux* before Antonia's thin fingers are wrapping around my biceps and towing me off again, an exasperated Gustav tailing us. It's not my most clever message, but I hope it at least makes her smile as big as her dad is right now.

"Oh, and Miss Lukowski," Officer Everett calls.

The three of us turn to face him.

"Someone may be in touch with you. You know, in case you saw anything."

Antonia nods. "Of course. We'll help in any way we can."

He gives us all a once-over before loading back into his patrol car.

Gustav hustles Antonia and me into the backseat, nodding to our driver before crawling in and slamming the door.

"We'll help by contacting our legal team," Antonia mutters as she watches the officer pull away. She whips to face me. "Do you really expect people to believe you're just out alone for a leisurely walk? What were you thinking?"

I sink into my seat.

"You set that place on *fire*, Lena."

"How was I supposed to know that Callum lit so many candles before his show?"

She massages her temples. "You dated long enough to know his pre-show routine."

I flatten my cheek against the cold glass of the window. "I need another drink."

She shakes her head, yanking out her phone. I already know who she's dialing, and it's the last person I want to speak to.

My manager. My *mother*.

CHAPTER FOUR

LENA

"DO you have any idea how hard this is going to be to cover up?" My mother paces behind her gaudy mahogany desk. "The media is having a heyday."

I pull at the snag in my mulberry silk skirt, most likely ruining it for good. If my closets weren't full of a hundred other awards show and sponsor gifts like this one, I might be a little more remorseful watching the fabric go to waste. Besides the unnecessary gifts, the royalties of my singles alone could afford me to stock my closet with these too-expensive skirts for the rest of my life.

Settling down into my seat, I send off an SOS: *My mom is about to murder me* text to my best friend, Joss, trying to buy some time. I am so not ready to be berated by my mother today. Three dots appear, then vanish, replaced by a headstone emoji and three simple letters: R.I.P.

Thanks, Joss. I know she loves me, but she's like the hardest person ever to get ahold of.

"Are you hearing me?"

I lift my eyes to meet my mom's, her deflated lips pressed into a flat line, no doubt in need of maintenance injections soon. When they're in this in-between stage, it reminds me of the face I remember her having when I was little. The one that looked more like mine. Back before my career consumed both of our lives.

"Callum got what he deserved," I say.

"I'm going to pretend you didn't say that."

"It's not like he *died* or something. A couple of minor burns and some superficial damage to a dingy dressing room are hardly things that should make the news."

"It's a historic building, Lena, and it wasn't isolated. The heat charred that whole wall. Discolored it. Ruined the original wallpaper." She leans over her desk. "Did you know that wall is shared with a restaurant? They had to evacuate because they didn't know where the smoke was coming from."

I try to fight the stinging sensation biting at my nose and eyes. *Don't let her see you cry. Not today of all days.*

Her eyes cut into me sharper than her tone when I don't respond. "Have you seen the tabloids? Antonia, please read her the headlines."

Antonia clears her throat, obediently reading from her tablet. "Lena Lux *Rekindles Flame* with Callum Porter at Allister King's Music Hall."

She falls silent, and my mother urges her on with an impatient roll of the wrist.

"Lena Plans *Hot* Night for Callum at King's." She swipes across the screen, pulling up another article. "Lena and Callum *Heat* Up King's Music Hall." Another swipe. "Lena Lux: Callum's Queen at King's."

I brush a stray hair from my forehead. "We should be pressing charges. Those headlines are slanderous." I look from her to Antonia to where Gustav's tucked into the corner by the door. "Right? They can't say those things as though they're facts. There's no proof."

"You were *allegedly* spotted entering his dressing room and then photographed exiting the building. When was the last time you were able to go *anywhere* without a pack of paparazzi trailing you?"

I lift a shoulder, wishing I knew. Performing has its perks, but losing all anonymity as a teenager is not one of them. My mother doesn't understand my recently developed aversion to being in the limelight while offstage. She tells me my fans would be disappointed if they knew how ungrateful I am and that it takes some people multiple decades to build what I've accomplished in less than one. Is it so bad to want to save some aspects of my life for me? I imagine she'd be squawking a different tune if the roles were reversed.

My mother sighs. "Lena, this is bad. Maybe even worse than your little outburst at the Grammys. I still don't know how your record label let that one slide."

"I didn't trip that girl. The train of her dress was too long. She just wanted attention."

"You knocked her over."

"Not on purpose," I counter.

"Maybe if you'd shown some restraint at the bar that evening you'd have been able to stay upright." She pinches the bridge of her nose, her inky brows furrowing. "Regardless, she screwed up her ankle. We had to pay for her medical bills."

I pick at my chipped manicure. "You know people will try to suck any finances out of us that they can. They'd bleed us dry if we let them, even if it's an accident."

"Was the Callum thing an accident?"

"He deserved it."

My mother's stare is stony.

I roll my eyes. "So maybe I overreacted this once."

"Overreacted?" She rubs her temples as Antonia ducks behind her screen. "Lena, you covered that boy's dressing room in an accelerant and lit it on fire."

"I spilled a drink next to a candle."

"You threw a bottle of alcohol at him."

I try to keep my breezy shell of nonchalance intact, but it begins to crack as panic sets in. The damage wasn't intentional. I didn't mean to scare anyone. Throwing the bottle was more out of frustration than anything.

I stare at my hands folded in my lap. "He called me a sell out."

"You can't weaponize a beverage because some gap toothed fool from England called you a name." She sinks into the chair behind her desk, her voice softening in a way I haven't heard in forever. "Honey, why did you show up there anyway? We both know things between you two didn't end well."

I shrug.

Why did I go? It's a loaded question.

Because I was in the area. Because I made sure my recording schedule and location would line up with his coastal tour dates.

Publicly confessing I lit the fire would be an easier feat than admitting I'd done something so completely desperate

23

to be in the same vicinity as my ex. But he isn't just another ex in my long line of failed flings. He's *the* ex. The one that, despite his imperfections, was supposed to work out. And somehow... he didn't. I shouldn't be shocked I lost him. Sure, Callum could have been a better boyfriend, but I'm not void of blame either. Between work and my strict social schedule, I hardly had any time left for him. How could he not move on after that kind of neglect?

She heaves a sigh, flipping open her laptop and sliding on her blue blocker glasses. And just like that, my mother vanishes, and my manager is back. "Antonia, how do we spin this?"

Antonia scrolls her screen, shaking her head, her plum lips pinched in concentration.

Mom rolls her eyes, pulling out her phone and shoving to her feet. "Well, think of something. I need to make some calls."

Part of me hopes she's blowing things out of proportion —again—but deep down I know this time we can't smile or pay or talk our way out of it. Things are royally screwed up, and there's no one to blame but myself.

CHAPTER FIVE

DECKER

"I'M happy for you two. I needed a little pick-me-up after the news about the restaurant." I clap a hand down on my brother's shoulder as his wife, Nora, rests her palms over her still-flat belly. "You guys will be great parents."

Nora reaches out and places a hand over mine. "I'm so sorry. We know how excited you were about Gable's. It's a shame it happened, and to such a beautiful, historical place." She shakes her head, sincere sadness overtaking her previous joy.

As much as I'd like to wallow about it and the fact that I just finished fantasizing about hiring someone to restore its vintage interior, redecorating a historical landmark and bringing it back to its—lucrative—former glory wasn't my sole goal. It's what an investment like that could do for the other aspirations I have, the ones that go beyond the 50-yard line and way past the end zone. It wasn't just my retirement plan that burned up with Gable's; it was the security it was meant to provide for a slew of castoff dogs, too. Ones who need more than just a little love and a warm bed, but medication, special food, the works. Gable's was supposed to fund that dream for the long haul.

I suppose my hesitation did me a favor. I never pulled the trigger on the investment, and given its current state, I should be more grateful than anything. My indecisiveness saved my butt and my wallet for once.

Nora's smile trembles as she pushes her braids out of her deep brown eyes. *Oh no.* I will not have the pregnant lady crying on my account. I pat her hand. "The good thing is, I never had a chance to sign the papers."

"But you said that was your retirement plan. What about the shelter?"

"The shelter will still happen. There will be more opportunities." My face strains into a smile as I attempt to convince both Nora and myself that my dreams haven't gone up in smoke.

It works because she smiles and returns to her spot at the counter next to my mom, where they graze on cheese and crackers.

I raise my beer to them both. "Restaurants are a dime a dozen, but it's not every day my big bro becomes a dad."

Ian grins at me, scratching beneath his full, dark beard. "We were all sure you'd beat me to it."

"Just not as potent as you, I guess." I laugh and sip my drink, grateful to be in the offseason and with my family all in one place. During football season, I hardly see Ian. At least not since he was traded from the Las Vegas Rollers to the Kentucky Miners five years ago. Las Vegas was fun to visit, and a short flight. Kentucky is quite the trek from

California and a lot colder. I can understand why he keeps a second home a few blocks down from Mom.

He chugs his can, tossing it into the ill-placed trash bin nestled beside the island. It hits the edge of the beige laminate counter and bounces to the floor.

"No wonder you guys couldn't clinch that win in the playoffs," I tease.

"Decker!" Nora shoots me a disapproving look. "That game's still off limits. It's too fresh."

"It's been like six months," I say.

"Exactly." She frowns.

I cock my head at her, wondering if Ian is as sensitive about it as she is, but he ignores my insult, gesturing toward his missed target. "Mom, you know they have ways to hide those now."

Our mom combs her fingers through her faded hair, shaking her head. "Don't even start on the trashcan thing. This is where you two grew up. You weren't complaining then."

"At least let us pay to update it if you won't let us get you a new place," I say.

This woman is more stubborn than me, and that's saying something. Deep down, I know why she's averse to change. It's the same reason I'd keep these threadbare rugs, the knicks in the walls, and the closets cluttered with years of memories. Dad lived here. This was his place as much as it was ours. If we plaster and paint everything, what will we have left of him?

She sighs. "When Ian wins the Super Bowl, then we'll talk, but—"

"Yeah, gotta catch up to your lil' bro," I laugh.

Nora clucks her tongue.

Our mom rolls her eyes. "But for now," she says, tugging Nora under her arm, "Ian, you focus on providing for your growing family. And Decker—"

"Yes?" I glance up from my phone screen.

"You just focus on making that animal shelter a reality. Don't worry about my kitchen."

I drop my gaze. "Maybe it's a sign."

She turns to face me. "A sign for what? Don't you give up now. Gable's is a setback in your string of plans. Nothing more."

I raise my brows, dousing the streak of panic that's cropped up with the rest of my drink. Hearing her talk about the shelter out loud makes me feel so... out of touch. Still, I can't help but think if there were someone advocating for them, maybe more dogs would find a comfortable place to live out their last few golden years. It keeps me spurring on, no matter how ridiculous of a dream it seems. A professional football career pays well, but with the cost of living and leasing and medical supplies rising, I need a sure thing. I need a backup plan. Growing up with my family's financial restraints makes you think ahead about things like that. If I always have some stream of income, I'll always be able to use it how I want, and right now, paying to keep my family and well-deserving animals comfortable is how I want to do that.

"Hey." Her tone is one I've heard my entire life. The stern one that forces me to listen even when I want to do anything else. "I'm older. Wiser, some may say. This is only a little hiccup. Something better will come along. Trust me."

She makes it sound so simple, like it's destined to happen. Gable's Restaurant and Lounge isn't the first time I've gotten ahead of myself. I should've learned my lesson after that last brand deal fell through. The restaurant was supposed to be my Hail Mary to make up for that loss. Regardless, it always hurts to say goodbye to a good thing, especially before it comes to fruition. Not only does it suck Gable's was damaged last night, but another historical landmark as well, the one on the other side of the wall. Allister King's Music Hall.

Mom has too much confidence in me and my ability to produce. I know she doesn't know any better because we've never really talked money together. It's not something I feel comfortable with. I know what kind of budget we grew up on, the kind of Christmases we had. My parents always made sure my brother and I had enough while they constantly put themselves second. Dad missed out on so many games and memories because the only way to cover our expenses was for him to work multiple jobs. As selfish as it sounds, it's something that took me years to understand and finally forgive him for. It's a guilt I still carry with me.

The minute I signed my pro contract, I promised myself they'd never go without again. And now that it's just Mom, there's no way I'm not providing for her. She's always cared for me, believed in me, no matter how farfetched the aspiration. It's the least I can do.

Mom crosses to the pantry, then the fridge, and then to the crooked cabinet door that hides the mixing bowls. As soon as she starts pouring ingredients, measuring with her heart, I know what she's making. Her famous chocolate chip cookies. Nora picks at the chocolate chunks as the two get lost in baby conversation. My mom always wanted a daughter, and even though it's through marriage, Nora is her first. I've only ever brought one girl home, all the way back in high school. Even then, I've never seen her take to someone like she has to Ian's wife. Ian and Nora have something I could only ever dream of. My family gives me a hard time about hopping from girl to girl, but the thing is, I don't enjoy it. Contrary to popular belief, I don't do it for sport. What these two have is something to be envious of. It goes so much deeper than the surface level stuff everyone seems to get caught up in. When Ian falls short, Nora picks up the slack and vice versa. It's a give and take, a team effort. They operate as one unit. It's something I don't think I'll ever find, and after the most recent head-lines regarding my latest romantic involvement, any sane girl would run in the opposite direction.

Shaking my head, I try to push my failures and recent tragedies from memory. I finish my bottle and watch as my mom rests her cheek atop Nora's shoulder, which she can barely reach. How that petite woman birthed two giants is beyond my understanding. Our dad was almost six feet tall, but I'm still not certain how that and a couple inches over five feet math up to creating two professional athletes towering six foot four and beyond.

Mom beams up at Nora as she starts mixing in the chocolate chips. She looks so *proud*. Just as proud as when I helped secure the Kings' Super Bowl win at the beginning of the year.

"Don't even think they're gonna name that baby Darlene, cause they're not," I tease.

"What's wrong with my name?" Mom huffs as she stirs her little heart out.

"We haven't even discussed names yet, Decker. Don't shoot her down already," Nora says.

My phone pings again. *Jason Lancaster* flashes across my screen. What does my manager want? The first weekend in months, I step away from work, and he can't seem to remember. I sigh, unable to hold back from scanning my texts. The words *new collab opportunity* leap from my screen. Has he been taken hostage by some multi-level marketing schemer or what?

"Need another?" Ian points to my drink.

I shake my head as he grabs a beer from the fridge and a bottle of water for his wife.

"If the baby's a girl, you never know," Nora says, opening the bottle. "Darlene would be unique, or we could always find another way to work your name in."

"Or maybe somethin' with James in it, after dad." Ian throws out the suggestion casually like he's suggesting we order pizza for dinner, like it's not the most gut-wrenching reminder that this baby will never meet her grandfather.

My mother's eyes well with tears as she wraps her daughter-in-law in a tight hug. She's always been a proud parent to my brother and me, but the admiration she has for this couple right now is something I've never witnessed in my thirty years.

Despite my closet full of football trophies, multiple championship rings, and a nod for one of Vista City's "Sexiest Bachelors" from a local magazine, none of them can top the arrival of her first grandbaby.

My chest feels hollow as I consider that. I can work

myself to the bone, winning awards and championships and titles, but at the end of the day, what do I have if there's no one to share them with? He's not much older than me, but I feel like he's decades ahead. While I'm out with whatever girl catches my eye that month, Ian has Nora. He has consistency. Someone to go home to that loves him for more than his accomplishments. Football wins and business aspirations pale in comparison to what my brother has—a family. He's steady, dependable, and despite his high profile career, he's predictable. All of the things that always seem just out of reach for me. As much as I wish I were successful in the same areas, I won't begrudge my brother true happiness. I may have more championship rings, but Ian is the one who always seems to win. And that's fine.

CHAPTER SIX

LENA

A MAN'S tanned face pops up on the video chat screen. Immediately, my mother's over-lined lips spread into a smile so wide you can see every bleached tooth in her head.

"Jason Lancaster. How are you? Looks like the Cozumel sun has been kind to you," she coos.

"I've got a reservation in twenty." He leans back. Droplets of water roll down his face from his dark hair, and I realize he's in a pool. I'm no stranger to working vacations, but even I know pool time should be sacred.

Antonia leans forward, clearing her throat. "Jason, this is Lena."

"I know who Lena is." A grin finally flashes across his face. "Doesn't everybody?"

I lift my hand in a small wave, mimicking my mom's smile, trying to remember everything we've gone over.

I'm in town for work. I want to see a Kings game. I love football.

I've never been much of an actress, though I've done my fair share of cameos, and I'm not sure if that last sentiment is something I can fake. I don't know the first thing about football. It's kind of something I pride myself on. Regardless of how many box seats and suites I've been offered by vying admirers, I've never dated an athlete, and I don't plan to.

Antonia leans toward the screen. "Lena is a huge Vista City Kings fan. Last time we spoke you mentioned you've been working with Decker Trace."

Decker Trace? Why does that sound so familiar?

She pushes a stray curl from her forehead, clearing her throat. "Lena is currently in Vista working on her newest recording endeavor, and she was thinking about collaborating with a player for one of her philanthropies."

My mother chimes in, her face filling the screen. "And she was dying to stop by the kickoff game. Ever since she was a child, she's just loved The Kings."

I can't hold back my scowl, and I'm relieved to see Antonia is just as annoyed as I am. Trying to wiggle our way in by leveraging a charity opportunity is fine by me, at least that feels authentic. But me being a Kings fan? That's a lie if I've ever heard one. I've never paid much attention to football, but my dad has been an Orlando Pit Vipers fan his entire life, so I grew up wearing Pit Viper purple, not Kings blue.

"And you were hoping I'd be your in?" Jason sips some fizzy cocktail over on his side of the world.

Antonia begins to speak, but my mom interrupts again. "We're having trouble securing tickets."

"I find it hard to believe Lena Lux is struggling to get in *anywhere*." He arches a brow.

"Our main concern is the charity." Antonia tries to regain control of the conversation. I nod, playing along, but my mother shoulders me aside.

"Jason, let me cut to the chase here." She eyes me before diving back into her story. "My daughter has been absolutely smitten with Decker Trace ever since she laid eyes on him on *Late Night with Lanza*. She was hoping you could maybe... put in a good word for her, at the very least."

My jaw drops as the last horrible piece of this deranged puzzle falls into place like some dissonant guitar chord. How could I forget? Decker Trace is the meathead who wolfed down my worms backstage at Billy Lanza's show. If I never saw him again, I'd die happy. Outside of football, he's mostly known for breaking hearts, and more recently, for winning some idle bachelor award. And the award isn't even international, it's local. I tried to search him after I met him, just to see what kind of crap human he really is, but other than those facts, his online presence is minimal. He posts about his dog a lot. That's it. The things I know about him are few. He's a gummy worm stealer who treats dogs better than women and likes to throw a ball around. Definitely not my type.

Jason's eyes dart to my sliver of the screen. I run my fingers through my bangs, replacing my look of shock with a smile I hope translates as more bashful than flustered. The fact that I didn't realize I'd met Decker, let alone stalked him online, is a bit concerning. I make a mental note to pencil in a spa day sometime soon to recharge the batteries and whatever mush is left of my brain. Antonia clears her throat, pulling Jason's attention back to her as she adapts our plan to accommodate my mother's curve-ball. This woman deserves another raise.

But why does it have to be Decker Trace? Even from our conversation backstage—though calling it a conversation would be an exaggeration—I can't say I was impressed. He hardly looked my way, and I didn't encourage his ego by glancing his after our little food fight. Thick biceps and even thicker-headed isn't really my type, anyway. He's far from what I look for in a man. If I were to choose one human who embodies "my type," it's Callum Porter, hands down. Musically inclined, covered in tattoos, and an arsenal of swoony one-liners worthy of any multi-platinum record. Maybe that's why nothing ever works out. Pretty words don't equate to a functional relationship.

When it came to Decker, he'd been less than poetic, to say the least. Beyond his lack of charm and veiny forearms, the only thing I remember about him is that he downed the last bits of my requested treat with complete disregard for anyone else. If I were to give him a star rating, it'd be next to zero for that alone. Give or take a point for the way his eyes lit up when he flashed that irritatingly confident smile.

Someone offscreen summons Jason, snapping me out of my stewing.

He glances over his shoulder, then leans into the camera, lowering his voice. "I don't know. Antonia. I'm not really in the business of matchmaking."

Antonia narrows her stare. "Jason, after I worked over-time to help resolve your last client's outburst, you owe me.

I saved your butt, and you lived to work again. I think the least you can do is arrange something so she can meet her crush."

I cringe, but quickly recover, giving Jason my best pleading eyes. It isn't abnormal for me to have to play along with my mom and Antonia, regardless of how much I despise this plan. Just another day at the office.

He sighs. "Might not be a bad look for Decker to be seen with you a few times."

I can see the gears in his head turning, eerily similar to the way my mother's had.

"I think we both know it's best to keep these matters private," Antonia adds quickly. "But if it feels right, maybe you and I can discuss how to present the relationship to the public."

Relationship?

A sly grin spreads across Jason's now-dry face as he steps out of the pool. "I'll be in touch soon to coordinate the details."

My mom gives him a cheesy thumbs up, and then his screen goes black.

As soon as I'm certain I'm in the clear, my smile drops, and I whip to face my mother. "I'm not doing it."

"You will," she says, closing the laptop.

Antonia shifts from one scuffed ballet flat to the other. "It won't be for long. Just until the headlines clear."

"I'm not going to date Decker Trace." The words scrape against my throat as they rush out.

My mother's eyes widen, something lethal overtaking them. "Lena Claire Lukowski, you're the one who—"

"I can understand how this is a very emotionally

charged circumstance for you both." Antonia steps in, her voice steady as she turns to face me. "Lena, just think of it as something casual. We will have you start with drinks so you can feel out the situation. Just you and him, so it's low pressure. That gives you potential for face time with the public if someone happens to spot you. It never hurts to get those rumors rumbling. Plus, you can see if he's a creep and whatnot first."

She raises a brow as the cogs in her head kick into overdrive. Her wry smile almost makes me grin, too. My mother huffs and rolls her eyes, but Antonia holds up a hand to keep her at bay.

"We don't want you to do anything that's uncomfortable for you, but the reality of the situation is we don't have many options, and we need to work fast to cover your tracks. Who knows, maybe he'll surprise you." Antonia's eyes are full of sympathy as she pats my shoulder, glancing at my mother. "Don't you agree, Blythe?"

My mother's phone buzzes across her desk, and she scoops it up. "I have to take this." She exits without another word.

"Lena, please just trust me on this one. I know you're not fond of him despite what your mom told Jason, but this might be the only way."

I sigh, pressing the heels of my hands over my eyes. "I know. I know. It's fine. Just schedule it."

Even without looking, I know the weight that had been collapsing down on her has lifted. I've complied like I always do.

"Great. Okay. I'll call Jason to schedule your meeting with Decker." Papers shuffle as she collects her things and pads toward the door. "Just give it a chance, okay? It'll be over before you know it."

That's the last thing I hear before she and Gustav exit, leaving me all alone, asking myself what I've just agreed to —or, more accurately, was coerced into doing.

But they're right, I have no other choice.

CHAPTER SEVEN

DECKER

"NO."

"Decker, it's just drinks." Jason's voice crackles across the line.

I run a hand through my wet hair. "Nothing is *just* something. If someone sees—"

"You act like I'm setting you up with some ogre. It's Lena Lux. Half the world would kill to drink the sweat from her tour costumes."

I grimace as I run a towel over my damp hair before swiping it across the foggy bathroom mirror. "She's not really my type."

He laughs. "Keep telling yourself that. I already set it up, so it's a done deal, unless you want to back out."

"I wanna back out."

"Honestly, I thought this would be an easier sell."

"Have you met her?"

"I don't know what you want me to say, Decker. We've got to get you back out there if we're going to grow your career opportunities. It's not always going to be about football." He sighs. "And since Vital Reign Athletics backed out after the whole Ada Lane breakup, it wouldn't hurt to give everyone a distraction."

The mention of Vital Reign rejecting me stings. It's not like we'd signed a contract—it never got that far—but according to Jason, they'd been very interested in working with me. Vital Reign is the most popular female athletic wear brand in the United States. Not only that, but it's women-owned and operated, too. It started from the ground up right here in Vista City. They recently announced they'd be branching out into men's wear. Of course they don't want some perceived "womanizer" as their first male spokesperson. When their correspondence stopped coming, I knew my personal life was to blame, though they never explicitly said that. I can't blame them, but I wish everyone would stop listening to the lies. I wish they'd stop making me out to be something I'm not.

"Not everyone cares who I date," I try.

"Have you read what they've been saying about you since Ada—"

"I think anyone who has internet access has read the rumors."

"Then you know how delicate your social standing is. Just be glad you aren't some spotlight showboat. If you actually had an online presence, you would've been immediately canceled after that whole relationship."

"We went on like five dates. Wouldn't call it a *relationship*. It wasn't serious." I squeeze a glob of paste onto my toothbrush and scrub until my gums burn.

"Does she know that?" The words settle heavily

between us before he continues. "You can't ghost Hollywood's girl of the moment, then be photographed in public cuddling up with a bottle service waitress without a few people getting their panties in a wad."

"It wasn't like that. I—"

"I don't make the rules, Decker. People will see what they want to see."

I sigh. Although I hate to admit it, I know he's right. Vital Reign sure saw whatever they wanted to and ruined my fallback plan—and all plans dependent on it—because of it.

I can see why people are infatuated with Ada Lane. I was too on our first two dates, but then the newness wore off. Even though she was just as attractive on date three, I was less mesmerized by her talent, her sweetness. Dates four and five were more for her than for me. When you're in the spotlight, you have to be careful of how you handle things. The problem is, I've never been very careful.

"I just want to focus on my career," I finally say.

"And this is part of it. Consider it a stepping stone." Jason sighs. "What if you snap your femur? Bust your head open?"

"That's why we have padding."

"Padding did nothing for you last year. How's that knee?" His words have bite. "All I'm saying is, we both know you can't do this forever. I'm doing what you asked me to do. I'm helping set up a future you can look forward to. One with investment opportunities and a roster of connections for networking. We scratched Ada off that list, and we're replacing her with Lena. Everything that girl touches turns to gold. You can only hope a speck of that rubs off on you."

I check the clock. It's almost one a.m. Tired of arguing, I give up. "Where am I supposed to meet this *golden girl*?"

CHAPTER EIGHT

LENA

GUSTAV PULLS out my chair with a screech, nodding before retreating to a nearby corner of the room. Our table is situated toward the back of the restaurant, behind some decorative fountain with abstract shapes pouring streams of liquid into one another. It looks like a modern art piece that should be in a gallery, not stooping to create some privacy barrier in the middle of a restaurant. The rest of the place matches its motif with abstract neutrals and pops of red stretching from floor to ceiling, where massive, twisted gold chandeliers hang. The whole place is too upscale for a casual meeting. Stuffy, even. The kind of establishment I now realize refers to their cheese fries as *pommes frites au fromage* and dumps truffle flakes on top, like that somehow makes it fancy. It's familiar and contrived. If I've been to one, I've been to them all. Did Decker pick this place? And if he did, is it because he likes it or because he thought I would? Or worse. Did he think this would *impress* me? The thought of Decker wanting to impress me makes me feel a lot of things. Annoyed. Amused. Flattered.

I sip my ice water, wishing it were something stronger. As though she read my mind, a server stops by, placing a bottle of complimentary champagne in the center of the table, sent by the manager or something. She smiles at me, popping the cork and pouring some into the flute in front of me. I smile and sip as she deposits the bottle in the center of the table and freezes, her eyes fixed somewhere over my shoulder. I turn and follow her gaze until I see what she's gawking at. Decker Trace's massive frame is heading straight for us.

When he pulls out his chair and sits, he gives us both the same megawatt smile. The waitress quickly pours the champagne into his flute, her hands trembling as she sets the bottle back on the table. I smile at her, hoping to ease her rattled nerves. She returns it, then promptly scurries away, too shy to stick around beyond that. I was hoping I could get an appetizer, but when Decker winks at me, I'm grateful to have the bubbly to help me through this.

"Starting without me?" he asks.

"There's still time to catch up." I down the rest of my flute, buying time to think of what Antonia would want me to say. I bite back a tart response, and instead smile sweetly. "The night is young."

"Isn't that the name of one of your songs?"

"It is," I say, pouring myself another glass.

"Is quoting your own stuff a normal occurrence for you?"

I grind out another smile. "I didn't know I was meeting with a fan tonight."

"Speaking of fans, I had no idea how much you liked the Kings." He leans closer. "I'm flattered."

My teeth feel like they're going to crack as I clamp my jaw tighter. "I love football."

"Well, you're in luck because I got you something."

He brought me a gift? That's almost thoughtful.

The waitress returns as Decker reaches into a pocket concealed in his jacket. He pauses the motion, rattling off a few appetizers for us to share. I'm surprised when he chooses all the ones I've been eyeing.

When she leaves, he scoops out his gift. But it isn't so much a gift as it is a permanent marker. I deflate as he grabs his drink napkin and scrawls his name across it before sliding it my way.

"Thought you might want that." He winks.

I stare at it, unflinching.

"For the philanthropy thing. I thought you might want it for that."

I snatch it from him when he waves it in my face. "You want me to give someone your napkin?"

He shrugs. "It's signed."

I roll my eyes.

"You can keep it for yourself if you want," he says.

I let out a long breath. He's just as insufferable as I remember. Did Antonia and my mom truly think this was going to work? Regardless of what they think, I can't do this to myself. I *won't* do this to myself.

"Thanks, but I think I'm good." I push from the table, grabbing my handbag and stepping away, but something catches my hand. When I turn around I find Decker at the other end of it, his eyes softer, his face settled into something less cocky than it was five seconds ago.

"Wait. I'm sorry, I—" He lets me shake free and runs his hand over his hair. "Here." He grabs up the napkin, flipping it over and placing my champagne flute on it. "Let's just pretend I didn't offer you my autograph. Sit down. Stay. Please?"

I glance back at Gustav, who is waiting for his cue to escort me out, but my mind flashes back to my mom and Antonia—to the entire reason I'm meeting with this big oaf —and I find myself sitting again. "Fine. My publicist will kill me if I don't at least see this date through, anyway."

"Date?" He perks up.

I shake my head. "Meeting. Whatever it is."

I push a swath of hair behind my ear, unable to meet his eyes. Did I really call this thing a *date*?

"I mean, we could consider it a date." He clears his throat, and when my eyes meet his, he backpedals. "If you want to. We don't have to. I was just thinking that Jason might leave me alone about my personal life for a bit if I told him we had a promising date."

"I feel that." I slam down another flute, placing it back on the overturned napkin. "Do you ever get sick of people meddling with your life?"

His brow knits. "I mean, Jason's pretty nosy, but I don't know if I'd call it *meddling*."

I watch the last few drops of champagne run down the sides of my glass like tears, my veins already buzzing as the alcohol fills my empty stomach. "I think my publicist— well, her and my manager both—wanted this to be a date."

"Would that be so bad?"

47

I throw my head back in a too-loud laugh. "Since you're a fan, I think you already know the answer."

He arches a brow, leaning in. "I don't mean to burst your little bubble, but I've heard maybe three songs of yours."

Is it weird to find that endearing? It feels nice, like a fresh start. I lean in too, lowering my voice. "Good. Because let me tell you, all of my songs are written about guys whose beginning and end started just like this." I tap a finger hard on the table. "Organized for one opportunity or another. Only made the mistake of completely falling for one of them."

Decker's eyes trail to where my pink nail digs into the soft wood.

Our waitress brings the appetizers, and he orders another bottle of champagne for us.

I waste no time scooping piles of steaming food onto my little plate. "Did you honestly think we called out of the blue for a random charity collaboration?"

"Crazier things have happened."

The champagne fizzes up, overtaking the conversation. "They were hoping you'd be like all the other suckers and fall for their little scheme."

His brow wrinkles as I shove a piece of fried calamari in my mouth.

"So you're saying that all of your relationships have been *planned?*"

"Most of them. And not planned, per se, but *suggested.* Heavily encouraged for whatever that partnership could offer."

"So your publicist and your manager arrange your dating life?"

"Yeah, and my manager's my mom." I snort like it's funny.

He presses his lips into a tight line, and I notice the auburn tint in his stubble in the low light. "You know, that's kind of sad."

"Thanks."

Just when I begin to regret opening my blabbering mouth, he says, "So what's one more?"

"What?" I say, chomping on a steaming, artisan cheese-smothered *pommes frite*—a pretentious cheese fry.

He picks up a few too, shoving them in his mouth, thinking as he chews. "If both our teams want to see *this* happen, then why don't we make it happen?"

"Because I don't like you."

"So? Business isn't always about liking people. If that were the case, I probably wouldn't be here either. You aren't exactly a ray of sunshine yourself."

I stick out my tongue.

He ignores the gesture. "I think there's something we can both offer each other to, ya know, help one another along."

I arch a brow. "So you want to use me?"

"No." He leans closer. "I help you. You help me."

"Why do you need help? I've seen how lucrative some of those football contracts can be. You don't need me."

"What about after football?"

I lean forward, too, narrowing my eyes. "Greed isn't a good look on anyone, Decker Trace."

"I'm not *greedy*." He scowls, spitting the last word like

it's poison. "I've just got things—people I want to take care of."

The judgment I imposed on him falters for a moment. It's easier to say you're going to share until the money is in your hands or your bank account. I've been in this business long enough to know that once someone makes their first million, the appetite for more becomes insatiable. Why would Decker be any different? I've been down this road. Someone wanting a piece of the life I've built, of all the time I've lost, sinking it into my career. I've had photos and documents hacked by those I thought I could trust. I've had stories made up and sold to journalists. All of that betrayal for a quick dollar. Why should I share my success —myself—with someone else simply because they think they have something to give me? Am I so desperate to cover my tracks that I'm willing to take this gamble?

"People to take care of? That's a pretty convenient excuse." I shake my head, tossing down my fries just as the waitress pops up and refills our glasses before setting the chilled bottle on the table and flitting away. "Anything I've got, I earned it myself. I don't need you to do a single thing for me."

"Just think about it."

"No, I'm good."

As desperate as I am to regain control of the headlines and salvage my reputation, I can't stand the thought of it being *him* who saves me.

He lifts his hands in surrender. "All I'm saying is maybe it's time you make a choice for yourself. It sounds like your rebellious streak is pretty limited, like you're afraid of going too far out on the limb without their approval." I scoff, but he doesn't stop talking. "You can start and end this thing on your own terms, and in the meantime, I might be able to get a little face time at your side. Redeem myself, maybe."

"Redeem yourself?" A laugh squawks out, no doubt given extra gusto from the drinks.

He nods. "I know it might be hard to believe, but I'm not perfect."

I roll my eyes.

"Besides the fact the entire internet hates me for how things ended with Ada Lane, I'm getting old, Lena."

I can't help but laugh at the way he says it, like we've gathered here tonight to choose a casket for him. "You're not *that* old."

"Older than you." He nudges my elbow that's propped on the table. "And in football years, I'm almost ancient. At least my body is. After last year's injury, I didn't recover the way I thought I would. It might not hurt if people know me for something other than that."

My first instinct is to laugh at the phrase *football years*, but then I see the sadness in his eyes, the way they won't meet mine when he discusses his injury. My heart squeezes in my chest. I once had surgery for vocal nodules, and by the grace of God, I made a full recovery. I can't imagine what I would have done if I'd had to sacrifice my career because my body couldn't handle it anymore.

I want to tell him that I understand where he's coming from, that I can sympathize, but someone approaches our table. Gustav steps out from hiding, edging toward us ever so slightly, ready to put distance between the newcomer and me.

"Hi," the young girl says timidly.

I turn toward Gustav, who has begun advancing, and shake my head. His brute force won't be needed. This girl is maybe thirteen, her long hair is cut just the same as mine, dyed to match too, if her contrasting roots are any indicator, and beyond that, the pink in her cheeks tells me she's too nervous to be a threat.

"I'm sorry, I..." She takes a deep breath, thrusting a pen in my direction. "Could I... Could I please have your autograph? I'm a big—huge—I'm a huge fan."

I put the napkin down, facing her so she has my full attention. "Sure. And what would you like me to sign for you?"

She freezes, glancing around, her eyes wide. "I thought maybe... I don't know."

"Here." I take her pen, grabbing for the closest thing to sign. Decker's napkin. "What's your name?"

"Sophia," she says, brightening.

"Oh, so now it's okay to sign napkins," Decker mutters to me.

I kick him under the table, and much to my dismay, it only makes his smile wider. "Sophia. I love that name. Love your hair, too."

The girl beams as she watches me draw my signature heart that appears somewhere on every album cover. Quickly, I flip Decker's name so it's flat against the table, giving myself the blank side for my autograph. I scribble out the lyrics *don't forget to love yourself* and punctuate it with my stage name, *Lena Lux,* before handing it back. Her eyes are wide as she reads it before flipping it over, her gaze trailing up to bounce between Decker and me.

"I don't know if this is rude." Sophia clears her throat. "But I just want to say I'm glad you found someone else. I never liked that Callum guy. And his music is weird."

My face heats. Some days I'm not sure why I liked him either, but talking about him now only reminds me of the fact I'm probably wanted for arson—if anyone knew it was me, that is. I feel myself spiraling, but I quickly recover. "That's sweet. You know, he and I are still great friends, but I understand his music isn't for everyone."

Decker scoffs, earning himself another swift nudge under the table.

"How long have you two been together?" she asks.

I panic.

Decker is more than a little amused as he sits back and waits for my answer. If only I could reach across the table and slap him, I would. But I consider the whole Callum fiasco, everything that's happened recently. He made some good points, and although I hate to admit it, so did my mom. If she and Antonia insist on orchestrating every aspect of my life anyway, what's the harm in me jump-starting their plan?

"It's pretty new," I say, groping across the table for his hand.

After what feels like too uncomfortably long, he grabs my hand and gently presses it to his lips. My smile falters as he rubs it against his sandpapery cheek, so I settle for a firm face pat instead.

"It's still a secret," Decker says.

Sophia looks as though she's about to burst from excitement. "I won't tell anyone."

Decker nods, and I flash her one more smile before she says goodbye and departs back to a table with her parents, almost skipping all the way.

"Lena with the game time decisions. I knew you couldn't resist a redemption arc."

I roll my eyes and shake my hand free. "I'm not sure you can be redeemed."

"I wasn't talking about me." Decker drops his smile and leans closer. "I give her two hours tops before she paints the internet with our love story."

I make a gagging sound. "*Love* is a little bit strong of a word."

He casually tosses a piece of calamari into his smug mouth. "Everyone loves me."

"I'm glad you think someone does."

"You will, too." He shifts in his seat. "Like, platonically. Eventually."

"Sure. Well, if you can love a business partner, then maybe you're right."

"Oh, we're partners now?"

"Business partners," I clarify.

He sticks his hand out. "You got it, partner."

I hesitate, choking down the rest of my flute before gripping his hand and shaking.

"So what do you have planned this weekend?" he asks, leaning back like we didn't just agree to sign our lives away for the next... however many months. Years? The thought makes my stomach churn.

"You're eager, aren't you?"

He frowns. "I'm making small talk. Besides, we should know at least a little bit about each other if we're gonna pull this thing off."

I shove a fry into my mouth, answering between chews. "I'm recording. Well, re-recording something. For a remix."

"Remix?"

"It's nothing major. We just wanted to give a more upbeat alternative version of the stuff from my first album for the ten-year anniversary." I swallow down my bite and realize I've said too much. "But no one's supposed to know yet, so please keep that to yourself."

He pretends to lock his lips, then leans closer. "Your secret is safe with me, *babe*."

I grimace. "Ugh. If you insist on having nicknames, I get to pick mine."

"That's not really how nicknames work."

"Fine. Then I at least get to approve it."

"Fine," he agrees. "Any more demands?"

My eyes meet his over our plates as the waitress stops by to silently pour us both another glass of champagne before disappearing again.

"I suppose we should set some boundaries," I say.

"Like what?"

My eyes trail to the table where both our hands rest, our fingertips mere inches from one another from when he grabbed my hand just moments ago. "Like no PDA."

"How do we convince people that two grown adults are in a loving relationship without touching each other?"

I cock my head. "Do you want to kiss me or something?"

His eyes drop to my mouth before falling to the table-top. "No, maybe not on the mouth. But like... Your fore-head or cheek or *something*."

"Fine. Just give me a warning before. And only in front of cameras or if other people are watching." He lets out a low chuckle, and I watch as his big hand engulfs his cham-pagne glass and lifts it to his lips. "We might as well add holding hands to the list since you kinda already forced me to do that."

He groans. "I grabbed your hand for like five seconds to convince that kid. I was acting. And apparently, I'm pretty good at it cause she believed it."

I think about that. Although I'm fairly certain my young fan wouldn't bat an eye, regardless of how convincing it was or wasn't, because who in their right mind lies about a relationship? The answer is: you'd be surprised.

He continues on. "Okay, so no kissing. Maybe fore-head or cheek, if given a heads up first." I nod, and he clears his throat. "Holding hands or maybe a hand on the lower back. Got it."

My champagne burns my throat as it froths back up into my nose. "Wait. What? Lower back?"

"It's, like, a normal thing. If we're in a crowded place, and we're navigating through, it's easier if you do it with your hand on your girl's lower back."

I grimace and tip the champagne back until it's gone. It punches me in my senses like it's seeking revenge. "Sure. Why not? That's half my pictures with my exes anyway."

"The paps love the lower back move."

"I'm sure my manager and publicist will have something to say about the guidelines." I trace a finger along the edge of my glass, hoping that if I focus on the movement hard enough, he won't be able to see the sadness cropping up at the thought of Callum. Something I'd hoped the champagne could bury for the night. "They're gonna lose it when they find out I just jumped in without consulting them. It's not just me who has to approve of it."

For this to work—and to not circle back and bite me in the rear—I know I need to tell them. We need a contract in place. An airtight one only my mother and our trusted legal team could come up with. I wish that weren't the case.

"Why?" His voice rises, and I can't help but to meet his eyes. "Isn't that why you agreed to do this, Lena? So you can approach it on your own terms? Forget about their approval."

He isn't completely wrong about part of the reason I'm agreeing to this right now. I'm sick of needing approval for half the things in my life, but I hesitate, still debating if I should tell him about the King's fiasco. Everything surrounding that night feels so wrong. Part of me wonders if letting him in on my motivation would alleviate some of the burden. Antonia would definitely advise against it, and my mother would probably keel over at the mere thought of me offering up a confession. Which makes blabbing to Decker all the more appealing. I wrote a song about urges like this once. It was titled *Self Sabotage*.

I clear my throat. "It's not seeking their approval, it's respecting their roles in my life so I still have a functioning work environment when all this is done. *That's* why I agreed to do this." I shift in my seat, scanning our surroundings as though anyone can hear us over here in our corner.

He leans closer, lowering his voice. "When is this done anyway?"

I think for a moment, but I already know the answer. "It only ends when we both feel like we've met our goals."

"Which are?"

The words flow as easily as the champagne, pouring out of me before I can stop them. "Evading arson charges and whatever you've set your sights on for your next big career move."

"Arson?" Decker sputters, bubbly dribbling down his chin as he mops it up with the back of his hand. His eyes go wide. "Does this have anything to do with the music hall and Gable's?"

I nod, biting my lip so hard I'm shocked I don't taste blood.

"Is that what all this is about?" When I don't answer, expletives hurl from his lips as he runs a hand through his wavy hair. "I thought your publicist told my manager you needed to partner up for a charity thing. Because you were getting bad press after a breakup."

"Well, kind of." I sigh and ease into the story of the beginning of my downfall two nights ago at the music hall. When I finish, Decker is silent for a long time. Too long.

"You realize *that* was my 'next big career move.'" He quotes the last sentiment with sharp strikes of his fingers.

"What was?"

"Gable's Restaurant and Lounge. It's for sale. I was

going to buy it." He shakes his head, flags down our passing waitress, and asks for an old-fashioned.

My stomach sinks. Not only did I ruin countless other people's plans that night, but now I can put a face to a victim of my destruction. My eyes sting, and I wonder if I actually feel bad for him or if I've had one too many drinks. I watch as he stares at his hands, wondering what to say next, wondering what *he's* going to say.

Finally, he pinches the bridge of his nose, his lips parting as he processes the news. "You do realize you somehow managed to destroy two historical landmarks in one night?"

"Ugh. Why is everyone so caught up about the landmark thing? I didn't mean to." Which is true. I wasn't aiming the bottle at the candles, I was aiming for Callum's head. That's why I get paid to sing and not to play offense on a field. "It's not like anyone died."

"How can you be so casual about this?"

I chew my cheek, biting back a fresh surge of emotion. My only option is to be casual. If I'm not, I might cry, and once the tears start, who knows if they'll stop. My choices are limited: detach and keep it cursory, or lean into my feelings and fall apart in public. As nonchalant as I'm trying to be, I can't squash the panic beginning to rise at the thought of him abandoning our plan. If he backs out, it's my fault. Not only do I have to see him disappointed in me, but I'll have to face a very disappointed—and probably very irate—manager, and that's the last thing I want on my list of failures for the week. The way Decker is staring across the table at me now reminds me of the millions of times my mother has disapproved of something I've done. I hate it. Something crumbles in me under his rigid gaze, and suddenly, I'm back to seeking approval from people I shouldn't be seeking it from.

"Does that change things? You don't wanna be my fake boyfriend anymore, do you?" I lean forward, my head feeling heavier than normal with all the golden bubbles I've been guzzling. "You're gonna tell someone it's my fault, aren't you?"

"I should."

"Should. Could. *Will*." My tongue feels thick as I form the words, and I force a smile at our waitress as she drops off his drink and hurries off again. "It's fine. It's probably time I take a career break anyway. Nothin' like a little prison down time, ya know what I mean? It's a shame I don't look better in orange." I pour myself a half glass and knock it all back in one swallow, trying to force away the lump building in my throat and the blur creeping in at the edges of my vision.

Decker watches, not a word leaving his lips as he grips his lowball glass. My nose stings, and my eyes grow hazy with booze and unshed tears. He sighs, chewing his lip as he scans the room before leaning forward and grabbing my hand. I squeeze my eyes shut, embarrassment heating my face when two tears trickle down my cheeks. Great. Just what I need. Here I am, sitting in the presence of this oaf, drunk-crying my dumb little eyes out.

Could this week get any worse? Not only have I committed what I assume Antonia and my mom would consider a cardinal sin—confessed the cause of the fire— but I jumped the gun. I made a choice without them, and here I am, getting shot down for a fake relationship by some man I never wanted to associate with in the first place.

Decker shifts in his seat, glancing around the room and awkwardly patting my hand. "Hey, it's okay. I'm not gonna tell anyone."

"Okay? I burned down half your restaurant." I dab my cheeks, a little wail slipping from my lips.

He hunches forward, lowering his voice. "Can you keep it down?"

I snuffle.

"You charred a single wall, and it wasn't mine," he says, straightening back up.

"Not yet."

"There are other investment opportunities. I'm just glad I hadn't pulled the trigger yet. Maybe it's a sign. Maybe I need to look into something else."

"Like what?" I sniff.

"I don't know. I didn't really have a backup plan." He lets out a bitter laugh as he brings his drink to his lips. "If it makes you feel better, you can pay me back."

I pull my hand from his. "Look, I know it's common knowledge that I've amassed a little bit of wealth over the years, but I don't know if I can get my team on board with—"

"No. Not money. This." He gestures between us. "Lena, I know I don't have to tell you this, but being seen with you is never a bad thing. Everything you touch turns to gold."

I dab my cheeks with my napkin, taking a deep breath as I listen to him.

"So, if anything—" he leans back, his hands out to the

side as though he's having some major revelation— "I'm all in. You scratch my back, I scratch yours."

"Ugh. I'm immediately writing that out of our rules. Don't scratch my back."

He smirks and leans forward. "Anything for you, *babe*."

CHAPTER NINE

DECKER

"HOW WAS YOUR DATE?" Ian asks, his wiry beard consuming the edges of his smile.

I bite back a grin as last night resurfaces in my mind. How upset Lena was when she essentially confessed to a felony. How good she'd make an orange jumpsuit look despite her protests. Honestly, it's not something I'm proud of, but I've seen a lot of girls cry, and somehow Lena still made it look good. Even if she did burn down my prospective retirement plan. Last night was weird and productive, and I'm still trying to convince myself it was real. If it weren't for the headache I accrued from all those drinks, I'm not sure I'd believe it happened.

The August sun is relentless as we cross our mom's backyard. I take stock of the sun-bleached patio furniture she's had since I was in grade school and the fence she zip tied together five years ago. Despite both of our offers, she won't allow us to invest anything in it. She's stubborn to a fault, and this backyard proves it. I only hope she gets over the whole "stop trying to buy me stuff" thing by the time she's retirement age.

"Fantasizing about Lena? I asked you how your date was," Ian repeats.

I elbow my brother hard, handing him the keys to mom's shed. "It wasn't a date."

He laughs. "That's not what everyone is saying."

"And you of all people are listening to rumors plastered all over social media?" I shake my head. "I'm disappointed in you. Mom would be too if she could hear you." I take a deep breath. "Just let me be the one to tell her I'm hanging out with someone again."

"Oh, she already knows. Saw it online this morning." He bugs his eyes. "She thought you were done messing around with your personal life, and then you pick Lena Lux to date?"

I can't keep the scowl from my face. "What's wrong with Lena?"

"I don't know. Why don't you ask one of her hundred exes?"

Something about that sends a blitz of irritation through my core. Whether it's for Lena or me, I'm not sure. Maybe for us both, for always being labeled as one thing or another. Who's to say she's what everyone assumes she is? I know I'm not.

"Maybe I don't plan on being her ex," I sneer.

Ian lifts his brows. "Maybe you should tell Mom that."

"Okay, mama's boy." I shake my head. "I just turned thirty, and you're like a hundred. I don't think we have to tell her everything."

"I just respect her enough to mention certain things."

I swing open the door to the shed and begin rummaging through, not willing to argue that his notion of sharing our personal lives with anyone has nothing to do with respect as much as it does with approval. It's been years since he's handed me a beating, and I'm not sure if he could anymore, but wrestling across our mom's suburban backyard isn't on my agenda today.

"What'd Jason say?" Ian asks, taking the hedge trimmer from me.

"Haven't talked to him yet," I say, grabbing Ian a pair of work gloves.

"Didn't tell mom *or* your manager? That's a dangerous game."

I ignore him, diving deeper into the mildew-stenched shack.

"At least if you drop dead tonight, we have a short list of who's at fault." His chuckle booms, needling under my sunburned skin.

I give him a sarcastic laugh. "I told you. It's new. Haven't had time to call anyone yet."

He straightens up and turns toward me. "Funny, coming from the guy who is constantly glued to his phone, texting the flavor of the week. Maybe you and Lena are a good match. At least you both have a similar track record."

Before I register what I'm doing, I give him a dead arm and run toward the house. For a split second, we're middle schoolers again, fighting in the yard over which one of us broke the rules to a dumb game. It's freeing to remember, and part of me wishes I could go back. Even if money was tight, I didn't care. I had no image I felt pressured to uphold. Things were simpler then. I didn't have to worry about my appearance, or enraging the internet, or pretending to date some girl to help my finances after my inevitable retirement and my dog shelter aspirations.

Lena. It's shocking she's willing to pretend at all. It's not like she needs to. She could get anyone she wants, and she knows it. It probably contributes to her bratty attitude. I smirk as I think about her clear blue eyes rolling after every single remark I made while we shared *pommes frites* and champagne. Without that attitude, pretending could be hard. Thankfully, despite her being more than my type, that attitude will keep us both in check. Besides, I could probably learn a thing or two from her business savvy, and that's what I have to keep in mind.

I'm putting my rocky personal life on hold in favor of something fake, so maybe, after Lena and after football, I can have something real to build my life on. Sponsorships. Endorsements. Commercial cameos. Outside of a secure financial future for myself and my family, being seen as someone who can hold on to a girl for longer than a minute isn't a bad thing. If I can tolerate Lena's sass and flippant behavior long enough, she might just be the single best thing that's ever happened to me.

CHAPTER TEN

LENA

I RATTLE my iced matcha latte until the drink settles enough for me to finish it.

"You seriously have nothing to say?" My mother fumes.

Biting down on the straw, I gaze up from the sprawling contract she's laid out before me.

No—I want to shout—*I actually have a lot to say.* But because most of my comments have nothing to do with her current conniption fit, I keep them to myself.

"Thank God Legal was able to work something up on short notice." My mother paces as Antonia becomes one with her tablet, scrolling and typing furiously.

Antonia pops her head up. "Jason just messaged that he's faxing over Mr. Trace's paperwork now."

"Thank God." My mom comes to a standstill, hands pressing into the freshly signed documents littering her desktop as she hovers over me. "This is why we have employees, Lena. This is why we've hired Antonia. She's the one who is supposed to orchestrate how we reveal details of your personal life to the public."

I shift in my seat, jaw clenching. I wish we didn't have to release any of my personal information to the public at all. No one is entitled to know a single thing about my personal life—her included. If it wasn't for Callum's unfaithfulness and my misplaced hope he'd take me back, I wouldn't be in this mess.

I sigh. "I just wanted it to feel organic."

"Then Antonia would have planned it that way."

"You can't plan organic," I argue.

She rubs her temples. "Antonia, please talk some sense into her."

Antonia lowers her tablet, stepping around the chair parallel to mine and dropping herself down to sit beside me. She gives me a sheepish smile as she leans forward. "I think what your mother is trying to say is that when we started this *interaction* between you and Decker, we were under the impression we would spearhead any and all leaks to the public, as we always do."

"Maybe Decker was just too cute for me to resist. Too *charming*." I snort. Sure, he's attractive—anyone with eyes can see that—and he thinks he's charming, but the thought itself is ridiculous. Decker *so* isn't my type.

"Sarcasm has no place here right now." My mother sighs, attempting to swallow down her irritation. "We just feel it's best that we handle things for you. You have so much on your plate with your career, the least we can do is assist with your personal life. Lord knows we can't help you on stage."

"You've got that more than covered," Antonia chimes in with a bright smile.

My mom nods.

"Well, I'm sorry for being overzealous, but it's not like this situation is any different from my past relationships. I just expedited the process a bit." I shrug.

My mom's eyes widen. "Lena Claire, this is *so much* different from your past relationships. This is your future we're talking about." She shakes her head, her mouth agape. "You started a fire. This is the relationship that will determine whether or not Antonia is worth her salt as a publicist." She smiles and tilts her head toward Antonia. "And I know you are."

Antonia shifts in her seat and places a hand gently on my knee. "Listen, Lena. I'm sure Decker is great, and we've all seen him, but given the reason we reached out to him in the first place, I'm going to have to agree with your mom. You need to let us handle this if we truly want to move past the whole music venue snafu."

I plunk into my chair, knowing the odds are not in my favor. They never are in this office. "I promise from this point forward, I'll let you two plan all my dates, posts online, whatever. And I'll do what I always do—focus on my career."

My mom sinks behind her desk as Antonia bolts to her feet and whips out her phone.

"I'll get ahold of Jason again. We need to trade contact info." Antonia pauses briefly, lowering her phone. "Did you get Decker's number?"

I shake my head, feeling a little embarrassed. How did

I expect to pull this off without my "boyfriend's" phone number?

Perking up, Antonia lifts her phone to her ear. "Good. We'll get everything in place and pass on the pertinent info to you."

I breathe out a sigh of relief. Despite what Decker and I discussed about feeling out of touch with my own personal life, I can't help but to be happy to hand this over. Why shouldn't I let them do their jobs and handle this thing? Focusing on my career has yet to disappoint me. Relationships, on the other hand, are always disappointing. Even after my vocal nodule scare a few years back, I learned that I can overcome, and that my career will still be there. I can't say the same about men. Dating Decker for real would be the worst thing I could do for myself after such a horrendous breakup with Callum. I never want to go through that again. I never want to put myself in a position to set myself up for that kind of failure again. Real, fake, or anything in between.

My mind kicks into overdrive as I consider what I've done. What do I do if Callum decides he wants me back but finds out I'm "dating" someone else? I instantly hate myself for considering it. He's a cheating degenerate who doesn't deserve a single thought. My heart aches. A cheating degenerate that, for some unknown reason, I wish hadn't dumped me.

I set my empty plastic cup on a coaster and press my palms into the cool wooden desktop. It's grounding. Pretending to date Decker will keep my mind off Callum, which in turn will keep my mind on work. It's a win-win. And I get to help the needy, since apparently Decker *needs* help sorting out his future. I do feel bad for ruining his restaurant plans. If nothing else, that's reason alone to try to pull this off. To atone. Plus, of all the relationships my mother and Antonia have ever suggested, Decker is the safest. He and I seem so completely different that there's no chance of making the same mistake this time. This time I won't be falling for someone so careless because I won't be falling at all.

My mom and Antonia huddle behind a tablet, engrossed in something.

"Can I go now? I'm supposed to be at Living Truth soon." I try not to let them see how antsy I am to leave this awkward conversation.

"You're volunteering at the church today?" My mom frowns, reaching over Antonia, who obediently lets her tap across her tablet screen. "It's not on your schedule."

So *that's* what they're looking at.

"I didn't have anything else tonight, so I wanted to squeeze in some time there. I wasn't sure when I'd be able to otherwise."

My mom sighs like it's the biggest inconvenience in the world that I want to help serve food to hungry people at a church. "We were hoping to set up an *actual* dinner date with Decker. To get you two in the public eye a bit more."

"Decker could always join her," Antonia suggests.

Great. Just what I need, my quiet place interrupted by Decker.

"And who would see them while they volunteer?" My mom scoffs. "If we don't get them in the public eye soon, what's the point?"

Antonia's eyes widen as my mother's delicate nostrils

flare ever so slightly. It's a warning sign, the look that has always let me know one of her signature fits is about to happen. Instinctively, my body tenses, bracing for impact.

"The kickoff game. They'll launch at the football season's kickoff game." The words fly from Antonia's lips.

"That's too far away," my mom counters.

"It's only a week or so away, right?" I ask quietly.

Antonia nods and turns toward my mother. "I want Lena to feel prepared. I really want to sell this relationship, so before we throw them to the wolves, they need to spend some time together."

"In the backroom of some church?" my mom rolls her eyes.

Antonia lifts a shoulder. "Wherever. They need to at least appear comfortable together. Lena's plans can work in our favor just as much as a dinner alone could. I'll call Jason. Decker is neck deep in practices, but I think he should have tonight off. If I remember correctly, the Kings have Sundays free."

I know my mom is about to lose it, but I'm so happy. I wish I could wrap Antonia in a hug and squeeze her until she turns blue. Relief replaces my looming anxiety. Not only because I don't have to cancel my plans, but because she's allowing me time to ease into this chaos with that oaf. If I have to meet with him, at least it's on my turf.

CHAPTER ELEVEN

DECKER

I CLIMB out of the back of Lena's black SUV and thank Gustav as he shuts the door behind me before jogging to catch up to Lena, who looks like she's on a mission. My hair's still damp from the rushed shower I took when Jason called to let me know we were *"officially doing this thing."* I just agreed and got ready. It was easier to go along with him than to tell him she and I had already decided to *do this thing* last night and that we talked guidelines and everything. It's weird how fast it happened, and it's better to let him think he's still steering this ship. This *relationship.*

Lena walks ahead of me, hips swaying as she puts distance between us. Only the faint scent of vanilla and something else lingers in her wake. I dodge a dumpster and a few trash cans, but she doesn't wait for me to catch up. It's like she's trying to lose me. Maybe she is. I hate to tell her, but one of my strides is about two of hers. If I wanted to be beside her, I would, but she wants space, and I respect that. I wouldn't be too happy either if someone encroached on my plans.

My foot lands in something sticky, and the sole of my high top peels away with a nauseating sound. The irony is not lost on me—America's Pop Princess being smuggled through the least glamorous place imaginable. She pads down the alley on grimy sneakers. Seeing her in those ratty things instead of her usual designer heels is jarring. Not only because they're less than pristine, but she's shrunk a few inches. She's even shorter than I realized. We weave through another alley, Gustav—her bodyguard—leading the way. It feels silly having someone here to protect Lena when I'm sure I could handle anything that comes our way myself, but I'm no stranger to security detail. It's his job, so I won't argue. Besides, I'm not sure how far I'd be willing to stick my neck out for her, anyway. I doubt she'd do the same for me, unless it was to save her own butt, from what I've gathered.

"Where are we going again?" I finally ask.

Lena whips her head around, dark hair obscuring her smirking face as she nods toward a steepled church towering ahead. It feels out of place with all the new buildings crammed around all sides, but there's something comforting about it withstanding all the updates surrounding it, stained glass and all.

"To help make food," she says simply. "For people who are hungry. People who can't afford enough food."

She says it to me as though I couldn't possibly know what it's like. What she doesn't realize is that there were a few years my family could have benefited from a place like this. We always scraped by, but there were times I had to watch my parents go without. They never took handouts. Too proud. I can't say I agree with their logic, but we live and we learn, as they say.

"Gotta keep up appearances," I say, sizing up the brick building.

She scoffs, and I don't look at her when she flips around to scowl at me. Gustav reaches a metal door and props it open for us both as I file in silently behind her.

We weave down a dark hall, Lena guiding us like she's been here a million times. She's greeted with broad smiles from the staff members, and even calls a few by their first name. What's different about this place is that no one rushes her, no one asks for an autograph. Their smiles may be a little brighter when she looks their way, but for the most part, every person we encounter treats her as though she's any other human on the street.

When we make it to the kitchen, hairnets and gloves in hand, I realize she wasn't joking about making food. A nice lady with pink lipstick and flowery perfume takes us to a table buried in potatoes and hands us two peelers. I pull out a chair and sit, examining the sterile-looking room. For a church, it sure doesn't feel very inviting in here. Everything is white and wallpapered. Gray linoleum flooring runs from wall to wall. It's like someone lost all the crayons in the box except for the most boring colors. I'm no interior designer, but this place could benefit from some flowers or a different paint or *something*.

I turn back toward the mound of vegetables and realize Lena's watching me. "What?"

"You just look uncomfortable, that's all." She arches a

brow, whisking her peeler across a potato. "Feeling a little out of your element?"

If I didn't know better, I'd say that she's enjoying the thought of my discomfort. "Why? Are you in yours?"

She shrugs. "Kind of, I guess. I like this place. I try to go to every Christmas service here. Sometimes I rearrange my work schedule so I won't miss it."

"And when it isn't Christmas, you just sit in the kitchen and peel root vegetables?"

"Not always. Sometimes I go out to meet people, but a lot of times I just like to stay behind the scenes. Work with my hands instead." She holds up a half-peeled potato and wiggles it. "Get some dirt under my nails or whatever."

"Hard to do that with the gloves on."

A corner of her mouth lifts at my joke, and then she sighs. "It's probably weird I don't just stand out there and say hi. And not to toot my own horn, but it does make people really happy when I do meet and greets."

"Of course it does. You're Lena Lux."

She eyes me coyly. "But I think it's just as important that their food is made with love, ya know? And I feel like I can provide that. Maybe some people would think it's selfish not to just go out and let everyone have an autograph or whatever, but I like to think I'm helping just as much this way. I have more to offer than a pen on paper."

Her words burrow into me. She's right. We're so much more than our careers, than what people witness from the outside.

"So, this is your philanthropy?"

"My mom and Antonia only call it that because it sounds better. I just volunteer when I'm in town. We make donations to all kinds of places I never even get the chance to visit, but this place calls you to serve. To be active. So I try to make time."

I arch a brow, still shocked by all her—very unbratty—answers.

"Is it your first time in a soup kitchen?" she asks.

I hesitate, then nod.

She breathes out a laugh and continues to peel her potatoes.

My brows dive down my nose. "What? I do other stuff."

"Like what?" she asks, not looking up.

"Well, for one, I give money to the local animal shelter and other rescue centers." I scramble to compile my list of decencies, debating whether or not I should tell her about my dream of opening my own shelter. "And I tried to foster a pup once."

"Tried?"

A smile breaks across my face as I push a pile of discarded peels into the bin nearby. "I failed." Tugging off my gloves as carefully as possible, I whip out my phone and show her my lock screen. Princess gazes up at Lena with that mottled gray stare. "I never stood a chance."

Lena brightens, her eyes finding mine for a moment, and I realize just how blue they are. She's hardly looked at me today, and for a moment, we're smiling at each other, like she doesn't have some weird thing against me for the way we met or that she ruined my retirement plan, like peeling potatoes next to each other is as natural as her being on stage or me playing on a field.

Her enthusiasm gives me the bravery I'd been lacking.

"I'd never had a dog before. Saw a post online begging for someone to foster her because she was set to be euthanized. She was older, needed some expensive meds to keep her comfortable while she waited to die after her previous owners neglected her. Left her outside. Hardly fed her." I chuck my peeled potato into a bowl and grab a new one. "She's the reason I was hoping to invest in Gable's. Thought maybe it'd bring in some steady cash after my football retirement."

"To pay for her medication?"

"No. She doesn't need it anymore. She beat the odds." I smile and swallow a deep, steadying breath. "I want to open a shelter that specializes in end-of-life care for senior and sick dogs. Was also hoping to offer financial help to people who are willing to take in a dog with medical challenges. My pup had so much life left in her, and she wouldn't be here today if those people had given up on her."

Lena is quiet for a long moment, and when I finally look up, she's smiling at me.

When the silence crawls on, I clear my throat. "I know it probably sounds weird—"

"No. Not weird. I think it sounds amazing. Like you have a purpose. Not everyone finds that." She smiles again. "What's her name?"

"Princess."

She stifles a little giggle.

"And before you ask, yes, I did name her."

Lena bites down on her bottom lip like she's holding in another laugh.

"What? What's wrong with Princess?"

She shakes her head, and I nudge her with my elbow until she breaks. She laughs again. "Nothing! It's just... a feminine name. I figured you'd be the type to name her Tequila or Vista or Field Goal or something."

"Field Goal?" I can't help but laugh, too. "That's a terrible name."

"You seem like you'd go for something football related. Not *Princess*. I'm just surprised, that's all."

I smile to myself as we pile the peeled potatoes into a big silver bowl. "Glad to know I can still surprise people, I guess."

"Are you a creature of habit or something? All out of surprises? I find that hard to believe."

I eye her as I rotate my potato under the peeler. "Regardless of what you believe, I guess these days... yeah. I kind of am. Traveling takes it out of you—as I'm sure you know—so I guess I kinda just like stability at home as much as I can manage."

She nods emphatically. "You have to find stability where you can, it seems. I try to keep up with a routine, but recording this week has blown all that out of the water." She flicks her peeler, sending a strip of potato skin flying to the floor. "We added extra sessions because I wasn't happy with the way the new song was coming along."

"I thought you said you were rerecording?"

She eyes me. "A man who listens, who doesn't love that? Yeah, well, if I'm being honest, I don't think it needs an update. Maybe *that's* what's giving me the most trouble with it."

"Don't fix what ain't broken," I recite.

"Exactly." Her lips part into a wide smile before each

corner falls again. "But I have to listen to my label, and they want to freshen it up, so it's my job to come to a consensus with them." She groans and leans back into her seat. "I'm gonna be stuck in the studio forever."

I give her a sympathetic smile, but I'm so unfamiliar with her world, I can't offer any words to soothe her. Despite how grating she can be, I wish I could.

CHAPTER TWELVE

DECKER

GUSTAV DIRECTS me down a narrow hall, past plaques and framed metallic records flanking either side of us. This is the last place I expected to be after practice today, but when Jason called with new orders from Lena's team, I couldn't turn them down. Not if I'm really going to give this thing my all. I've been in recording studios before for team promos and whatnot, but seeing the names and faces lining the surrounding walls is intimidating—reminders that in this place, I'm out of my element. These musicians are legends, people who have changed lives with their lyrics alone. At the end of the hall is a door, and right beside it, I see a familiar face, although it's several years younger. Lena Lux's first platinum record gleams back at me, and just through this door, I'll get to see her again for real. Something in my stomach wobbles like pre-game nerves as Gustav pushes the door open to a dimly lit room. I hesitate, but when he lifts a meaty arm to show me in, I obey.

This place has a vibe to it. It's a whole mood on its own. My eyes adjust to the single lamp in the corner, throwing shadows across the space. In the low light, everything looks beige and gold and monochromatic. It's warm and pretty inviting, considering one half of the room looks like the inside of a computer. A window looking into another room lines one wall and casts just enough light for me to see the two smiling faces perched in white leather chairs in a corner near it. I smile back, wondering if they can even tell I'm looking at them. Gustav joins the two, leaving me to stand awkward and alone, debating if I should follow. Someone sneezes, and I jump. Straightening my shoulders, I recover quickly and turn toward the sound. A man sits in a swivel chair behind a board lit by pinpricks of colorful light, his hands skimming over it, adjusting the series of buttons and dials as he stares out the window. I follow his sightline to the other side of the glass until my gaze lands on a very serious Lena. I can't help but smile as she taps out a rhythm, nodding along in her clunky headphones, her brow furrowing and knitting with every beat. It's always refreshing watching people doing what they love. She lifts her hand and gives a signal, and the man on the board flicks something on. Music pours from speakers dotting each corner of the dimly lit room.

Lena closes her eyes, and when her lips part, the gentlest sound emits. First a murmur and then it swells into full-on lyrics. A tingle races over my skin and up my arms. I run my hands over my forearms, trying to swipe away the sensation, but the goosebumps stay put. I'm mesmerized. It's amazing to see her in such raw form, despite all the high-tech recording equipment. She's hitting every note. This girl is living, breathing autotune. To me, she sounds best this way. Forget the finished albums. All of the high-tech additives just bog everything down.

"She's good, isn't she?" someone whispers somewhere below my shoulder.

I whip around to find a little woman with slick, dark hair.

"I'm Blythe. Lena's manager." She extends a hand. "And mother."

I take it and am shocked at how firm her grip is. "It's nice to meet you."

"Did you think you'd meet the parents so soon?" She elbows me in the ribs like we're old pals as she sidles up beside me. I'm lost for a response and am grateful when she continues. "You know, this is her tenth take. She can be a bit of a perfectionist. I said we were good at eight, but she wanted to try again. And then again. The pressure from her label must be starting to get to her." She shakes her head, pressing her fingers to her lips as she stares through the window ahead.

"She's very talented," I finally say.

Her mother nods and watches her daughter through the glass.

As the song begins to dwindle and the final instrumental comes back in, Lena opens her eyes, lifting them to the window, searching through the glass. What she's looking for, I'm not sure. Approval most likely, if there's anything I've picked up about her. My stomach does that pre-game wobble again as I consider that maybe it isn't a *what* but a *who*. Is she looking for me?

I get my answer when her eyes finally land on me and go shockingly wide before narrowing. She mouths something at me and pulls off her headphones, stepping out of the booth just as the song completely fades. Briefly, she disappears out of her room's exit before reappearing through some seemingly hidden door in the room I'm in.

"Look who's here," her mom simpers, gesturing to me like I'm some game show prize.

I lift my hand to wave, but Lena grabs it and shoots it down.

"Yeah, I see," is all she says as she yanks me to the edge of the room like moving ten feet away will award us more privacy.

I shake free once her mom's eyes stop tracking us. "Nice to see you, too."

"What are you doing here?" she whispers.

"Watching you record, I guess."

"You guess?" She crosses her arms. "When I told you I'd be stuck here all week, I didn't think you'd *stalk* me."

A laugh bubbles awkwardly out of my mouth. "*Stalking?* You should be so lucky."

She glares up at me.

"I got an invite. How else do you think I got the address? Someone named Antonia contacted my manager, and—*bam*—here I am."

"Ugh. Of course she did. Apparently, this information wasn't *pertinent* to tell me." She brushes a loose hair from her big eyes, checking our surroundings.

When the guy sitting behind the window glances our way, she grabs my hand, a wide smile finding her lips like he just flipped some switch for it on his board. Her skin is soft and warm in my palms, but her grip is rough. Cold. Squeezing. *Ow.* For such a little person, she feels like she could do some damage. I shake one hand free and boop her on the nose with a finger. Her smile doesn't falter, but her eyes turn murderous before averting toward the board guy again, who is no longer looking at us.

She shakes her hand free and immediately flicks me in the chest. She's fuming, but when she speaks, I know it isn't entirely my fault. "They know I never invite my boyfriends to the studio. Not even the real ones."

"I'm sorry, I thought you knew." After yesterday, I figured she'd maybe even want me here. I shove my hands into my pockets to keep from fidgeting. "I didn't mean to intrude. *Stalk you.* Whatever you want to call it." I offer her a smile, but I wish I could hide somewhere or teleport to my car and drive home. Or maybe curl up and die or something. "Plus, aren't you the one who was less than thrilled to be *stuck here?* I thought maybe I'd bust you out. At least for a little bit."

At that, I swear Miss I-Hate-Decker perks up.

"Well, I guess," she lifts her wrist and checks her chunky gold watch, "I'm due for a break anyway. Are you hungry?"

"I'm always hungry."

She smiles up at me, and this time, it seems more genuine—more relaxed—than any of hers I've seen. "Good."

CHAPTER THIRTEEN

LENA

DECKER'S CAR isn't as flashy as I anticipated. Sure, the little silver coupe exudes luxury, but it's an older model. Most guys I know make a million, go out and buy the fanciest one on the lot, and still trade them every year for the newest model. Or hire a car service. Maybe Decker doesn't make as much as I thought he did, or maybe he's just more financially responsible. I glance at him from the corner of my eye, his angular jaw ticking as he scans the intersection before crossing through the fresh green light. I don't realize I'm still staring until he stops at another red light.

"What?" he asks.

"I thought you had a bug on you or something." I flick my gaze out the window, but not before I catch his smug expression. Another car pulls up beside us, and I recline in my leather seat, grateful he at least paid for the upgraded window tint to block out any prying eyes. Half the people in this city don't care about running into a celebrity. With so many living here, it's a regular occurrence. The other half, however, will eat up any tiny morsel of gossip they can sell or use to go viral. It's hard to know which one you'll meet, so I've found it's better to avoid interactions if you can.

"Not wanting to meet any fans today?" he asks.

"Not if I don't have to."

He scoffs.

"What?" I ask, adjusting my chair back to an upright position. "Have you met some people in this city?"

"Just a few."

"Then you already know how brutal they can be."

"Oh, I do." He sighs as the traffic light turns and we accelerate forward. "At least from behind their keyboards."

This piques my interest, and I can't help but to pry. I want to hear his take on the swirling rumors. "Oh, do you? I'm all ears."

He glances over at me and rakes a hand through his dark hair. "I'm surprised you haven't heard."

I shrug, not willing to give up the fact that I've *definitely* heard. "I don't pay much attention to online gossip."

"Smart. I wish I had that self-control." He smiles at me, and I can't help but smile back.

"Oh, it gets pretty easy when half the things you read about yourself are lies."

"Tell me about it. I should probably consider myself lucky for it to have taken so long, but I guess I didn't realize how many superfans Ada Lane has. She's only been in like three movies."

"So you played Ada Lane?"

"I didn't *play* her. We just weren't compatible."

I hoot a laugh, my hand flying over my lips to stifle it.

"And she got her feelings hurt, and..." He trails off when he sees my hand is still pressed to my lips. "Are you laughing at me?"

I shake my head. "No, no. I just... It's funny when the player finally gets played."

His eyes harden, fingers squeezing the steering wheel. "I'm not a player."

"I may not always read the tabloids, but what kind of girl would I be if I didn't do a little research on my boyfriend?" I spin to face him, my seat belt cutting into my collarbone. "I assume you've heard what everyone's saying. So, did you really stand Ada up and then ghost her?"

He scowls at me. "What happened to the whole 'tabloids tell lies' thing?"

"You're avoiding my question. Did you or did you not?"

"I screwed up the time."

"Uh-huh. If that's true, then why not reschedule?" My eyes narrow. "Did you ghost her?"

"It's kind of a long story."

"I have time. I'm on break."

He sighs. "I forgot we agreed to meet up and went to my buddy's birthday thing instead, and there was this bottle waitress—"

"You stood up your date to hook up with someone else?" My jaw nearly hits the floor mats.

"No. Nothing like that. There were some photos taken that didn't look good. That's it. Never saw the waitress—or Ada—again. She sent me a few fuming texts I didn't know how to respond to, so I didn't. And that was that."

"That's it?" I ask, waiting for the final blow.

"That's it."

"Wow. I was hoping for something a little more exciting. If you're going to get dragged across the internet, you might as well make it count." I eye him up and down before turning to face the dashboard again, ignoring the sympathy that's sprung up. "You have a stain on your shirt, by the way."

There's a long silence as his eyes dip to his chest, then rise again. Only the GPS squawks at him to take a turn in a few hundred feet.

Finally, he asks, "Has anyone ever told you that you're kind of mean?"

"Has anyone told you that maybe you're too sensitive?"

He rolls his eyes as he pulls into a parking spot. "Stay here, I already ordered."

"Ordered? How do you even know what I like?"

"Be right back." He presses the lock button on the door and bolts from the car and into some little deli I've never even heard of.

For a split second, I wonder if what I said to him was too harsh. However, if there's one thing I know, it's that men who aren't gentle with women's emotions don't deserve gentle treatment. If the big oaf can't handle getting a little crap, then maybe he shouldn't be dishing it out.

CHAPTER FOURTEEN

DECKER

"MR. DECKER! Your order's here. Two sandwiches today, huh?" Niko yells from behind the counter, craning his thick neck in an attempt to look out the glass front door. "Got someone special waitin' for ya? Who is it today?"

I ignore the insinuation and grab the two paper bags from his hands. "Nah, one's for Princess."

"Which princess, huh?"

"You know which one."

"Surely you don't mean a *pop* princess." An ornery smile unfurls below his bushy mustache.

My jaw goes slack, but I quickly recover. "Niko, you know you can't believe everything the internet says. Half of it's lies. Take it from me."

He laughs as he rips down some little papers hanging behind the counter. "Sure, sure. You just never know with you, huh, boss?"

Shaking my head, I can't help but smile at his antics. I've been coming here for years. He practically has my order memorized. It's not a restaurant I see Lena liking, but I had a craving today. Beyond that, I kind of want to see how Miss Pop Princess reacts to a couple of greasy deli sandwiches. I don't know why I'm denying this very real, not-real relationship right now. That was the whole point. It was our agreement. Pull this thing off, get everyone to believe that it's the real deal. It's one thing to fool strangers online or for five seconds at a restaurant, it's a totally different thing to lie about it to someone's face that I've known for years.

I throw a chunk of cash in his tip jar—extra today, mostly to make myself feel better about the lies, but he deserves a bonus anyway. Maybe he'll use it to finally spruce this place up. "The only Princess for me has four legs, you know that."

"That I do, boss! That I do!" He waves as I back out the glass door, the little bell ringing overhead as I exit.

Lena jumps when I throw my car door open, her phone dropping into her lap.

"Geez, give a girl a warning," she says, adjusting her seatbelt.

"The warning was when I left and said *be right back.*"

No wonder Gustav follows her everywhere. This girl has gotten so used to it, she's almost forgotten she's sitting in a strange vehicle in a not-so-great part of town. I'm surprised he let her go along with me so easily.

I plop the bags in her lap and buckle up. "We're eating at my place."

"Better than the car, I guess." She leans forward, nodding toward Niko's Deli as I throw the car into reverse. "Or in there."

"It's not so bad."

She stares at me incredulously. "One of the windows is duct taped."

I follow her sightline and realize she isn't wrong, but that doesn't compromise the quality of Niko's food. Everything I've ever had there is worth the drive, the duct tape, the extra layer of dust coating the fake grapes hanging from the ceiling of the waiting area. Not even the grease-coated floor could deter me after what I've tasted.

"If I weren't starving, we'd be going somewhere else." She huffs and sits back, checking her watch. It's endearing that she's holding her phone, yet for some reason, she still refers to her watch. "Plus, I need to get back soon."

I nod. "Work waits for no one."

A knock on the passenger window nearly sends Lena scrambling over the center console. I press the lock button just as some wild-haired and wilder-eyed woman reaches for the handle, crying and begging for a photo with Lena. A few others join in the frenzy at the mention of Lena's name, and soon there are people tugging at both our doors. Lena gasps, squeezing my hand until reality slugs me across the face. My pulse ratchets up like I'm in the middle of a big game. Without another thought, I throw the car into reverse. The growing horde chases us across the parking lot until I peel onto the main road and weave back into traffic.

"You should get your money back for that window tint," Lena quips, letting out an unsteady breath.

From my peripheral, I can't help but notice how her eyes dart from the passenger mirror to the rearview. She may be making jokes, but it's clear she's shaken. Case in point, her hand is still firmly locked around mine, fingers cinched tighter than a jockstrap. A small part of me wants to make some snide remark just like I know she would, but instead, I stay completely silent. I don't draw attention to her iron grip. I don't let go, no matter how numb my fingers may be. I let her hold on, not just because it's the anchor I know she needs, but because I think I need it too.

Guilt slices through the unexpected warmth budding in my chest as I consider all of the other—much worse—scenarios. Seeing her this way now—frightened, vulnerable, her composure shattered—it makes my stomach churn. I did this to her. The seemingly unflappable Lena Lux has been thoroughly rocked, and it's my fault. As I speed down the road, not sure where I'm going, I know one thing for certain. I never want to see her this way again.

"I'm sorry. I shouldn't have left you alone," I say.

"I was fine when I was alone. It's when you showed up that everything took a nosedive." Lena turns to face me at the exact moment she must realize she's still holding my hand. Jerking free, she busies herself with smoothing her dark hair. "Can't wait to see how everyone spins that little fiasco online. I wonder if they'll solely focus on the fact that I ignored my fans or that I was with a new guy."

I flex my hand to regain the feeling in it and turn toward Lena. Her empty stare pierces the windshield.

I clutch the steering wheel tighter. "Are you okay?"

Another breath quivers from her lips. "I shouldn't have told Gustav to hang back. People like the ones we just saw are literally the reason I hired him."

"So why didn't you bring him?"

She sighs, her facade of composure restoring itself one

snarky word at a time. "Because it's awkward enough spending time with you one-on-one, but it's painful when there's a third wheel."

"Painful? Ouch."

Her lips twitch into a smile. "Thanks, though."

"For what?"

"For getting us out of there. I froze up."

I don't admit to her that for a split second, I did too. "What kind of boyfriend would I be if I didn't protect my woman?"

Lena rolls her eyes.

Flipping on the blinker, I careen into the turning lane.

"This isn't the way to the studio," she says.

"We're still doing lunch at my place." I glance over at her, hoping for some kind of response, but her lips are pressed into a tight line. "If that's okay. I can take you back. I understand if you're too—"

"I'm not ready to go back yet."

I nod and accelerate back toward where we came from, watching out the windshield as the buildings slowly go from endearing—albeit a bit rusted and chipped—to stiff and modern. Bleak. No personality. I sigh as we turn onto my street and head toward my building. It's the tallest one on the block. Sleek. Industrial. Cold. Nothing like the cozy little house I grew up in. It may have been falling apart half the time, but it was home.

The year I signed with the Kings, this building was brand new, the best in the city, and I bought a condo right then and there. I was twenty-two, a fifth-round draft pick, and eager to start my career and spend whatever was nego-tiated in my rookie contract. That was when I realized I'd finally made it. The years I'd invested my all and let my parents pour whatever time and little money they had into my dreams had finally paid off. They did it for Ian, and then they did it for me.

This building was proof of my success beyond the jersey and the paychecks. But the longer I live in this place, the more I realize how different I am from who I was when I chose it. Every day I'm here, I crave something simpler more and more. Somewhere with a yard to mow, for Princess to spend her golden years in. For now, it just makes more sense for me to be in the city, close to where practice is. Where the stadium is. Where my life is.

I peek at Lena from the corner of my eye. That's one thing we have in common, I guess. Both of us are on the road for work quite a bit, at least part of the year. I wonder if she gets tired of it the same way I do. Although, I'm grateful my travel stints are typically only a few days. Up until my injury last year, I loved it. Now, I'm not so sure.

I clear my throat. "So, where do you call home?"

"Like the city or what?"

"Wherever you consider home."

She thinks for a moment. "Well, I'm from Florida. And I love Florida. My dad's still there. So I guess that's home. But work is mostly here, so I spend the majority of my time in Vista."

"Why doesn't he come to Vista City?"

"He visits sometimes, but won't move here. It's kind of a long story." She's quiet as I pull into my building's private parking garage and find my spot. Then she sighs. "He thinks I work too much. My mom disagrees. They don't like being around each other much anymore, so he stays in

Florida, and we stay here. Or there. Or wherever my next show is. You get it."

"So, are they divorced?"

She shakes her head. "Probably should be, but no. Not yet."

"Do you think you work too much?" I ask.

"Not really. It's work. It's a lot of dedication, but I love music. And if you love what you do, it's not really work, right?" A faint smile finds her lips as her eyes meet mine. "At least that's what they say."

"But what do *they* know? *They* all think we're dating." I smirk, pop open my door, and round the car to open hers like the gentleman I am. At least when I have a girlfriend— even if it's pretend.

"We *are* dating." She latches onto the bag in her lap and wiggles out of the car. A finger pushes into my chest. "And don't you forget it."

I laugh, shutting the door behind her before guiding her out of the garage. "Kind of hard to forget when everyone has already started whispering about it. Even the deli guy was gettin' in on the gossip."

"Really?"

"Oh yeah, he was way more into this than any of the other rumors."

She's quiet for a long moment as we hop into the elevator. "Well, now I definitely need to know what these rumors are. I should know *something* about my boyfriend."

"You know a few things."

"Like what?"

I shrug. "I don't know. You tell me."

She turns to face me, leaning back into the mirrored

wall of the elevator. In this reflective box, there's a hundred of her, and it strikes me just how beautiful she is. Not a single bad angle.

She presses her lips into a tight line, squinting at me like I have the answers written on my face somewhere. "Your older brother plays for the Kentucky Miners"

It's cute how pleased she looks with herself. The elevator dings and I step out to guide her in the right direction. "Okay, so you know something about Ian Trace. What about *Decker* Trace?"

"I know he speaks about himself in the third person." She makes a gagging sound before dissolving into giggles. "What do you know about me? Huh? Time to put you on the spot."

"I know you like sour gummy worms." We approach my door, the welcoming echo of Princess's nails clicking against that hardwood floor on the other side. "Probably *too* much."

I unlock the door and crack it, then turn to face Lena whose mouth is hanging open, her dark brows angled sharply down her nose. She looks like she wants to fight me, but as soon as she hears Princess whining on the other side, her face relaxes, her demeanor shifts, and her pretty blue eyes shine up at me. Then she's shoving me out of the way and falling to her knees in my doorway.

CHAPTER FIFTEEN

LENA

"HOW DID I forget about *Princess?!* What a sweet baby." I can hear how shrill my voice is, though it's hard over the panting and slobbering of the pooch in my lap. "She's so much squishier in person!"

"Baby? She's eleven. She's a grown woman. Pay her some respect."

I shoot daggers at him over my shoulder before turning back to Princess. "Don't listen to him. You are a beautiful young lady."

This earns me a sloppy kiss right over my mouth and Princess a scolding from Decker. I can't help myself. I pull out my phone and snap a quick photo of her squishy little pitbull face. As she stares up at me, I stroke her velvety head, my nerves finally fully regulating from our run-in with the pushy fans earlier. There's something so therapeutic about loving on a dog. If I ever have a chance to stay put somewhere longer than a few weeks, I'd love to have one of my own.

Decker extends a hand to me, his eyes warm as they catch on mine. I grip his hand and push to my feet. Suddenly, I'm closer to him than I've ever been, and the gravity of it all hits me full force. I'm alone for the first time with my new fake boyfriend. I take a step back, just far enough that I haven't lost sight of his deep green eyes, but enough space that the heady scent of his cologne has some room to aerate. Surveying my surroundings, I realize how clean the place is. Most of the guys I know struggle to keep anything straightened up on the home front. I wonder if he has a maid. He's handsome, clean, *and* has a sweet pup? Before Callum, I would have been all over a guy like this. If he weren't a pro athlete. And if Callum hadn't ruined men for me forever.

"What?" Decker asks.

"Nothing. This place is just like... super clean."

"Are you surprised?"

"Kinda. You have a maid, right?"

He shakes his head and walks toward his expansive kitchen, Princess clipping his heels. Everything is stainless steel and creamy marbled surfaces. Dropping the bags of food on the counter, he says, "Nah. Why would I pay someone for something I can do myself?"

I raise my brows, a little surprised by his answer. *Why? Because you can afford to*, is what I want to say, but I don't. It's none of my business. As long as he doesn't treat me as his maid, who cares?

"Doggy daycare is all the hired help I have, with the exception of my days off. I'm not here long enough to make a mess usually." Reaching into a bag, he pulls out two hoagie-shaped wads of paper and drops one in front of me.

"Besides, Miss Princess here is the messy one. It took me almost an entire year to teach her to put her toys away."

"You *taught* her to put her toys away?"

He takes a huge bite out of his sandwich and nods. "She's a smart girl."

I reach down from the stool I'm perched on and pat her blocky, gray head.

Decker picks off a piece of ham and tosses it to Princess before standing and leading her toward the door. She bounces and barks as he hooks a leash to her pink collar. "So the real reason we're eating here is because Miss Princess needs a potty break. Wanna join?"

"Miss Princess." I smirk and check my watch. "I don't have long, so I think I'll stay and eat."

He nods, guiding Princess out, and locking the door behind him with a click. Gotta love a guy who protects his home.

And his woman.

I take a huge bite of my sandwich, stuffing the sentiment down along with the urge to roll my eyes. I am not *his woman*. I'm disappointed that I'd even let the thought cross my mind. Even for a split, sarcastic second. I take another bite. I have to admit, this sandwich is good. Like *really* good. When I'm sure they're both gone, my curiosity gets the better of me. I grab my hoagie and set off to peruse my new surroundings.

I traipse across the dark hardwood floor, my footfalls echoing with each step. The place is nice, though it could benefit from some warmth. Everything is cool shades of gray and black, glass and metal, and concrete. Even the floor is stained so dark it might as well be modeled after a blackhole. It's not that I don't like the industrial feel, it just isn't my first choice. If we were actually dating, I'd have an interior designer in here in no time with some curtains and paint, and some velvet throw pillows at the very least. Continuing down the hall, I finish off the last few bites of half my sandwich.

It was never my intention to snoop, but when I find his bedroom, I can't help but peek inside. And then I'm at his window, peering out into the courtyard, straight down at him playing with Princess. I never imagined someone who seems to treat their dates so coldly could be so warm to an animal. I have to admit, it's a little bit endearing. He pats down her sides, which sends her into a spiraling frenzy. She barks at him, jumping at his face as though she can reach it. Even from here, I can see his eyes crinkle as he sinks to the ground beside her, raining kisses all over her head. Then he stands and faces his window. I duck behind the wall, dropping to the ground to crawl from the room. I don't know if he was looking up here, but if he was, I won't be caught spying. That's the last embarrassing thing I need right now.

His bed is made, his comforter a frosty white. I wander over the thick black and gray rug to his closet. As I pop open the door, I'm immediately met with a scent that is just so... Decker. It's like he's standing here with me right now. Whatever cologne he uses, it's *good*. Woodsy and bright and masculine. I back out of the closet and click the door shut, moving on to my next mission: find said cologne. A girl has to know what cologne her boyfriend wears, right? Even if it is all a lie.

His bathroom is attached to the master bedroom, and

when I enter the room, it's in a state of disarray. Dirty clothes litter the floor, towels are hung over knobs and shower rods. Now *this* is what I was expecting from his entire place. It's nice to see he isn't some weird male drone at least.

Decker is human, after all. Look! He's dirty too!

I pop open the mirror. Behind it is a little cavern housing bottles, lotions, and cotton swabs. I pick up a cologne bottle, one of many, and read. It says something about the vetiver on it, and I give it a sniff. The title is etched green glass with gold details, and it looks expensive, but smells even more so.

I move on to the drawers—I've never been able to help myself when left alone. Besides, I need to know what I'm working with here. If there're any concerns I should have, I need to know now. Those concerns come in the form of a junk drawer, but not just any kind of junk. It's all pink and gold and shiny and looks distinctly *female*. Upon closer inspection, I find used lashes and lip glosses, concealers and powders, all of which are different shades of God's brightest rainbow. Little gold earrings and silver bracelets rattle around in the bottom. These things belong to women. Yes, wo*men*. Plural. He's made a lost and found for all of his... companions.

It might as well be a time vortex because suddenly I'm pulled back to the moment I realized my ex was being unfaithful. One crystal-encrusted earring that I'd never wear, floating aimlessly in a kitchen drawer. For some reason, I believed him when he said his maid had lost hers, and I allowed him to gaslight me for another few months. Never again. If I could go back in time and smack myself—

and him—I would. This drawer is just the reminder I need.

When the front door shuts down the hall, I slam the drawer closed and race back to the rest of my waiting meal. It doesn't matter how sweet a guy is with his dog, he's still a guy. And if there's one thing I've learned lately, it's that no matter how sweet someone seems, they can still turn around and slap you in the face. Every man has a drawer of secrets in some capacity. They're all hiding something. Decker and Callum are one and the same. They're guys who love the attention of women. I can't blame them, but I refuse to be the next conquest—for real, at least.

"Lena?" Decker calls.

"I was, uh... using the bathroom!"

He unhooks Princess's collar, his brow knitting when I finally waltz up to the expansive island. "You know there's a half bath right off the kitchen."

"No, but I do now." I offer a smile and jump back on the barstool to finish my sandwich.

He eyes me suspiciously as I sink my teeth into the other half of my sub. It's even better than I remember it being five minutes ago, but despite the delicious distraction, I can't keep my mind off of the drawer. Who does that? Who collects that crap like some kind of serial killer? I wonder how many more habits he has like that, habits that could embarrass me publicly, could make me look even more like a fool than my little music hall encounter with Callum did. Habits that could destroy my already threadbare reputation. All this tells me is he's way too wrapped up in his past for anything meaningful. Which means he's probably the type to string girls along. What a dog. Princess strolls over and licks my leg. No offense to her, of course.

Decker leans over the island, unwraps his sandwich, and takes a bite so big herbed oil dribbles down his chin. An awkward silence rises between us as I watch him stare down at his food, his jaw clenching and unclenching with each chew. Nothing but the sound of mastication and Princess's clicking claws fill the space. As much as I don't want to talk to him, I need to get back to the studio soon, and if I don't build some kind of rapport with this monstrosity, I can pretty much kiss my cover-up goodbye.

All it takes is a few weeks, Lena. Maybe a couple of months at the most. Play nice. Save face. Keep everyone happy and move on.

Swallowing my bite, I clear my throat. "So."

His green eyes meet mine from behind his sandwich. I can't help but feel like he's nervous for some reason.

I forge on. "What do you like to do for fun?"

"Besides practice?" A gusty laugh bursts from his lips. "I'm kidding. Karaoke."

I freeze mid-bite. "Karaoke?"

"Yeah. Me and the guys go to The Malted Mule every Thursday."

"Every week?"

"Well, we try to. We can't always make it, obviously, but in the offseason, we do. And if we don't have a Thursday game during season, we go." He grabs a napkin and finally wipes the oil from his chin with pink cheeks. "Those usually suck though cause we don't drink much during season."

"Sober karaoke?" I stifle a laugh.

He lifts a shoulder, taking another bite.

"Yikes." The laugh I'd been holding in finally explodes from my lips, and I try to rein it in. "That's not what I was expecting."

He runs a hand down the back of his neck, his rock-solid shell of confidence starting to crack. "It started when Aleki's girlfriend was a waitress there. Before they were dating."

"Aleki?"

He arches a brow. "My buddy. Maleko Aleki. He's on our O-line."

"Sorry, not a big football girl here, despite whatever my mom led your manager to believe."

He frowns at me. "So you just let them say anything they want about you?"

I grab a napkin and subtly dab my own chin. "I've learned to let it ride. Everything's easier for me if I just let them take the wheel."

He snorts.

"What else am I supposed to do? Go out at all hours of the night doing karaoke?"

"Better than getting bossed around by a bunch of people who are using you."

I drop my sandwich, unsure of how to respond. Sure, my mother benefits from my job—I'm the reason hers exists —and yeah, I'm paying Antonia a hefty sum to keep my career and appearance afloat. But all of it's worth it. I've gotten what I've always wanted. Writing my own music and performing has been my dream ever since I picked up my first guitar, and if the articles and sold-out shows are any consolation, I only stand to gain more popularity.

Whatever they're doing—what *I'm* doing—is working. Who is he to say otherwise?

"Better than keeping a weird drawer of secrets in my bathroom," I counter.

His eyes go wide, his jaw dropping. "Using the bathroom... Snooping in the bathroom... Synonymous, apparently."

"I should know something about my new *boyfriend*," I mutter, rolling my eyes.

"Then ask," he says firmly.

My buzzing phone cuts through the tension, and I check my watch. I already know who's calling, and I don't think I'm going to like the conversation. Expletives fly from my mouth as I answer. Sure enough, it's my mother, matching my colorful language with a spectrum of her own.

"Let me guess, they're summoning you back," Decker says when I end the call and drop my phone to the counter.

"Part of being successful."

He shakes his head, not dignifying my less-than-clever jab with a remark. Decker Trace knows a thing or two about success, and as he leads me out of his opulent condo and down the hall, back to his car, it's hard to stand here and deny it.

CHAPTER SIXTEEN

LENA

I JUST WANT one day without Decker. Is that too much to ask?

Mixing some self-tanner into my vanilla lemon lotion, I pray it'll overpower the unpleasant scent of the fake tan. I've been slacking on my self-care lately, which means I haven't made time for my typical bronzing spray. As I wait for it to dry, I text Joss—my best friend since forever and the only person who has a knack for keeping me calm in situations like this—for the fiftieth time today, desperate to tell her about what my mom and Antonia have tasked me with. Even if I can't let her in on the full secret, according to my contract. I stare at my screen, hoping she'll finally respond. She's notorious for opening texts and never replying. After text number fifty-one—okay, maybe that's an exaggeration—it becomes clear I won't be hearing from her anytime soon. Sighing, I drop my phone to the counter.

Folk music drifts from a bluetooth speaker nearby as I

hum along and dig through my makeup kit, my fingers already caked in the shimmery residue that coats everything inside this pink bag. Despite the fact that my Vista City home has ample space and a smattering of full vanities spread throughout the three floors—just a few of the reasons it's one of my favorite properties—I still find myself crawling onto my bathroom counter and into my sink to get ready. It's a habit I formed when I started wearing makeup in middle school, and I can't bring myself to break it. Something about it is comforting. These days, it's refreshing to be granted a little time to myself, even if it isn't long. I revel in the moments I can step away from everyone and be alone, but now that I have Decker, those are practically nonexistent.

An ethereal song echoes through the marble-tiled room. It's haunting, beautiful, the type of song I wish I'd written. I itch to step up a third and harmonize—something I rarely get to do as a solo act. Giving in to the urge, I let my hum swell into something more. Singing centers me enough to flawlessly apply my eyeliner on the first try. I release my bangs from their Velcro roller, still miffed by the bleached chunks that flank my fringe. I wonder what my mom would say if I showed up at our next meeting with pink ones instead, or if I went absolutely feral and cut them out. A twisted satisfaction unfurls at the thought. My aesthetic is something that's been fine-tuned throughout the years. However, as much as I'd love to watch her lose her mind, bringing any attention to myself outside of my fake relationship is the last thing I need.

When the playlist ends, I reach for my phone just as a notification rolls onto my screen. I deflate when I see Joss is still MIA. It's an email alert. Something new from Antonia. My eyes roll out of my head when I open it. It's an outline of ideas for my "candid" photo shoot today. Something she cooked up to help Decker and I "soft launch" our relationship and to ensure we have plenty of coupley photos once we go full-public with this stunt. A bitter laugh bursts from my lips. This is the farthest thing from candid. This much meddling makes everything I do feel so counterfeit. Sometimes it feels almost *yucky* how contrived half my life is. And yet, people believe it. And I benefit from it. When Antonia gives me the go-ahead, and I scatter all these meticulous breadcrumbs across social media, I know my followers will gobble them up. I know Antonia's plan will work—they always seem to be foolproof—and I know everyone online and in the media outlets will collect these bite-sized nuggets of information and speculate until I fully launch—aka: "hard launch"—my *fauxmance* with Decker. It's all so perfect. Too perfect.

A second later, I get a text from my mom. In true Blythe Lukowski fashion, she's stepping into Antonia territory with a few photo suggestions of her own to inspire Decker and me. Three dots appear, and then her text pops onto my screen.

MOMAGER

Remember, the goal of today's post is to merely get people talking. Don't give away that it's Decker just yet. No face, no jersey, nothing too specific to him. Antonia says we need to drive up speculation until you're trending online. I had a few things in mind. Standby.

As if Antonia needs any help doing her job, screen-shots of other people's couples' photos populate our text exchange one after the other, and I quickly mute our chat. What happened to the whole "this is why we have employees" thing?

I glance at the time. Decker should be here any minute. Something deep inside me flips. Whether it's my heart or guts, or nerves, I'm not sure. I feel so completely out of touch with myself lately, but the thought of Decker —despite how insufferable he can be—does something to me. Leaning over the sink, I check the blend of my blush and wipe a smudge of berry lip gloss from the edge of my mouth. Then I check my teeth. I tell myself it's definitely because I'll have a camera in my face soon and definitely not because Decker will be in my house in a few short minutes. If I have to pretend with someone, at least he isn't bad looking. In fact, he's pretty cute, if you're into that giant, beefy kind of thing. Despite having a relatively attractive partner for this whole ruse, after my breakup with Callum, I wish I didn't have to pretend at all. I wish I were far, far away from anything to do with falling in love —even if it's the pretend kind.

A spore of hope sprouts on my moldy, out-of-commission heart. What if everyone has already forgotten about the whole King's Music Hall thing? What if I no longer have to pretend that Decker Trace has—*barf*—captured my heart? To see if my wishful thinking is more than a simple fantasy, I do some online searching. First, I enter Allister King's Music Hall. All I find are articles about "rebuilding the historic dressing rooms," and not far below is every single article Antonia read to me last week in my mom's office.

My fingers type at their own accord, and I check on Gable's Restaurant and Lounge. In the photos, its back wall is still in shambles, but luckily, the owner was cleared of the insurance fraud he'd been accused of when the place he'd been trying to sell for months went up in flames. I click the screen off before I can read any more. I never meant for someone to get accused of a felony, but I also never thought throwing a drink—okay, a bottle—at someone would spark such a dramatic fire. And while I'm on the subject of improbabilities, I never expected Callum to be unfaithful to me either. When I showed up in his dressing room that night, ready to forgive him, I was convinced he'd take me back. Instead, Callum laughed and doubled down on the sentiment that we were never a good match. As if his words didn't sting enough, he said he worried for my sanity that I still hadn't come to terms with it.

An overwhelming weight presses down on me as that night replays in my head. The next thing I type is not something I'm proud of. I wish I were a stronger person. If I were, maybe Callum Porter's most recent comings and goings wouldn't be filling my search screen. My stomach sinks as I scroll through. Instead of whisperings of our "reconnection" and our "hot night at Kings"—though those articles are present—what I see is speculation. Speculation about some girl he's been seen out with. A girl who remains nameless. Only a picture of him sitting across from some blonde, gazing into her eyes—a blonde who has her back to the camera, of course—in a way that makes my chest feel like someone has taken an ice pick to it. I instantly miss the way he used to look at me. The ice pick lodges deeper. Is this her? Is this the girl he left me for? The one he cheated on me with?

A burning fury overcomes me, and before I can think twice, I'm logged into Instagram, uploading a photo, and clicking post. If Callum was working on a soft launch of his newest conquest, then I'll soft launch harder. Thirty seconds later, large, mottled gray eyes stare back at me. Princess is incredibly photogenic. Within seconds, comments start flooding the photo.

They all say the same thing. Heart emojis, dog emojis, a few words here and there about how cute she is, and then I find the one that sparks the kind of speculation I was hoping for, the kind of theories Antonia and my mom were wanting to garner from my photo shoot today. But I've taken matters into my own hands and expedited the process. Everyone online is speculating about my ex, why not me too? It's my turn to show that I've moved on. Kind of.

I chew my lip, scrolling through the comment section as people reply to one another.

LuxLuver365: So cute!! You got a dog?!

SadGirl_247: Call me a weirdo, but as soon as I heard Decker Trace and Lena might be a thing I started following him on here too. This is def his dog.

LenaLux4Lyfe: I second this. I only follow Decker because of the rumors. Can confirm it's his pup, she's the only thing he posts about. Her name is Princess.

LuxLuver365: LENA, ARE YOU TELLING US WHAT I THINK YOU'RE TELLING US??? EEEE!!! I'M LITERALLY DYING OVER HERE!

Listenin2Lena: Lena deserves the kind of man who has a soft spot for animals. And the dog is SOOO CUTE too!

LenaLux4Lyfe: She's cute but have you seen HIM?!

The rest of the conversation is a series of drooling and heart eye emojis.

Like clockwork, my phone explodes with messages and calls. Antonia, followed by my mother. I honestly thought it'd take them longer, but with my social media on their minds today, I should have expected this. I should have known they were scouring my grid to see how to change it up with my next phase of life—my fake dating phase. I'm honestly still shocked they let me manage my own accounts. After this though, who knows. I silence my phone, brush my teeth, and try to pretend like my mom isn't going to murder me later.

Ten minutes later, there's a knock at my door followed

by another phone notification from my doorbell camera. Decker's here. Flying through the house and down the stairs, I try to check my surroundings. Is there anything embarrassing I forgot to put away? Though I love this place, it's not where I spend the majority of my time typically. When I'm in town, I'm at the studio or doing a show or whatever other engagement that's been planned for me. Nothing is out of place in this house. It hardly even looks lived in. The brief moment of relief is soon batted away by a lurch in the pit of my stomach as I throw open the front door, but I'm not met with Decker's insanely green eyes. Instead, it's those gray ones I posted to my feed a few moments ago.

Decker gestures to his phone screen. "What's this?"

I squint at it as though it isn't obvious. "Whoa, wait. Are you following me? Stalk much."

He steps around me, tucking his phone into his pocket and rolling his eyes as I shut the door. "You don't follow me?"

"I don't wanna damage your ego, but no. I didn't know if we were ready for that kind of commitment."

Decker kicks off his shoes, checking out the space as he crosses to my sofa and plops down. "You don't follow your *boyfriend* on Insta? Shame."

He looks so out of place splayed across my lilac couch, a testament to his position in my life. I shake my head. "I was waiting. You know my followers would check to see if we follow each other, and if we did, that would pretty much seal the deal on our relationship."

"And posting Princess doesn't?"

"That was kind of the point."

He stares at me for a long moment, pulling a lip into his mouth as he mulls it over. "Okay, so you made your move, now what's mine?"

Something inside me lifts. "I guess we move forward with these dumb candids, and you can have the honor of posting our first selfie after the game this weekend."

"The kickoff game?" His brow knits. "Why?"

"I figured Antonia had at least contacted Jason." Shoving a beaded throw pillow out of the way, I ease onto the other end of the couch and face him. "I'm going to your game. That's our hard launch. That's when everyone will know that we're... serious."

"Hard launch?"

"It's a phrase people use to announce new relation-ships. I didn't make it up. Don't ask me."

He laughs dryly.

My jaw laces tighter than a corseted dress on a red carpet. Why do I let him get under my skin this way? "Look, I know it's not ideal, but we're both benefiting from this, in case you forgot."

"Oh, I haven't forgotten." He slides his phone across the couch. "It's probably time we at least exchange numbers, then."

The temperature of my cheeks spikes when I meet his eyes. I must be as pigmented as cherry candy now. His lips slip into a cockeyed grin. No wonder he has quite the repu-tation with women. Just a tilt of his lips can wipe away any irritation he may have caused. A stupid little flutter rolls through me when my fingers brush his as I take his phone and begin to type. As soon as I'm done, I slide it back over like it's on fire to avoid any more unnecessary touching. As he lifts the phone to his face, he clicks on my name.

"What are you doing?" I ask.

"Making sure everyone knows where we stand in case they see our texts." His eyes lift to mine briefly before falling back to his screen. "I figured we need to have some kind of exchange on here in case someone reads over my shoulder or something." His fingers fly over his keyboard before he flips it back to face me. "There."

I stare in horror at the words *Lenny-Pie* surrounded by an assortment of hearts and other emojis. "Lenny? That's a guy's name."

"Seems pretty neutral to me."

"Wait. Isn't that the guy who likes bunnies from that Steinbeck book?"

"Oh, she's a reader?"

"Don't sound so surprised. I think it's more shocking you know who Steinbeck is."

He raises his phone and taps his thumb across the screen, ignoring my dig. "You know, for being your boyfriend all of one week, it's like I hardly know you. Do you like Lenny-*Bunny*? I can change it."

"Ugh. That's worse. That book was horribly sad. We had to read it in eighth grade, and I never recovered."

"Don't they say 'sad is your aesthetic?'"

I roll my eyes. "They that don't actually know me do."

"Fine. Then no Lenny-Bunny."

"Thank you."

"Lenny-Pie it is."

His fingers fly back over the screen, and I can't help

myself. I slide across the couch and grip his thick forearm, lowering his hands. Something zips through my fingertips and up my arm at the feel of his warm skin.

My heart pounds in my chest as our eyes meet. His gaze drops from mine to my lips momentarily, just long enough for me to realize that I'm *so* close to him. Closer than I think I've ever been without actual cause, like yelling at him for showing up unannounced at my private recording session.

"Please don't name me after a man. Something tells me people won't quite believe us if they think he and I are synonymous to you. There isn't anything sexy about Lenny. I've seen the girls you've dated, and none of them look like a Lenny-Pie. You're supposed to at least find your girlfriend sexy. Even if it's fake."

"Who says I don't?"

All at once, my heart catapults into my stomach like it's mad at it. Did Decker just say I'm *sexy*? It's a compliment I'm no stranger to, but it feels different coming from him. I'm nothing like the girls he's been cuddling up with in rumors and photos. I'm not even the cutesy girl-next-door type like Ada Lane, his most recent conquest. I'm just Lena Lux—Lukowski—"the brunette with thick thighs and a voice of gold," as I was once coined by some online publication. Though I'll take "sexy" over that description if I have a choice.

My lips part, but words evade me as I stare into his eyes. Out of my peripheral, something appears, and before my brain can register what it is, Decker's phone makes a clicking sound. Then he leans back into the couch and stares at his screen like nothing happened.

"Did you just take a picture of us?" I ask, unsure of whether I should laugh or throw his phone across the room.

"Our first fight. Gotta document."

I roll my eyes. "That's hardly our first."

"Won't be our last either with that attitude."

I huff out a laugh, and Decker catches me out of the corner of his eye before smiling back at his phone.

"I have to admit we look pretty good together, though." He scoots closer so I can see the photo.

It's candid. It is *not* flattering. But it's kind of sweet he thinks it is.

"Here," I say, pulling up the stupid series of pictures Antonia and my mom have bombarded me with for inspo. "You can't post that. My team had some ideas—"

"Your team?" He guffaws. "I know they're pulling the strings here, but I feel like you'd know best. What's your signature *this is my boyfriend* pose?"

"Signature boyfriend pose?" I laugh, but not because it's funny.

He's as misinformed as everyone else if he thinks I have a "relationship pose." Sure, I've dated my fair share of men, but there's no signature anything. Each one is different from the last. The guy. The dynamic. Who I feel like I'm becoming. I want to be offended, but when he nods and leans in like he's truly listening, I can tell he's taking this seriously. Decker is strategizing. He's asking because he wants us to succeed, and in this moment, I feel like he's someone I can truly partner with. We both need our heads fully in the game for this to work. We have to be a team. If I flee at any slight offense, we'll never convince anyone. We'll never outrun the things that wove this "relationship" together in the first place.

I waver but dim my screen, forgoing the cache of poses from my pushy mom. If this is going to work, we need to be natural. We have to be ourselves. My stomach does a roll straight to the floor as I place my hands on his shoulders and begin to maneuver him. I pull my hands back, not sure if I should be manipulating him like he's some kind of photo shoot prop, but for all intents and purposes—the purpose of saving both our skins—I suppose he is to some extent. At least for today.

My faltering doesn't throw him off. Carefully, he places his strong hands around each of my wrists, plants my palms back on his shoulders, and smirks. "Go ahead. I'm yours. Do your worst."

Why do I feel like I might ignite at that sentiment? I push it aside, avoiding the way that he watches my face as I slowly drape my legs over his lap. My pastel pink shorts contrast with his navy jeans, the lace of my white top a contradiction to his casual olive t-shirt. Even the way we dress screams our differences. I run a hand through the back of his shockingly soft hair. His chest stills. Is he even breathing? Have I taken this too far? There's a jittery feeling zinging through my veins, something that goes beyond my typical show adrenaline. It's different.

Wait. Is Decker Trace making me—I pause, searching for the feeling—nervous?

I clear my throat and try to maneuver as gently as possible. "Sorry, you asked for the pose, and with Callum —" Saying his name feels so wrong as I sit atop the mountain that is Decker Trace. But I have to admit, it sure feels nice not to worry about crushing someone's thin legs under my own thick thighs. Beneath me, Decker's legs are firm, like sitting on warm tree trunks. Which is weird, because whoever thought tree trunks could feel so... good. "Of course we have to make it our own, but I would say this will definitely get some attention."

Decker nods along, staring into my eyes like my words are some playbook he's poring over.

Awkwardly, I reach out and wrap an arm around his barrel of a neck, trying to mimic the cozy lap pose that, at the time, had come so organically to Callum and me. "This was the photo everyone went nuts for with Cal—" I cut off his name, reminding myself I'll never move on if I keep speaking it. "With my last relationship."

"Callum?"

I nod.

"Screw Callum." In one fluid motion, his hands are wrapping around my bare legs and pulling me across his lap to face him like it's nothing. Like we do this all the time. Like it's *natural*. And suddenly I remember how *hot* it is when a guy takes charge. No wonder he's had no shortage of dates.

My mouth falls open in shock as I stare down at Decker, my legs perched on either side of him. There has got to be something in our guidelines that *straddling him* oversteps. Yet for some reason, even if it does, I'd allow it.

He smiles up at me. "This okay?"

I nod again.

His face brightens. "Good. I want to try something."

I watch his face as he sweeps a swath of my hair behind my shoulder. My pulse picks up at the feel of his fingers trailing over the bare skin there, and I can't look away from him. I've never noticed the array of greens in his eyes before. It's breathtaking. Instantly, chord progressions and disembodied lyrics swim through my head. I have an itch to *write about them.*

Oh, sweet Lord above, send help. What is happening to me? A familiar feeling flutters inside, which is immediately overshadowed by a sinking dread.

Lena Claire Lukowski, you big, dumb boob. You have a crush on him. You have a crush on Decker Trace.

How is that even possible? He's done nothing but annoy me since the moment he inconsiderately gobbled down my refreshments. My heart is a stupid, fickle thing. How dare it betray me for a pretty face and muscles? How can it be so ready to be crushed again? *Traitor.*

I turn my head, eager to break eye contact, but he pursues. My breath hitches when he leans his forehead into my cheek, and I wonder if he can hear my heart kick into high gear as his dark lashes graze my skin. I close my eyes, the scent of that vetiver bottle I unearthed in his bathroom filling my lungs. It's grassy and woodsy and, for a moment, makes me forget how annoying he can be.

As much as I wish I could stop myself, I can't hold back. Leaning in and going with it is my natural reaction. Is it the fact that his cologne smells way too good to be wasted on anything fake? Or that before they brushed against me, I didn't realize exactly how soft those waves in his hair are? I want to lean back. I want to add some distance between us. I want to take a cold shower and scour away this *other* want that's cropped up inside, but I can't. Not only do I find myself frozen, but if I keep backing down, no one will ever believe what we have is real. I take one long—probably creepy—whiff of his coconut shampoo before he's dropping his head and nuzzling my neck. Instinctively, I giggle. And then I hear another click of the camera.

CHAPTER SEVENTEEN

DECKER

LENA IN MY LAP IS... better than expected. She fits perfectly, all her soft edges sinking into me, molding to my body. The way she's looking at me now, and pressing into me, I have a hard time believing this thing isn't real. I can understand how she's left a string of broken hearts in her wake—even if a few of those were hers. The way she feels, smells—all sweet and sugary and like I walked into a room lined wall to wall with baked goods and lemons. I wish I could surround myself with it all the time. The way her cheeks flush when my nose grazes her neck. It would be easy to fall in love with someone like that. Someone like her, who loves my dog and can flip a switch from sweet to sour in an instant. Why do I like that so much? And then it slams into me harder than a 300-pound linebacker at the twenty-yard line. These aren't simply quirks I'm drawn to... They're pieces of her. I don't just like those things. I like her.

I like Lena.

Disappointment washes over me when she leans away. My body is instantly cold at her abrupt departure.

"Let me see." She grabs my phone, and all at once I remember *this is a photo op, Decker, you idiot.* That's it. Stop drooling over the way she smells and feels. She's not thinking anything more of it. This is a business exchange, and mixing business with pleasure is never a good thing. One of them always ends in a fiery crash. Still, I can't help but wonder if it would be worth it.

She clamps down on her pouty lip, chewing as she zooms in on the picture. "I didn't realize you had freckles." She leans in, and I hold my breath as she cranes her neck around to scope out the light smattering on my cheek. "It's either sun damage or freckles."

Sun damage? Attractive.

"Or both," I say, deciding that self-deprecation might make me feel less awkward. At least she's honest, I guess.

"It's just a little hyperpigmentation. I didn't even notice until now." She tilts her head. "You really should start wearing sunscreen."

"I do."

She jabs a finger into my cheek, drawing attention to the spots again. "You don't. It's okay. We can work on that. I have some extra upstairs someone just sent me to try."

"Someone sent it to you for free?"

"People send me stuff all the time, hoping I'll endorse them. I'm sure after this little relationship is over you'll have your pick of products too."

"Products like skin care?"

"I've also been sent beef jerky, deodorant, blankets, and electronics, to name a few. Some of them are decent, too." She nudges me. "When you open your shelter, I bet they'll send you doggy care things. The sky's the limit if a company thinks attaching themselves to your name will get them sales."

I raise my brows, surprised at how confidently she worked my potential shelter into the conversation.

Lena shifts away from me again, lifting the phone to examine the photo. "Don't act like you've never been handed something free for being part of the Vista City Kings."

She's not wrong, it's just that anything I receive complimentary, I haven't grown tired of yet. Even after almost a decade of being part of the Kings, it's still exciting to see what people want to send my way. "Not very often."

She rolls her eyes like I'm being modest, which maybe I am, but what's wrong with that?

"Half the stuff I have to donate. I can't travel with it all and don't need most of it," she says.

"You are quite the philanthropist, you know."

"Don't look at me like that."

"Like what?" Suddenly, I'm even more self conscious than I was over my not-freckles.

"Like I'm some saint for giving away free clothes and electronics or peeling potatoes in some backroom of a church."

"I mean, you're also well known for your financial donations."

She ducks her head, concentrating on the screen. "What if I told you that I just give my team a budget and they're the ones that make all those *timely donations* any time some tragic story pops up in the news? Would you still be looking at me that way?" When her eyes meet mine, there's pain in them, like she's somehow ashamed of the money she's made and her ability to give it away on a whim.

"A donation is a donation. Your intent to help is there. That's all that matters," I say.

"Don't make it something it's not."

"Do you like helping people?"

"Well, yeah," she says as though it's obvious.

"Then that's it. You're changing lives."

"I have five houses, at least twice as many cars, and a private chef. Half my fans can hardly afford their gas, and I know some of them can barely buy dinner."

This strikes a chord with me, one that I thank God I don't struggle with anymore. A chord that definitely won't ever be strummed again if my agreement with her pays off the way we hope it does. "I've been there. My family has been there. We've gone without, and we made it through, but a little help from others never hurts."

The turmoil in her eyes softens as she stares at me with... Is that pity? I never meant for her to feel sorry for me. She's got a softer heart than I realized, but I'm only stating facts. I want her to know from someone who has been there that help is help, regardless of who or what form it comes in. I didn't mean to kidnap the conversation.

Lena shifts her weight on my lap, tilting her head as sad eyes cut into me. "I'm so sorry, Decker. I didn't realize how... how you'd grown up."

I lower my gaze, locking in on her, hoping she really hears my next words and that we can get off the subject of my financially unstable childhood. "You're making a difference. Don't try to act like you aren't a good person. You may hate me half the time, but even I can tell you're good."

"Thanks." She lifts a corner of her mouth, erasing the pity that had begun to cloud her vision. Leaning back in, she focuses on her screen as she uses her fingers to zoom in on our picture, and in a blink, we're back to business. "This is honestly better than I expected."

"We should probably take a few more though, just to make sure it's the right one." I worry I sound too eager when she smirks and arches a sharp brow, and I scramble to cover my tracks. "Or maybe in case Antonia and your mom wanna see—"

"No. *We're* choosing this one." Her pretty smirk drops, and I lift my hands in surrender.

"I'm game. Next pose?"

She chews her lip as she thinks, finally handing my phone back to me. Without warning, she leans in and plants a soft kiss on my cheek, the stubble I haven't shaved in a few days an unwelcome barrier. I almost forget to take the picture. At the last second I snap it, just in time for her to miss the heatwave sweeping over my skin.

Really, Decker? You're blushing over a kiss on the cheek? How old are you?

The heated feeling intensifies as I turn to face her, my eyes drawing down to her mouth. It always looked soft, but I didn't realize *how* soft those lips could be. And now I know. There's no more wondering. The worst part is... I want to feel them again. In a very not-posed-for-a-photo op type of way. My pulse rockets as I consider how far I should push this, which is immediately replaced by a question. *Why* do I want to push this? And would she let me?

There's a war in my brain as I battle between leaving our boundaries firmly within our guidelines or trying to feel out if this attraction is more than the obvious physical.

Something about her is different. I can feel it. Lena isn't that bratty girl I met backstage. Beyond her steely exterior is a girl who cares—about her fans, about those in need, and even about Princess. She has layers. I've witnessed them. She's sweet and fiery, and I want more. After the impromptu cheek kiss—the one she initiated, might I add—I want to know if she could want more too. I drag my gaze up her face to meet her eyes. She's still staring down at me, smiling. She doesn't ask to see the photo. Then she reaches out and her fingers delicately graze my forehead. I don't flinch. I'm completely still, completely willing in this moment to let her do whatever she wants.

Her fingers linger at my temple. "Sorry, you had a piece of hair. I thought I'd—"

The front door flies open, and she jumps, nearly falling out of my lap. I steady her, and she shoots to her feet, staring down the man in the entryway. The contents of a cardboard box tower to his chin, but I can see him. My stomach drops as I finally register who he is.

"Callum? What are you—" Lena's voice sounds like someone is strangling it until finally it gives up and fades away.

Callum Porter treads onto the lush, cream and gold rug, not bothering to take off his shoes as he advances into the living room and drops the box on the coffee table in front of us, followed by a small set of keys. The scent of old cigarettes fills the room. "Sorry, love."

Love? The endearment seems a little callous considering the whole he-dumped-her thing. Callum's accent is thick. He sounds like a Bond villain. Kinda looks like one too.

His light brows crinkle as he scowls at me, then at Lena. "Did you two... Is this staged?"

Our wide eyes find each other, and I can sense the streak of panic ricocheting through her. It's the same alarm that's cropped up in me. The last thing we needed was her ex, of all people, to be the one to figure us out. How does he know we're faking it anyway?

Lena sways from foot to foot. "Callum, we—"

He holds up a tattooed hand, silencing her, his voice rife with accusation. "Did you tell me to return your things so you could prove to me you've moved on?"

Relief rushes over me.

"That was today?" she asks, picking up her phone and clicking on her calendar.

Callum gives her a look like he's not buying it.

She frantically scrolls through her personal schedule. He's making her nervous. In her own home. And I don't like it. I stand, wrapping an arm around her waist. At first she's so zeroed in on tapping around on her phone that I wonder if she even realizes I'm holding her. Seconds later, she glances up at me and relaxes into my side.

"Bit pathetic, don't you agree?" he says flatly, twirling a silver keyring around his finger.

She pulls her eyes from mine, rolling them before they pin Callum to where he stands. Still, she doesn't say anything. We all hover in silence, both of them sizing each other up. Examining them closer, Callum's look is confident, like he's won something. Smug, even. Despite my initial assessment, Lena's gaze isn't as stiff as I would expect her to give someone who cheated on her and riled her up enough to cause a reaction that required a visit from the fire department. There's something soft in her eyes, like whatever stern, sassy gaze she's going for has been overshadowed by a filter of tears. It makes me angry for her and a little disappointed that he still gets such an emotional rise out of her after what he did. I wish she looked as strong as I know she's trying to be.

She takes a deep breath, tucking her phone away. "I'm sorry. I've been so busy this week I forgot to add it to my schedule."

"Don't you agree, though?" His voice is sharp as he commandeers the conversation as though Lena never opened her mouth. "It does seem a bit odd with the timing. With you in his lap when I walked in the door. But good for you. I'm happy to see you pulling yourself out of that sad, desperate place I last saw you in."

He pushes his hands into his pockets, his eyes boring into Lena, who seems to have lost any fight she'd been trying to muster. If I didn't know any better, I'd say he's enjoying this. He likes to see her squirm. I can't help but wonder if this is what she had to deal with throughout all of her time with him. All those moments she thought they were happy together, he was talking to her like this and undressing other women behind her back. Lena can be difficult, but she doesn't deserve this. And if there's anything I've gathered from the last few minutes, Callum definitely never deserved her either.

Immediately, something ignites in me, and it takes

every shred of restraint I have not to punch him. My jaw stiffens. I clench it once, then glance down at Lena, who's still frozen, her head bobbing around my chest. She's got a distant look in her eyes, one reminiscent of the day we were mobbed in that deli parking lot. Her meticulously curated composure is cracking, and I won't let it.

I smooth my hand over the top of her soft hair. "Are you ready to go? We're gonna be late."

Her brows knit and unravel again. "Oh, yes. Yeah. Let me get my stuff."

I step forward, attempting to block Lena from his scrutinizing gaze. "I'll show Callum out."

Callum holds up a hand. "No need. I've been here plenty." He cranes his neck around, finding Lena again as he dangles the silver keyring in her direction. "I'll leave your keys atop the box. If you have mine, I'll take them now."

She deflates, and I can't help but feel embarrassed for wanting her while she so clearly is still stuck on him. If this is the kind of guy she goes for, I don't know how to compete. I can't stack up against a musician with an accent who is half my size.

"Yeah, sure. I'll just grab them while I'm upstairs." She disappears, leaving Callum and me alone.

I roll my shoulders back, letting my spine stiffen, my gaze harden. If he keeps talking to Lena in that condescending way, I'm gonna morph from a tight end into a defensive tackle real quick.

"Where are you two off to?" Callum's accent grates against the last of my nerves.

I don't blink. I don't look away. "It's a surprise." He lets out a patronizing laugh, and my jaw tenses again. "It's a bit ridiculous to think I'd tell you where we're going when I haven't even told her yet, don't you agree?"

He rolls his eyes, shaking his stupid blonde man bun.

I take a step closer, letting myself tower over him.

The tiny man stands his ground. "I've heard about your escapades."

"And I've heard about yours. Do your fans know you're a cheater?"

"Do yours?"

My hands tighten into fists at my sides. I know he's referring to Ada and the bottle waitress. How original. Maybe I've been with a lot of women, but I've never cheated. I open my mouth to spit the fire at him that's building inside, but he cuts me off.

"She's not all she's cracked up to be. You'll get bored with her soon. You'll see."

Movement in the upstairs hall pulls our attention. I bend down to his level, checking over my shoulder and lowering my voice as Lena appears at the top of the stair-case. "Your music sucks, by the way. If it weren't for Lena, your shows would still be empty."

He scowls as she lands at the bottom of the stairs, drop-ping the keys into his hand and turning to face me. "Ready, babe?"

I lean in. She's added some lipstick that makes her soft mouth look even fuller, and a delicious, sweet-scented cloud swarms around her. I plant a kiss on the top of her hair. "Ready."

Her brow folds, and I worry I've overstepped, but then her face brightens into a contagious smile. For a split second, Callum isn't there. It's just the two of us, but then he says something snarky that barely registers because all I can focus on is the turbulent blue of Lena's eyes.

"Gustav will be by to get it," Lena says, finally breaking eye contact with me.

We follow Callum to the door, stopping behind him to pull on our shoes. He gives us a once-over before exiting without a goodbye. The door clicks shut, leaving Lena and me completely alone once again. But this time it's different. I feel like we've been through a battle over the past fifteen minutes, despite never moving more than a few feet. Somehow—together—we made it out unscathed. She watches out the glass panels of the door as he shuffles through her meticulous landscaping and jumps into the back of a dark SUV. When it loops through the circular drive and disappears out of her gate, she begins to pull her shoes off.

"Whoa, whoa, whoa," I say, hoping to lighten the heaviness that was the presence of Callum. "You gotta wear shoes where we're going. No shoes, no service, as they say."

She shakes her head. "It's okay. We don't have to—"

"Do you have to work or something?"

"No, I have a free day today."

"Me too. So I'm taking my girlfriend out."

I can tell she's fighting back a smile. "And where are you taking her?"

"It's a surprise, *babe.*"

She rolls her eyes, a rosy blush covering her cheeks. "I panicked! I didn't know what to say."

I laugh at how cute she is when she's flustered, tossing an arm over her shoulders. "It's okay, really. Better than

Deckie-Pie, I guess." I take a deep breath. "That guy's an idiot, by the way."

To my surprise, she doesn't shake free of my arm, and she doesn't defend him. She quietly agrees and lets me guide her out the door.

CHAPTER EIGHTEEN

LENA

"WHERE ARE YOU TAKING ME?" I watch from the corner of my eye as Decker fights back a smile. It's kind of adorable how pleased he seems to be at my cluelessness. Or maybe he's excited. And I have to admit, I'm kind of excited too. It's been too long since I've done anything remotely spontaneous, unless we're counting my random not-a-date-lunch-date with Decker the other day. I tend to keep a tight schedule—especially while caught in the throes of recording—but inspiration has been lacking lately, and I need a break.

"You'll see." His smile presses further into his stubbly cheeks, and finally, he exposes his perfect teeth.

A feather-light flutter unfolds in my belly, and I have to turn away. I reach for the door and fiddle with the window button as I wait for the unwanted sensation to subside. Hoping to be whipped back to my senses, I press it, anticipating a deluge of fresh air, but nothing happens. "Did you lock me in here?"

"I'm carrying precious cargo."

"Who uses the child lock, anyway?"

"I do when a 330-pound man in my passenger seat won't stop playing with the buttons." He glances my way and must notice my confusion because he smiles at me again before pulling his attention back to the road. "Maleko. He was the last one to ride there. That's why the seat was so low. He's a fidgeter. Messes with everything."

"Is he your best friend?"

"Yeah, one of them. But only after you, *babe.*"

I roll my eyes. "You're gonna have to fight Joss for that spot."

"Joss?"

"My best friend since grade school." We come to a stop at a red light, and I can't help but smile as I think back on all of our years together. Church choir, sixth grade English class, climbing trees in the summer. "She's a photographer, travels worldwide for it now. I'm proud of her, but I miss her a lot. She'll be in town soon, though. She's doing my next album art. For the re-release."

"What's your favorite memory with her?"

His question catches me off guard, and I can't help but sneak a look at him as I jog my brain. "There's way too many, but probably junior prom."

"Was she your date?"

I smile. "No. I didn't go to any proms. After missing the one my junior year, my mom promised I would make it to my senior prom, but then she scheduled some last-minute event for me and—" I shake my head. "No high school proms. Joss knew how bummed I was and set up a photo shoot outside the venue where they'd held prom about a month earlier. Her sister took the pictures. It wasn't the same as going to the dance, but I appreciated the gesture. At least I got to wear my prom dress."

"She sounds like a good friend."

"She is." I smile at him.

He smiles back. "Old friends are the best. Keep 'em if you can."

"You said one of them. Who else is on that list? And don't say me." I arch a brow at him. "We're not there yet."

"Well, we better get there soon or no one will believe us, but I think asking questions is a good start. I need to know more about you."

"Need to?" I ask.

"Gotta know a few things about my girl. What if someone asks me something about you?"

He reaches over and pats me on the knee like it's Princess's head, but then he doesn't lift it. It lingers on my bare skin for a moment, my eyes falling to his grasp before tracking up his arm and meeting his gaze. We freeze there, and I'm not sure if either of us is breathing. His hand is as reassuring as his presence was when Callum was being so very *Callum* earlier. His body even more so before Callum burst in and ruined that too. *Ugh... Callum.* A car honks behind us and he yanks it away, gassing through the green light, leaving a cold spot where his palm once lay.

"Hmm... My best friends besides Maleko... and Princess, obviously. And you." He smirks, and I shake my head. "I mean, most of the team is pretty close. I spend a lot of time with Cole too."

"You seem to be pretty liberal with this best friend title."

He shakes his head. "I'm not. I just have a lot of friends. It doesn't mean I trust them all the same. Other than Maleko, it's my brother. Ian. Can't beat the ol' built-in-best-buddy, as they say. And probably my mom, too."

I bite back my smile. "Your mom?"

I expect him to at least blush at admitting he considers his mom a best friend, but he doesn't make excuses. He doesn't back down. "Family's important to me."

"What about your dad?"

He sucks in a slow breath through his teeth as we pull into a parking lot. "He passed away a few years ago."

"Oh, Decker. I'm so sorry. I didn't know."

"We weren't very close in the end. I wasn't close to my mom then either. We'd had a falling out. Not a great time in my life. But loss seems to have a way of pushing people back together. Well, tearing them apart or bringing them back together. Fortunately for us, it was the second option." He puts the car in park and turns to face me. "It's weird because as much as I miss him, I'm grateful that losing him somehow fixed my relationship with my mom. I just wish I could have made it up to him before he was gone, you know?"

I press my lips together, nodding. I'm not sure what to say. He's being so... open. For the second time tonight, he's surprised me. He's pushed aside his cocky, jokey exterior and shown me there's more going on underneath. I don't want to ruin it, so I take a note from his book and reach out, testing our guidelines like he already has so many times today. Placing my hand over his, I wait for him to pull away, but he doesn't. Instead, he stares at my hand before slowly weaving his fingers through mine. A jolt rockets through me, but I don't back down. I can't keep stepping back every time he steps forward. We're supposed to elicit comfort. *Love.* And this is a move in that direction. Besides, after the way he was there for me today in the presence of Callum-the-Terrible, the least I can do is be there for him now.

He gives my hand one squeeze before forcing a smile onto his face, but his eyes don't reflect it. "Ready, Lennie-Pie?"

I try to keep my smile bright enough for the both of us. "I don't know where you're taking me, but I guess."

"The correct answer is 'ready.'"

"Ready as I'll ever be."

He shakes his head, dropping my hand before pulling out his phone and typing something out. Shoving it into his pocket, he hops out of the car and makes his way around to grab my door. I pull on a baseball cap and a pair of aviators—real original disguise, I know—and step out. I don't know why I hadn't paid more attention to where he was taking me, but I'm not sure what I'm looking at. I don't know where I am. Painted brick and metal doors sprawl out before me, but there are no signs and hardly any other people except for a few that appear to be on smoke breaks, sitting on curbs and leaning against walls here and there. We're behind a strip of businesses.

Decker begins to walk toward a door, expecting me to follow, but stops when I don't move. "Come on."

"Where are we?"

"It's a surprise." I cross my arms and cock a hip, unwilling to go without some kind of explanation.

"Trust me. I may not know much about you yet, but I know you're going to love it."

I can't say no to his smile, and the smoke breakers around us are starting to stare. Quickly, I grip his hand in mine and let him lead me to a pink door with 213 painted above it. He knocks once, twice, three times, and finally, it flings open.

"Hey, man!" A guy almost as tall as Decker and nearly twice as broad pushes open the door and holds it for us with an outstretched arm, his mop of messy curls flopping with every movement. "Lena. Nice to finally meet you."

"Finally?" I nudge Decker, and his cheeks actually redden with a veneer of embarrassment. After his football retirement, he may have a future on the big screen. That is, if breaking Ada Lane's heart didn't get him blackballed from Hollywood.

"I had to tell him our secret, so he'd give us special treatment today."

I scrunch my nose at him in a faux-show of disapproval, channeling all the lovesick puppies from my mom and Antonia's inspo pics today. Decker taps me on the nose delicately with his index finger, and soon our lovers' quarrel has ended.

"Uh-oh." Decker's friend's gaze locks on something behind me, and I turn just in time to see someone running toward us with a camera, calling my name.

In a split second, Decker's body is blocking me from their view as he leads us into a storage room. His big friend slams the door and double-checks that it's locked.

"Thank you..." I search for his name and realize I never learned it.

Decker fills in the gaps for me. "Cole. Plays on our defensive line."

"Hi, Cole, nice to *finally* meet you."

He clasps his chest, his eyes dancing from me to Decker. "Finally? You told her about me?"

I don't wait for Decker to answer because suddenly I'm being steeped in the overwhelming scent of sweet, sweet sugar. "Oh my goodness, where are we? Have I died? Is this heaven? What is that smell?"

Decker's smile grows. "You'll see." He turns to Cole. "Are we good?"

"I'm sure my mom has no problem shutting down for Lena Lux, but I didn't exactly tell her, so if she says anything, this is your idea."

"Your mom?" I ask.

Decker leans closer. "This is his mom's place. She owns it. He just stops in from time to time and hijacks it, apparently."

Cole bats away the comment. "I'm an investor here."

Decker swats him in the gut. "And taste tester too, by the looks of it."

"This is the body of a two-time Pro Bowler. When was the last time you got voted into the Pro Bowl?"

Decker shakes his head, lost for a response. Something tells me this is their normal rapport, but I still make a mental note to look into the Pro Bowl and whether there's anything I can do to help him participate since—from what I'm gathering—it's a coveted event, at least for these two.

Cole smiles slyly, glad his jab landed as well as Decker's had. "Maybe someday you'll get voted in to do it too.

I'm sure Lena's fan base will have no problem spamming the polls 'til they get you in. Unless you break her heart."

I grab his bicep, running my hand down his arm until our fingers entwine. "Not gonna happen."

Decker looks down at me, his lips smoothing into a soft smile.

"Enough of the googly eyes. I'm still here." Cole turns and leads us to another pink door. "Well, the whole place is yours for the next fifteen, so better make it a quickie."

Decker shakes his head but wastes no time pulling me past Cole and through the pink door to what I now realize is a *candy shop*. The walls are striped with creamy yellow and powder blue. I feel a little like I've walked into a nursery, but something about it works with the pops of pink. It's warm and fun, and I'm absolutely giddy to be surrounded by rows upon rows of sugary goodness. Staring up at the cheesy, lollipop-shaped light fixtures, I let Decker lead. When the silence stretches on for too long, my eyes drop from the ceiling to him. He shuffles along, brows crinkled as he reads the tiny labels and examines each case. It's cute how focused he is on finding whatever it is he's looking for. When he freezes two steps later, I have to backpedal so I don't slam into his rear.

Decker gestures toward an acrylic box, smiling like he's won some grand prize. "I thought we could start here."

My jaw drops when I realize it's stuffed to the brim with multicolored, sugar-coated gummy worms. "You remembered my favorite candy?"

"How could I not? You almost murdered me over it." A wicked smile parts his lips as he turns and grabs a rose-colored plastic bag from a dispenser and hands it to me. "Here. Go crazy."

I eye him as I gently pick up the silver scoop, but I can't resist. Throwing open the bin, I shovel until the bag is so full my fingers strain to hold it. Decker swoops in, his hands cupping the bottom of it as we work together to twist and close it with a metallic tie.

"What's next?" he asks, pulling out another bag.

I slap my sack of sugary bounty. "This is it."

He arches a dark brow. "Anything you want. I'm buying."

He and I both know that him buying makes no difference.

I shake my head. "This is my favorite. It's all I want. What about you? What do you want?"

"Can't. Been trying to eat clean for tomorrow."

"Right. The kickoff game." Suddenly, the room is too hot, and I pace until I find a vent to stand under. "Gotta stay in shape for our debut."

"And what could possibly be my last season of football."

I freeze where I stand. Retirement? I know he worried about his body holding up for the remainder of his career, but I didn't realize he wanted to end it so soon. Retiring from something you love, that's brought you so many opportunities, is hard. I don't know if I could ever give up my job. I don't know if my manager would ever let me.

Decker trails after me, standing with me beneath the AC, his arm brushing mine in a warm contrast to the cool, blasting air.

I turn toward him, tilting my chin up until I find his

eyes. "What about all that champagne and cheesy *frites* we ate?"

The air kicks on higher, blowing my hair until a few strands stick across my face. Without missing a beat, Decker clears them away. "It was a special occasion. Didn't want to disappoint my new business partner."

I stare up into his eyes, examining his tan skin, his green eyes, how perfectly they contrast with his near black hair. When God created Decker, He really showed off. I don't care how creepy my staring is, I can't think about anything other than what a beautiful man he is.

"What?" Decker asks.

"I've never seen someone with greener eyes."

"Is that a compliment?"

I hold his gaze. "If you want it to be."

"Does my girlfriend actually find me attractive?" He leans closer, lowering his voice. "I want to hear you say it, Lena."

My eyes go wide as a thud pulls me from my trance. I scan the space for any sign of Cole or other eavesdroppers. And that's when I see it. The pink accordion shades may be pulled tight across the large glass storefront, but the one on the door is too small, leaving its margins completely open. Light peeks through the exposed glass along with someone's face. And then another face. And then a lens. The flash is blinding as the camera goes off. It's the guy from the back lot. The paparazzi.

Decker curses, stepping around me to block their view as the mumbling outside builds to excited shouts and screams. What have I done? Did I really think closing the door in that guy's face would deter him? Paparazzi are relentless. If there's one truth I know, that's it. Decker's warm hands grab my now-frigid arms and sweep me back to the storage room. I attempt to calculate how long I might have until this leaks—until it's everywhere. Before my mom and Antonia see that I've gone completely rogue. Again.

Decker paces as I sit on a box. "Do you think we can make it to my car?"

Loud music blasts from beyond the closed office door, and I can only assume Cole is behind it, keeping himself distracted.

I shake my head. "I've gotten stuck places before. I can call Gustav."

"Why don't we try to sneak out the—"

"I had a lot of fun with you," I say honestly, letting the gravity of the situation pull me back to reality. I can't just gallivant around like everyone else. My reputation can be ruined in seconds. With one click of a camera or one slip of unkindness from my mouth. I could lose everything. And now with Decker tied to me, our futures are in my hands, even if they're separate. I have to save both my butt and his. That's the only reason we've connected with one another. Like he said, it's for *business*. I can't lose sight of that, regardless of how much the lines have blurred today.

"We only have until tomorrow. Then we don't have to be so careful. Today we soft launch, tomorrow we hard launch, and all the rumors will come true. Lena and Decker, star-crossed lovers." I can't keep the sarcasm from my voice as I pull out my phone, dialing Gustav.

"Lena, I want you to—"

I turn away, holding up a finger to Decker as I explain

145

the situation to Gustav. I desperately want to know what he was going to say, but at this point, whatever it is isn't going to fix our situation. Gustav tells me he'll be here in twenty to extract me. My mom has meetings, but Antonia will come along, and she agrees that Decker and I should leave separately. The sooner we split, the better. She rambles off more instructions, and I assure her I'll relay them to him.

"Can you leave in a way that makes it seem like we're traveling together? They want you to go first to divert attention. They said they'll pay Cole for staying with me." It feels silly to say, like I'm some child to be babysat.

Decker's hesitant but finally agrees. There's something that shifts in his demeanor, though. "I don't want to leave you here. I don't care what they—"

I hold up another hand. "Decker, please. I know this isn't how we saw the day going. But at this point, timing is crucial and I've already screwed it up enough."

"Because you said you wanted to do this on your own accord. *Our* accord."

I can't meet his eyes. "I know, but you said it yourself. This is a business deal, regardless of how unprofessional it feels. Business. I'm a musician, not a businesswoman. I think it's best from here on out that we listen to our teams. Stick to the plan."

"Stick to the plan," Decker repeats, running a hand through his thick hair. When he sighs, I know he'll comply even if he doesn't agree. "So when should I leave?"

"Probably now."

A hush falls between us until Cole meanders from his office.

"The paps found us. Can you stay with Lena 'til her ride gets here?" Decker directs his request at Cole, but doesn't look at him. His eyes are locked on me.

"Yeah, sure. Whatever you guys need." Cole looks confused, but bless him for being a good friend.

Decker backs away toward the exit. "Jason will send over suite details to Antonia. Not sure who will be in there tomorrow, but my mom never misses a home game."

"Your mom?"

Decker lifts a corner of his mouth into a wry grin. "Time to meet the parents. See ya tomorrow night, Lennie-Pie."

And just like that, he disappears.

"How long did you say you two have been seein' each other?"

My attention snaps to Cole. "We didn't, but it's still pretty new."

He sucks in his bottom lip, nodding as he processes it. "So tomorrow you're meeting Darlene for the first time?"

My body stiffens like I've been doused in laundry starch. Why didn't I ever ask Decker about his family, or at the very least, their names? I wanna knock my head against the wall for being so caught up in everything else that I never even got the names of his family members. So I nod, hoping that my apprehension passes as nerves. I try my best to commit her name to memory so I don't screw up at the game. *Darlene.*

"Calm down, girl. You look like you're gonna be sick." Cole gives me a once over and I force a smile onto my lips, a little embarrassed that I could pass for on-the-edge-of-vomiting, but mostly just grateful that he didn't pick up on my lack of knowledge about Decker's family. "No need to freak out. Darlene's seen a lot, and I mean *a lot,* throughout the years. Decker doesn't always seem to have the best taste in women."

I stare up at him.

"Besides you. *Until you,* I should say."

"They can't all be that bad," I say, trying to be the girls' girl all my fans claim I am. To be clear, I'm supportive of other women, but Vista City can be small in some ways. I've met a couple of the girls on his dating roster, and I have to admit, their beauty seems to soak in about as deep as their moisturizer. Though they were kind enough to me, I watched one dump a drink on a waitress because the bartender forgot the extra lemon peel in her cosmo. Not exactly the type I'd want to bring home to the family.

"Trust me. They were." He runs a hand over his buzzed hair, bugging his eyes. "You two seem much more natural together. Him and those other girls, I don't know. It felt forced. He'd pick 'em up treats from here and then tell me the next day they refused them because they'd ruin their cleanse or something." He shrugs. "You two seem to have a better flow, ya know? Most girls of his I meet are so rigid. Like, if they crack a joke or smile, they'll ruin their *aesthetic* or whatever. And Decker's a funny dude. His jokes deserve laughs."

"Did he tell you to say that to me?"

Cole's smile is broad. "Nah, but sometimes his humor's so cheesy I figured I'd give him a boost."

"You're a good friend."

He winks at me. "I try. That's why I'm happy he's finally with someone that looks at him the way you do."

My heart stutters like someone zapped it with a cattle prod. "The way I look at him?"

"Yeah, like you're not rolling your eyes at him all the time, even when he deserves it. I've literally watched his dates walk away from him when he cracked some subpar joke and laughed at it himself. Trust me, I can already tell you're genuine. You guys are endgame."

And I do trust him—though I feel a bit guilty because he shouldn't trust me—but I ask, anyway. "Then why'd he bring them home to meet his family?"

"He didn't. They always meet Darlene at the games. In the box." He must realize what he's said because he immediately starts to backpedal. Maybe if his feet weren't so big, he'd be able to keep them out of his mouth. "But she's going to love you. I have a feeling. Just wait."

He holds up a finger before darting away just in time to miss me deflate. I remind myself it's a good thing Decker's going through his typical relationship motions by having me meet his mom in the suite without him present. If he did it differently this time, people would get suspicious. I brush a piece of hair from my eyes, and my mind can't help but to wander to earlier today. When I was on his lap, and he was bold enough to clear my vision himself. Before Callum walked in and wrecked my life again.

"Here." Cole returns from the storefront with a pink box in hand, a golden ribbon tied tightly around it.

I take it from him as a knock resonates from the back door. My chest tightens.

Cole checks through the peephole. "There's a big dude out here. Sunglasses. Shaved head. Tight shirt."

"Gustav," I say, relieved.

He arches a brow.

"My security detail."

Cole nods and pops open the door as I push to my feet to leave. He greets Gustav before turning to me one last time. "Chocolate-covered dates with sea salt sprinkled on top. They're Darlene's favorite. She's the only reason my mom orders them."

I take the box as Gustav leads me out. "Thanks for everything, Cole, and good luck tomorrow."

Cole fills the doorway, his white teeth blinding in the bright sun. "Same to you."

CHAPTER NINETEEN

LENA

THE CLICK of my heeled boots echoes through the concrete hall like I'm completely alone, despite the horde of people around me. Stiff fabric chafes my thighs. The skirt is cute, but whoever picked it out didn't take mobility into consideration. Maybe it's my oversight. I grabbed the first skirt and shirt that were laid out before me after I finished my meetings today, and I changed in the back of my ride. So here I am, sporting Kings blue, and I have to admit, I kind of love it on me.

"It's the Truman Family Suite," Gustav repeats.

"Yes, I remember." We pile into an elevator, and I squish to the back. "Remind me who the Trumans are again?"

"They owned the team before the Barclays took over," he answers.

I nod like any of this makes sense or matters to me, but all I can think about is what I'll say to Decker's mom and if these date treats are still as fresh as they were yesterday when Cole packed them into this pink box for me. My phone vibrates, but my hands are full, and my skirt's too tight to yank it out of my pocket. I wish I'd thought about that before I put it on. At this point, I'm a little nervous about how I'm going to sit comfortably. I'm praying the suite isn't entirely glass front. There's usually at least a counter up front, right? It's going to be a long night if I'm fielding both making a good impression and not flashing my team-colored bum to everyone in the stands. The elevator doors open just in time to pour in enough cool air that the sweat threatening my hairline never fully forms.

"Will you hold this, please?" I hand Gustav the candy shop box and pull out my phone, a stupid smile spreading across my lips when I see who it's from. "It's Decker," I announce. Antonia told me to make displays public tonight, and if everyone couldn't tell from my mile-wide smile, I want them to know that it was my (fake) boyfriend who did that. The good thing is, in my line of work, sucking it up and faking it is truly how you make it, or at least make things easier. My brain is already conditioned to respond that way. What a good little actor it is. At least that's what I tell myself.

I read the text to myself because what normal girl reads their boyfriend's texts out loud? That would be overkill. Antonia said *public*, not obnoxious.

DECKER

Can't wait to see you in Kings blue later.

My belly flips, and I check around me to see if anyone's noticed. Which is silly because how could anyone ever see the knots my guts are tying themselves in right now?

DECKER

> But I'll be honest, I've never seen anyone look better in it than me.

There it is. My eyes roll as I continue on.

DECKER

> Kidding. Won't be able to text for a while though. Mom's name is Darlene, loves sincere compliments, eye contact, and collecting baskets. And those little date candies Cole said he gave you.

> Also thought maybe we should put in some face time tonight after the game since we'll be "official." I'm having a few people over after. If we win, probably a few more than a few. Good luck with Darlene, Lennie-Pie.

I try to commit the list of his mom's preferences to memory, but I can't get over the fact that he's right. Tonight's the night that we become *official*. The internet won't be buzzing with rumors anymore, it'll be swarming with pictures and more speculations and now *proof*. Proof of this carefully orchestrated lie by way of photos of me, standing in a glass box, chumming it up with *his mom*. Something heavy presses down on my chest, squeezing out my air. I've been through this before, so why does it feel so different now?

"If you're gonna puke, at least miss your shoes. I know those cost you a pretty penny." Before I turn to see her face, I already know who it is.

"Joss!" I squeal, throwing my arms around her shoulders, effectively causing a pileup of the throng of people around us with my unexpected stop. "I thought you were in New York this week."

She knocks her head back, flopping a lock of purple hair out of her eyes. Last time I saw her it was pink. "We wrapped early, and I busted my butt to get here. Antonia told me she had an extra ticket."

God bless Antonia for always being aware of what will keep me calm in high-stress situations and utilizing it. If I look good, she looks good, and she knows it.

"You could have texted me," I say.

"Yeah, but this is more fun." Joss grins, then holds up a hand to block her mouth, her blue and gold bangles jingling down her arm as she lowers her voice. "Plus, I heard you're meeting the mom, and I love seeing you flustered."

"Gee, thanks," I say flatly.

She giggles. "Thought I might be able to help ya out if you try to embarrass yourself like you did with T.J. Mills's mom freshman year of high school."

"Really? You're going to bring that up right now?"

"That's what you get for forgetting to tell me you're dating a pro athlete."

"It's a long story." I check my watch, and my stomach somersaults. We're fifteen minutes late. They're probably waiting on me. They probably think I'm rude.

"Can't be that long of a story. It's barely been a couple weeks according to everyone online."

"Maybe if you answered your phone for once, you wouldn't have to rely on gossip to hear about your best friend's new relationship." I scowl.

"Hey, Miss Career, you're the one who encouraged me

to chase my dreams. There's only so many hours in a day." She laughs like it's funny.

My frown doesn't budge.

She groans. "Fine. I'll admit it. I've been a crappy friend. You always make time for me, and I shoulda done the same for you. I'm sorry." She pouts. "Forgive me?"

I roll my eyes. "Always."

Throwing an arm over my shoulder, she pulls me in for a little squeeze, her plump lip popping back into place. Gustav slows his gait, stepping around us as we close in on our destination, and I take one leveling breath as he pushes open the door.

The luxury skybox is as luxurious as a football stadium will allow. The lighting is warm, the accents are gold, and little pops of Kings blue are spread throughout the space. Pillowy leather seats flank an aisle of wide stairs that lead down to a sprawling glass front. Nothing about it screams *sports stands* to me. As I perch at the top and stare out, part of me wishes I could sit in the bleachers snacking on popcorn and hot dogs with everyone else. The catered food along the wall looks delicious, but sometimes a beer and something greasy hits the spot. Of course, if I asked, I'd have my choice of both brews and munchies, but I've found people like you more when you don't come off as demanding in any way. When you're content with what is offered, it gives everyone less to gossip about. I'm not afraid to ask for what I want, but given my current circumstances and the sole reason I'm here, I'll stick with the buffet they've laid out.

An elbow sinks into my ribs, and I turn to Joss who gestures towards the seats. A woman with faded brown hair smiles up at us, and I immediately recognize the soft-angled nose. It's Decker's nose. This is Darlene. I've never been one to be nervous to meet the parents, so why now? Maybe because I have to full-blown lie to this poor woman's smiling face. The growing guilt is immediately washed away when I remember the fact that Decker is totally okay with me lying to his mom. Something about that makes it feel even more wrong. It makes *him* feel wrong. Without a second thought, I paste on a smile and start her way, the pink box clenched in my hands.

"Darlene?" I begin.

She nods, her cheeks full and pink, a glass of red wine sloshing in her hand. Pasting on my politest smile, I switch into interview mode. If I can captivate audiences, surely I can charm one person. But why are my palms sweating so much?

"So glad to finally meet you. A little birdie told me these were your favorite, so I couldn't pass them up."

She fumbles for a moment, trying to find a place for her wine glass until finally, I awkwardly offer to hold it as she takes the box from me and lifts the lid. A dramatic gasp drops her jaw like she's just cracked open some long-lost treasure chest. "Oh, Lena. You're too sweet. Thank you." She wraps an arm around me, crushing the box between us as I try my best to avoid dumping her wine all over her.

I stiffen instinctively. Meeting people is always a toss up of reactions. From tears to speechlessness to oversharing and groping, I've endured it all. Typically, when people grab me this way, it's unexpected and unwanted, and Gustav is on it, pulling them off in no time flat. Though unexpected, there's something warm about her, and I find myself feeling charmed by her ability to be so *motherly*. Sometimes I wonder what my life would be like if my mom was more mother than manager. Forgetting about the crushed box, I lean into the hug, squeezing her right back.

"I'm so glad you could make it." She says as she steps away, giving me a once over. "You're even more beautiful in person. That blue suits you, Lena."

Tucking the box beneath her arm, she takes back her wine glass, her other hand resting on my back as she steers me toward the food. People clear a path for us, and I do my duties nodding and greeting everyone with the biggest smile. Joss pops up out of nowhere with a small plate of desserts, completely forgoing any of the appetizers or entrees in favor of her sweets. She introduces herself to Darlene between bites and heads off to the open bar for a cocktail. I follow along with Darlene as she makes suggestions about what's worth eating and what I should avoid, and then she offers to grab me a cocktail too. Though I decline, she insists because her glass is empty too. She tells me she'll grab me one of Decker's favorites, which I pretend to know.

I descend the stairs with Darlene on my heels, taking a deep breath as we approach the window. It's time. This is what we've been waiting for. My stomach flips a little more with each step closer to the glass. After this moment, we're all people will be talking about. Decker and I. The fact that I seem so chummy with his mother. And as always, those trivial little things—what color my drink was, my outfit, and how many times I didn't smile. Naturally, my made up lips press further into my cheeks as though it can wipe away the nerves. As excited as I am to bury the whole

King's Music Hall fiasco, I'm officially—and publicly— stepping into unknown territory. New territory. *Decker's* territory.

Darlene and I sit, and she shoves a plastic cup into the built-in drink holder in the arm of my chair. Which reclines, by the way. I might as well be in anyone's living room across America in a chair like this, but instead, I'm being stared at by thousands of eyes as though I'm in the world's biggest fish bowl.

"Spiced rum and Sprite." She points to the swirling liquid in the cup. "Deck's favorite."

I shake my head like his drink choice is the most endearing thing and lift it to sip. It's not bad. It's also my first time trying it, but she can't know that. "I will say it's growing on me. Better than the old-fashioneds he's been ordering lately."

She guffaws. "Honey, he only orders those after a day he wants to forget or to impress you. Hopefully it's mostly been the latter."

I try to bite back my smile, but it's no use. Darlene lights up, nudging me with her shoulder as she sips her red wine, her lips already tinged with purple. "Did Decker tell you about his first game here?"

I weigh my responses, knowing full well he never made a peep about it to me, but wondering if it's something a girl- friend should know. "I'd love to hear your take on it."

She beams brighter and launches into how a twenty- two year old Decker was so nervous he was puking on the sidelines. No wonder he never mentioned it. I smile along and laugh, making sure to infuse all the admiration I can into my reactions. Despite being a semi-gross story, it's commendable he went on to play and win like none of it happened. I'm grateful when her next few questions are about me and not about our relationship. Darlene listens intently, swiping a hunk of crusty bread through some type of cheese dip as she nods along.

The noise beyond the suite builds with applause and music. Joss bobs along with the Kings cheerleaders, who have begun some sideline dance routine as she takes her seat beside me. Craning my neck to watch the dancers, I accidentally make prolonged eye contact with a few fans. I smile and wave as they excitedly reciprocate. More whoops echo through the stadium as both teams take their places on the field, filling the sidelines. I check for number 27, but I can't find him.

"There he is," Joss says, pointing to a spot below.

Darlene and I both snap our attention to where he stands on the sidelines, his helmet poised to be placed over his thick hair. As though he can feel our eyes, he turns toward us, smiling and pointing in our direction. The jumbotron across from us snaps to a shot of him just as one of those green eyes closes in a wink. And then his helmet is covering his chiseled features, and he's jogging into place. My cheeks feel warm, and I'm shocked at how well I've programmed my brain to respond because there's no way this sensation is genuine. Cocky and inconsiderate Decker Trace could never make me feel this way. Though the more time I spend with him, the more I start to doubt my judgment. As much as I don't want to admit it, I may have been wrong about him.

Joss bumps me with her shoulder, and I cover my face to hide my blush. When I come out of hiding a split second later, I know I'll never be able to hide again. Now my face—my reaction—is blasted over the jumbotron, one of my songs about young love blaring from every speaker in the stadium. On the screen, Darlene sits beside me, a glass raised over her head as though she's toasting us. This is it. Decker and I are officially official.

CHAPTER TWENTY

DECKER

THE LOCKER ROOM blasts with music and the victory whoops of my teammates. In my opinion, we should have won by more, but at least we won. I executed every play exactly as we'd studied, so overall I'm happy with how our season has started. Plus, I didn't embarrass myself in front of Lena. If the rest of the season plays out like tonight, maybe this is the year I'd finally be comfortable retiring. The deals will roll in thanks to my affiliation with her, and it'll be like she never pulled Gable's out from under me.

"Lena comin' tonight?" Maleko yells over the music, stripping out of his towel shamelessly and pulling on a pair of briefs.

"How many times have I told you to change *before* you start yelling at people?" I run a towel over my freshly washed hair, not telling him that the reason I decided to have a party is because of her. Because my manager insisted that the more people who witness me in a stable relationship, the better. However, the thought of seeing Lena again isn't a bad one. "And yeah, she is. Why?"

"My girlfriend wants to meet her," he says, wrapping his long, thick hair in a towel and plopping it on top of his head, just like he does in all his shampoo commercials. He's the face of one brand specifically, and people go wild for a big guy with a pink towel. Don't ask me why. "Plus, I gotta make sure I approve."

I laugh, shaking my head. Maleko is the nicest guy I know. People he's decided he dislikes are few and far between. He sees the good in everyone.

"Did you see Lena's skirt?" Ty, our safety, interrupts.

Maleko and I both turn to face him.

He scrubs a towel over his blond head, then throws it over his shoulder. "What I wouldn't do to—"

"Watch it. That's my girl." I grab my towel from where it hangs and snap it in his direction, nailing my target. He cups his groin and retreats back to his locker.

My girl. The claim on Lena came so naturally, I didn't have to think twice. It eased from my lips like it was true.

"Disrespectful," Maleko spits. "He's probably still mad about that personal foul."

"Yeah, or because he's a clown."

"That too." Maleko smiles.

My phone lights up, rattling against the metal shelf of my locker. It's a text. From *Lena.*

> **LENA**
>
> Where am I supposed to meet you again? Antonia wants us to be seen leaving together. Holding hands.

"Yo, why you smilin' like that?" Maleko takes a step closer, stretching to see my screen.

"Mind your business." I turn so my back is toward him and take a few steps.

"I never seen you smile so stupid over a girl before, bro."

I turn, and with one reach, I bat the towel off the top of his head. I'm 2-0 with these cheap shots tonight. He frowns and rewraps it, but there's a smile threatening to crack through his surly expression. "Hey, nothing wrong with looking stupid if they're worth it."

I ignore his attempt to rile me again and fire back a text.

> ME
>
> Have Gustav bring you to the tunnel outside the locker room. I'll be right out. Some media usually waits nearby, but security keeps them in line. We can take my ride to my place.

> LENA
>
> Right. The party.

> ME
>
> Try not to be too excited

> LENA
>
> Can I bring Joss?

> ME
>
> Thought she was outta town

LENA

Look at you, Mr. Memory. Her shoot ended early in NYC and she flew back to see me for a few days. She wants to meet you.

ME

Of course she can come

LENA

Don't worry, we won't stay long. I have a fitting early tomorrow and need to rest my voice before my recording session after. No drinking, no yelling, etc.

ME

I swear I saw you holding a suspicious cup on the jumbotron

LENA

Well, I couldn't tell your mom no! I cut myself off after the two she shoved in my hand.

ME

It's hard to say no to Darlene

LENA

I noticed. Gustav is bringing me to you now. Put your game face back on. It's go time.

ME

See you soon

Suddenly, I'm rushing to pack my bag, eager to get out of the rowdy locker room. I ignore the hoots, questions, and promises to make things awkward from the guys who will be attending my party tonight. Despite my profession and my bright idea to date one of the most famous women in the music industry, I'm not someone who loves the spot-light. So a party is kind of a big deal. Hopefully it doesn't suck.

As I reach the exit, the blaring hip-hop music stops. The room is completely silent until seconds later, a sweet voice pours from the speakers instead. It's Lena singing some song about belonging together from one of her older albums. More shouts rise up over the music. I turn and brandish my middle finger high above my head for everyone to see. No one is intimidated. The guys laugh and carry on, singing along with her.

I push open the door and out into the hallway, coming face to face with Lena.

"Your friends have good taste," she laughs.

I roll my eyes, grabbing her hand and leading her away from the locker room. "I think they're all excited to see you at the party tonight."

"Or they like to see how much they can embarrass you. Your cheeks are *crazy* pink."

I duck my head, hoping to hide my blush as people shout our names from all sides. Slowing my stride, I walk in step with Lena as Gustav brings up the rear, people from various news outlets trailing him like baby geese. Lena smiles my way, a slow heat swelling inside me the longer we lock eyes. Suddenly, holding her hand isn't enough. The hallway narrows, funneling us onto a new path. Without thinking, my hand finds her lower back, gently resting on the smooth strip of skin her shirt doesn't cover. To my surprise, she lets me guide her through the cramped hall.

The blood whooshing through my ears drowns out any

idle chatter as our walkway expands once again, and her hand slips back into mine. We round the corner of the spacious concrete corridor and wait at the elevators. Someone with a media tag dangling from their neck steps forward, their camera flashing in our faces. My shoulders tense as they move closer, but Lena smiles, still camera ready until Gustav staves them off.

When they're a safe distance away, she swings back toward me. "Oh, this is Joss, by the way."

I turn to see a head of purple hair stepping out from behind her. I don't know how I'd missed her before. Joss leans forward, wobbling slightly. Someone definitely took advantage of the open bar.

"You're even hotter in person." Joss giggles. "Why didn't you tell me he had green eyes? I'm gonna die, they're so green."

Lena rolls her eyes. "Ignore her. She had a dessert plate and then drank her weight in spritzers."

"Dinner of champions," Joss says to me. "Speaking of which. Congrats on the win, big guy."

I know she's drunk, but I like her. She's funny. "Thanks. Nice to meet you."

The elevator pings, and we climb in. I guide Lena in first, dropping her hand for only a second so I can press my palm to the small of her back as we step across the threshold. The exact thing we discussed the night we made our guidelines. I swear both the camera flashes and media questions flare up at that moment, but we're saved from answering them as the elevator doors slide closed.

My hand drops, my fingertips grazing a sliver of her skin where her shirt has ridden up. Lena makes small talk with Joss, completely unaware of how she's affected me. My heart rate picks up like I'm back on the field. I clench my hand at my side as though it'll erase the feel of her smooth, warm skin. A rush of muggy air floods the elevator as the doors clang open at our destination. This time Lena grabs my hand and leads me out. I follow her in a daze as she and Joss catch up. When we come to our ride, Gustav helps them climb into the back of the black SUV.

I'm halfway in the door when Lena nudges past me and pokes her head back out. "Gustav, you can have the rest of the night off." Gustav raises a brow and grunts, his lips parting as though he just might speak, but Lena beats him to it. "Call up that lady friend you've been talking about, and I'll see you tomorrow as scheduled."

"He can come too. If you feel more comfortable with him being there." I turn to face Gustav. "We wouldn't want you to miss out. You seem like quite the party animal."

I swear, Gustav almost smiles.

Lena shakes her head. "No. We'll be fine. Plus, it's been so long since I've seen Joss. I just want to pretend like it's old times for a while."

"Pretend, huh?" I arch a brow, and she rolls her eyes.

Gustav shuts the door behind us and rounds the car to have a brief word with Ives, our driver. I opted for a chauffeur tonight in an effort to keep everything as low-stress as possible for myself. The game brings on its own kind of anxiety, but the thought of going live with our relationship makes me more nervous than I thought it would. It's exactly what I've wanted. I have more to gain than to lose from our partnership, but the thought of being thrown into the spotlight to be scrutinized settled onto me like a dozen linebackers sitting on my chest, so I opted to hand off driving duties to Ives, my part-time driver.

In the backseat, Joss chatters about her favorite parts of the game, which aren't really part of the game at all. Next to the uniforms, she says the touchdown celebration dances were her favorite part. I smile in response to Joss's rambling quips, and Lena does the same, but there's something distant about her expression. I can't help but notice she's a little stiff. I can feel it in the way her shoulder brushes mine. Joss is too tipsy to notice anything, like the fact that Lena hasn't made eye contact with me since we climbed in. Which is pretty typical for her, but this time it's different. Normally, I feel like she's off somewhere else, wishing she could be anywhere but with me. This time, though, it's like she's too nervous to look my way. Her eyes are darting, catching glimpses of me every so often, but nothing sticks. As Ives pulls up to my place, I reach over and squeeze her hand. For a split second I think she might pull it away, but finally, she turns to face me.

"Ready?" I ask.

She takes a deep breath, bites her bottom lip, and nods.

"Born ready, baby. Let's go!" Joss shuffles across the seats, barreling over me to get out of the SUV. Lena calls after her as she stumbles across the pavement, but Joss doesn't slow down. We both watch as she rushes toward the open elevator and dives in with a group of people carrying a cooler and a couple bottles of wine. I assume they're headed to my place. Which means Lena and I have no time together before we come face to face with another crowd. Lena calls after her again, but the elevator doors close, leaving Lena with a few choice words about her drunk bff and a hard roll of the eyes.

I hang back, helping her maneuver out as she slides across, careful to keep a hand on the hem of her skirt to anchor it in place. As much as I want to peek at her smooth, tan legs, I keep my eyes locked on her face. Her lips are red tonight, my favorite shade, and one that makes her blue eyes pop even more than they typically do.

"Ives, I'll pay you double if you park and come up to take Princess out. I've got something to show Lena before the night gets crazy," I call to him just before I shut the door.

His lips part into a smile that's all teeth as he watches me grab her hand. "Say no more."

After Ives pulls away, Lena drops my hand, but leans closer, her voice a whisper. "You have something to show me?"

"No. I just... I figured we should make a game plan real quick or something. Take a few minutes to get comfortable together before we're on display again. Collect ourselves or whatever."

I glance down at her, a little ashamed of my lie. Did I disappoint her? The notion is scrubbed away when her cherry red lips split into a grin.

"Smart boy," she coos, walking ahead to press the elevator button.

It's like every urge from the moment I saw her in that skirt consumes me, and my eyes dip down her back. Each sway of her hips is more mesmerizing than the last. And because apparently I have no self-control, I scan down her legs. They're smooth and tan, their length ending in a pair of sexy black boots. My eyes trail back up, landing on their target. Lena is gorgeous, anyone can see that. She has the face of an angel, but this is the first time I've allowed myself to fully indulge in every curvy aspect of her. And let me be honest, everything about her is an *asset*.

Suddenly, I'm staring at a pair of knees. I shift my gaze to focus on a crack splitting the ground below, wishing I could fall into it and disappear.

"Were you checking me out?" she asks, amused.

The elevator pings and opens, and I rush ahead of her as though there's anywhere to hide inside. "I just thought I should know what my favorite part of my *girlfriend* is."

"And have you decided?"

I swallow my embarrassment and turn to face her. "Her personality, of course."

She laughs and rolls her eyes.

We make it up to my landing and find Joss in the middle of a very tense phone call.

"Everything okay?" Lena asks when Joss finally hangs up.

"Since Graham moved in, nothing has been okay," Joss says through gritted teeth.

"I told you he sucks. He doesn't deserve you," Lena says with no mercy.

Joss slumps forward, defeated.

I don't know what to say, so I start toward my door, hoping they will follow, and they do, chattering about whoever this Graham is the whole way. When I get to the door of my condo, it's cracked. This is exactly why I don't throw parties. First, I check for Princess, who is happily perched on the couch, a group of girls scratching her head and fawning over her. She's in heaven, and thank God she's not out wandering the halls or worse.

Lena drifts past me, making her way through the crowd, acknowledging everyone in her path with a smile or a wave. It never ceases to amaze me how gracious she is. This isn't for show. This is her. For the most part, everyone ignores her like she's any other party goer. Most of the guys on the team are pretty high profile themselves. They aren't as starstruck as the handful of "plus ones" that have been dragged in tonight. Despite my profession, I've managed to mostly stay out of the public eye, though my dating life recently has kind of destroyed the low profile I'd worked hard to keep. Being associated with a big name like Ada Lane decimated that completely. In hindsight, I now realize it's my fault. I threw myself into the spotlight. Which means to right the balance of the world, I have to be associated with someone who has an even bigger name. That's how it works, right? I watch as Lena weaves through the jam-packed hall and disappears into my room. That pre-game wobble emerges in my stomach again.

She's in my bedroom.

Instead of continuing on to the kitchen, I take a detour. My heart thuds in my chest as I approach my room. Taking a deep breath, I ease open the door and spot Lena sitting on the edge of my bed, staring at her toes.

"Everything okay?" I ask.

She inhales deeply, releases it, then pops up to face me with a smile. "Your mom told me you painted the sidelines with your puke before your debut game."

"That's what you want to talk about?"

She shrugs. "I thought it was funny. And it made me

feel like I know you better than I do. Which is important since we're supposed to be falling in love."

My stomach tightens.

"Well, *pretending* to fall in love," she amends.

I step closer, standing over her and crossing my arms. "And that's what does it for you? You're gonna tell people you fell in love with me when my mom told you embarrassing stories about my younger years?"

"I mean, that does sound a bit romantic, doesn't it? Kinda like flipping through photo albums together and telling stories about all the years I've missed out on not knowing you."

"You're pretty nostalgic, you know."

"I know." Finally, she lifts her eyes so they meet mine. "If anyone asked, I think I'd tell them I fell in love with you when you took me to the candy store."

An unexpected laugh explodes from my lips. "You like candy that much?"

"It was just really thoughtful." She pushes to her feet so her nose is almost brushing my chest. "You better come up with a story, too."

A story. All of this is fabrication, I remind myself. "I guess I'd tell people that I fell for you the minute you made such a big deal over *sour gummy worms.*"

She rolls her eyes.

"It shows you have passion." I grin.

"Yeah, right. You need to know. People will ask." She stares up at me, a challenge in her eyes. "When did you fall for me, Decker?"

Her skin looks buttery soft in the dim light of my room. I want to reach up and touch it, but I refrain. It feels too... intimate. I don't know if she'd let me, but I want to. Every time she opens her mouth—even when it's to insult me—I learn a little more about her, like her a little more. If I were to answer her question, I think it would be kind of like that. I fell for her little by little until it was so completely undeniable, I had to confess. She watches me expectantly, her eyes dipping to my mouth. I chew my lip, wondering if I should tell her my newest piece to add to our fabrication.

A knock on the door pulls our attention, and before I know what's happening, Lena's hands are fisting the hem of my shirt, a rush of chilled air shocking my bare skin.

"Quick! Come here," she whispers.

Her warm fingers graze my obliques as she pushes to her tiptoes, bringing our faces just inches away. Without a second thought, I take her lead, closing the space between us and letting my mouth find hers. For a split second, she hesitates, her lips stiff against mine. And then they soften, parting ever so slightly to pull my bottom lip between hers. It takes me by surprise, finally awakening my rigid arms. They wrap around her waist, pulling her in as she tugs the edge of my shirt tighter. She sinks further into me, and all I can taste, smell, and feel is Lena. I can't deny how easy this feels. How *real*.

And then she stops. And steps back. Leaving me slack-jawed and wanting more.

"Sorry, sorry." Maleko's big hands flatten over his eyes like he truly interrupted something.

Lena giggles, stepping closer again and reaching to my face. She draws a thumb across my bottom lip, and my jaw snaps shut. "Sorry about the lipstick. Been waiting to do that all night. I couldn't hold back anymore." She turns toward Maleko. "It's okay. You can look."

He peeks between his fingers before shoving his hands into his pockets.

"I didn't know you were... that you were both in here... I didn't mean to—I'm sorry," he fumbles.

"Chill, Maleko. It's fine," I say.

"It's just that there's a girl standing on your island threatening to show everyone her backflip? And that it's just as good as it used to be? I don't know. She won't get down."

"Joss," Lena groans. She bolts toward Maleko, stopping in the doorway to flash him a quick smile. "Thanks. I'm Lena, by the way."

"Maleko." He inclines his head.

And then she's off to rescue her friend—or everyone else from her friend—like nothing ever happened. Like she didn't just kind of make out with me.

CHAPTER TWENTY-ONE

LENA

I THINK I just kind of made out with Decker.

I stomp down the hall, threading my way through the bodies clogging it. There's no time to think about what I just did. What he just did? My brain hurts as it racks itself for an explanation. I was only getting closer to him, so we looked like... Well, like what a couple looks like when they're alone in a bedroom. It wasn't an invitation for him to kiss me. That's not what I was hoping for, right? My brain is a jumble of lips and green eyes and his firm chest against mine. For pretending, that felt pretty real.

The kitchen is even more crowded than the hall, but I spot Joss easily. She's toddling along the surface of the island, dodging attempts from various very large men to snatch her down. Maybe she should have taken up football.

"Excuse me! Sorry!" I smile and try to act happy and bright when I feel anything but. Any little light that had been ignited moments ago with Decker in his bedroom has been extinguished. Why tonight, Joss? I'm used to her antics, and typically I find them entertaining, but not tonight. Not when the only reason I'm here is to make good on my deal with Decker, for both him and me. We're supposed to be the ones putting on the show. Even from the floor I can see that Joss is too drunk to be here. Her eyes are red and watery, almost like she's been crying, and maybe she has after her heated phone call earlier, but I know booze is the other culprit. The main culprit. Judging by the red spillage down the front of her once-white shirt, I'd say she's had quite a few more in the short span of being left unattended. Assuming that the rest of the drinks made it into her mouth, that is.

I grab her ankle. "Joss, my love! Time to go!"

She shakes me free, whipping into a wild dance.

Someone behind me snickers. The bass thumps, and the scent of beer permeates the air. It's a far cry from the spotless place I'd seen the first time Decker brought me here.

"Joss! I need you!" I try again.

She ignores me, dancing some teetering two-step to the other side of the island. Phones whip out in my peripherals, but a handful of them are swatted down as soon as they appear by large, grumpy-looking men. Kings players. And they like their privacy. I can respect that. Just as I'm about to mount the island too, one of the grumpy dudes steps closer, calling up to Joss. It's Cole. To my shock—and a little to my surprise—she listens to him. They exchange a few words, and within seconds, her face is split in a double-wide smile as she hops into his arms. His grumpy expression wipes clean when she lands a sloppy kiss on his cheek before bouncing out of his hold.

"Lena! You're here!" Joss says, tumbling in my direction.

"I sure am. And I'm ready to go."

She pouts, pushing a ratty tangle of hair from her eyes. "Already? We just got here. I was just getting to know Colt."

"Cole," I correct.

"That's what I said. Cold."

"I have a fitting in the morning bright and early and recording after. Come have a sleepover with me like old times? I'll have someone arrange for McDonald's breakfast to be waiting for us." I try my tried-and-true go-to: appeal to her drunk stomach that seems to be stuck in the ninth grade. And it works.

"Yes, please! Extra cheese, extra orange juice, extra hashbrowns."

I know what she's saying, but half of it is garbled, though her excitement is loud and clear. Grabbing her hand, I guide her toward the door, my phone at the ready. I have to get ahold of Gustav. We need to go. I've seen Joss like this many times before, and it's only a matter of time before her legs stop working. Decker is nowhere to be found, his bedroom dark at the end of the long hall as we pass it to reach the door. I'll have to text him too. I make a mental note to do that as I reach for the knob.

"Hey. You guys good?" Decker asks.

I turn to find him emerging from the dark hall. "Hey. I was about to text you. Joss is kind of hungry, and I need to wake up early for that fitting. I'll see you soon."

His brow twitches almost undetectably, and then he smiles. "See you soon."

"KISSSSS!" Joss hisses the command, her words slurring even more than they were moments ago. She laughs so hard she falls back into the door.

"Here. Let me help you guys out. I'll call Ives. He can drive you," Decker says, scooping an arm around Joss to stabilize her.

She leans over and gives me a wink and a clumsy thumbs up. We maneuver down the hall toward the gilded elevator.

"Thanks for the help," I finally say.

"Yeah. Thanksss." Joss squeezes one of Decker's pecks, and I have to admit, I'm almost as jealous as I am mortified.

"I'm so sorry," I tell him.

Decker holds back a laugh. "Don't apologize. You're not the one feeling me up."

His eyes linger on mine a little too long, and I wonder if he's thinking about minutes ago when I basically was doing just that.

There's a click and a flash and a four-letter word. We spin to see a photographer pop out from a nook by the stairwell, staring down at his camera, cursing the flash.

"We're not photo ready right now," I say sternly but sweetly. I always try sprinkling on the sugar first. Decker... not so much.

"Hey, dingleberry. This is a private building." Decker steps in front of us, but Joss is still attached to him, so she just kinda flops behind him momentarily in his attempt to shield us.

"He said dingleberry." She snorts, pressing a hand over her mouth.

"I was visiting someone," the photographer argues.

"Visiting hours are over," Decker grinds out.

"There are no visiting hours." The photographer sounds bored as he pulls a phone from his pocket and lifts it to face us. Apparently, it's his backup plan.

"There are tonight. You need to leave," Decker seethes.

He steps forward and Joss shifts her weight so it's resting on me as his arm slides from holding her. His shoulders square as he moves toward the photographer. As much as I appreciate him keeping the paparazzi away, I don't know what he's doing. Sure, this could be bad for our image—adults stumbling out of a party like they're some kind of drunken teenagers—*gasp!*—but we want people to see us. Our entire relationship hinges on how many people see us. On how many people believe us.

I want to use this to our advantage, to step forward and be the girl who calms the wild beast before he does something he can't take back. I contemplate how to do that while keeping Joss upright, but before I can resolve the issue, there's a gagging sound and a splatter. Something warm splashes over my bare legs. Joss's groan is enough for me to know what happened without looking at the carnage.

"Ah, sick! Your friend just puked on you!" the photographer says gleefully, swinging his phone in our direction.

I'm frozen like a vomit-drenched deer in headlights.

Decker mumbles a curse as the photographer carries on about how great this all is. In a second flat, the paparazzi's phone is in Decker's hand and then flying straight into the putrid puddle below.

I watch as the man scrambles to find something to retrieve his phone without touching it. It makes me feel a little bad, but not bad enough to ditch Decker and Joss and dig it out myself. Decker fumes as I stare at him wide-eyed. That may have been an overreaction, but it's not like the stranger can't retrieve the footage from his storage cloud later. Joss gags again, her hand pressing to her lips. She squeezes her eyes shut and then swallows.

"We need to get her back to your place," I tell him.

Decker nods and scoops her up. I only glance back once at the man behind us who has fallen to his knees, staring aimlessly at his soiled phone. In no time, we're back in his apartment, shoving past a wide-eyed Cole and down the congested hall to Decker's room. Gently, he lays Joss on the gray chaise by the window so her head is propped up and springs into action. I sit by her, pulling her hair into a messy ponytail as Decker disappears into his bathroom. He comes back with a trash can and two little trash bags, as well as a hand towel and a damp cloth for her face.

"Dr. Decker in the house," I say, a little bit impressed by his swiftness.

He flashes me a grin as he pulls out his phone. "You should see the guys on karaoke night. This isn't my first rodeo, Lena."

A moment later there's a soft tap on the door and Cole appears with a peanut butter sandwich and three bottled waters hooked between his thick fingers. "She okay?"

Joss peeks her eyes open long enough to see Cole,

another groan rolling from her lips as she presses her fingers to her eyes and covers her face.

"She will be. Trust me, it would've ended worse if she did the backflip." I take the trash can from Decker and move it to Joss's side.

Cole drops his goods on top of the dresser before heading for the door. "Just let me know if there's anything else I can do for her."

"Thank you," I say as he backs out into the hall.

"What time do you have to get up in the morning?" Decker asks me, his voice almost a whisper.

I eye Joss on the chaise, her body still, her breathing evening out. Is she falling asleep already?

"Like 5:00 a.m.," I say.

He scrunches his face. "Tomorrow's an off day for me, so I was planning on sleeping in."

"You can. It's not like you're going with me."

"You'll set an alarm, I assume. And I'm guessing it'll wake me up too."

"Wake you up?" My brows bunch. "I'm not staying here."

Shouts and squeals ring out from the kitchen, making me wonder what we're missing out on. Something scratches the door, and when Decker opens it, it's an alarmed Princess.

"No one can get any decent sleep here. I'm already up too late." I cross my arms and cock my hip. This was not part of the plan. This was not in our guidelines. We never discussed a sleepover.

Princess waltzes over and licks my leg. My puke-

181

covered leg. I back away in an attempt to save Princess from herself and to keep from hurling myself.

Decker frowns like I've just slapped him across the face.

I throw an arm in the dog's direction. "I'm not rejecting Princess. She's licking *my legs!*"

A strangled sound of disgust squeaks from his throat. As horrified as I am by the vomit and the dog and everything else, I have to hold back a laugh. Decker grimaces and scoops Princess up like she's not fifty-plus pounds, depositing her in the bathroom and shutting the door.

More screams echo from the kitchen as heavy bass rattles the walls.

"Lena, it's late. You need to sleep. Joss is already asleep. Princess isn't having fun." He runs a hand through his dark hair. "I'm not even at my own party. Just stay the night, go to your fitting in the morning, your recording session in the afternoon. I'll make sure Joss makes it home safe. Or she can leave when you do. Whatever."

I hesitate, but I know he's right, regardless of how much it stirs the nervous little butterflies in my stomach. What's the point in going home when all I'm doing is losing more sleep? If I'm ever going to nail this rerecording in the "new direction" it's supposed to be going in, I need to at the very least be rested. That and actually want to rerecord the whole thing, but the latter isn't going to happen anytime soon.

"Fine," I agree.

A smile splits his face. "There are towels in the bathroom closet. You can use anything in there you want. Should be a pack of new toothbrushes under the sink." He points across the room. "My shirts are in the dresser. Shorts, boxers, all that. Take what you want. Now go wash that barf off. I'll be right back."

He doesn't wait for me to protest, just disappears into the hall. A minute later the blaring music silences, the yells become murmurs, and eventually—as I finally duck into the bathroom and free Princess—there's not a sound coming from the party at all. He's killed it.

I debate not washing my hair, but once the warm water is pouring over my back, it feels too good not to scrub every inch of my body. It's been a long day, and the filth Joss so kindly spilled across my calves has left me feeling a little more than disgusting. Decker has an impressive collection in his shower. Shampoo and conditioner—none of that two-in-one stuff that's targeted at unsuspecting men. No wonder his hair is always so nice—as well as face washes, scrubs, and three types of body wash to choose from. Sure, I'll smell like a dude after this, but I've smelled Decker. My mind flashes back to yesterday, a warmth spreading through my belly as I remember the feel of him under me during our little photo shoot. Decker smells *good*, and anything smells better than Joss's stomach contents.

I step out of the shower and follow his directions to locate all the hygiene products I'll need. Rummaging through a cabinet, I find a bottle of expensive moisturizer and slather it across my face. At least he has good taste. In the mirror, I check to make sure every inch of me is covered as I rewrap my towel and prepare to go back out there, not knowing what I'll find. My eyes catch on the drawer. The one I discovered the first time I visited this place. Immediately, all the sweet and soft moments that had accumulated throughout the last couple of days together explode on impact. His souvenir drawer. It gnaws at me still. Why does he have it? Why do I care?

As I wring out my hair one more time over the sink, I try to convince myself this drawer is proof that Decker is no different from any other guy. That he's as bad as Callum, a cheater. Something wedges itself into that notion, placing distance between the two of them. The guilt follows. For a moment, I feel almost shameful for comparing them. The past few days, Decker has been nothing but sweet to me. Even at our highest peaks, the terrain that made up my relationship with Callum was bumpy to say the least. I made excuse after excuse for him, always trying to see the good. Always hanging onto those *sweet* moments. Moments that I later realized were more autocratic and self-serving than they were meant to serve me or our relationship.

I scrape my long hair into a messy, wet bun and knot it around itself on top of my head. Of course, Decker's turning on the charm. We have a deal. If we don't last until our teams tell us we need to, he won't reap any benefits. If I weren't a business arrangement, I'd just be another high five in the locker room, an earring in that drawer.

Though, if it weren't for the agreement we made, I'd never date him to begin with. My jewelry would never be cast off in here for him to sift through as he recollects his conquests. A little fire lights inside me, a different heat spreading within as I stew over this dumb collection of junk. I wonder if he laughs about it with his friends. Smells the crap in there when he's bored. A mix of disgust and fury builds inside until I'm marching out of the bathroom, no longer caring about my state of dress. When I fling the door open, the words about drawers and conquests are erupting out of my mouth before I can even form a rational argument. No matter. I'm ready for a fight. I'm ready to put him in his place.

Decker is perched on the edge of his king-size bed, a fan on his bedside table already blowing full blast toward his pillow. He stares at his phone, oblivious to the fact that I've entered the room, that my lips are moving. The fan is drowning me out. As my feet pound toward him, he finally looks up and stands. Only then does it register that the sole thing he's wearing is a pair of gray sweatpants. He's completely shirtless. I have to pry my shocked eyes from his bare chest, which only makes me angrier with him. How dare he distract me from the earful I decided to give him like five seconds ago? Princess perks up, tilting her head as I open my mouth, but Decker speaks first, his unblinking eyes focused on my face.

"Do you need clothes?" he asks quietly.

"I sleep naked," I whisper back.

"Oh." He swallows hard, his unflinching gaze still locked somewhere on my face.

I roll my eyes. "Yes, I need clothes, Decker. I'm not sleeping naked *with you*. Especially with Joss in the room, you perv."

His face twists, his voice rising to a ridiculous whisper-yell. "Perv? I'm trying to help you. I'm offering you clothes."

"You're the one waiting for me like that!"

"Like what?"

I allow my eyes to slip down his body again as I

squeeze my towel tighter to my chest. "Like that! Half-naked!"

"This is what I sleep in. It's time for bed. I can put a shirt on." He crosses to his dresser, pulling out two t-shirts and a pair of shorts. A Kings blue shirt and baggy black shorts land next to Princess. Yanking a shirt on, he heads toward the bathroom. "Whatever. I'm gonna brush my teeth."

I peer over at Joss, who hasn't moved an inch, then to the open bathroom door. When it clicks shut behind him, I drop my towel and pull on the clothes Decker's laid out for me like I'm in a race. I rewrap my wet hair into a bun, and then I'm back on my warpath, busting into the bathroom without knocking. A startled Decker stares back at me, his toothbrush halfway to his mouth.

"Why do you have this?" I ask, pointing to the drawer.

Slowly, he begins to brush his teeth, staring at me like I've sprouted three extra boobs or something. "What are you talking about? Have what?"

I roll my eyes and yank it open. "This! Why do you have a drawer of other people's stuff?"

I don't specify that these things clearly belong to women because I don't want to sound jealous. And then it hits me. Is that why I'm doing this? Is it truly because I'm repulsed by his former antics, or is it because I can't stand the thought of him being with someone else? It's not like I haven't been with other guys; that's the entire reason I'm here right now. Because I dated someone else and it ended in a literal fiery crash. More than the thought of him having other girls over, I think what bothers me the most is the possibility of finding out he isn't the person he's shown himself to be over our time together. The thought is enough to make me want to keep him at arm's length.

He smiles, his toothbrush dangling out of the side of his mouth. "You know, my mom said you would keep me on my toes."

He already talked to his mom about me?

I double down. "Answer the question. Why do you keep this stuff?"

He sets his toothbrush on the counter and spits in the sink, taking his time to rinse it down the drain. The peppermint scent knocks me over as he turns to face me, pressing the heels of his hands into the countertop and leaning back. "I didn't know what to do with it, so I threw it in a drawer. What if there's like an heirloom in there or something?"

"Then they should have cared about it enough not to leave it here." I snort. "Are you seriously making excuses right now? What if one of your buddies saw? No self-respecting woman would stay with a guy who hoards his exes' stuff."

"They aren't my exes." He runs a hand down the back of his neck, breaking eye contact. "I threw it in there because I can't remember who any of it belongs to."

Gross. "Then why keep it at all?"

He shrugs, eyes still locked on the hodgepodge below. "I don't mean to keep it, I just don't think about it. I can throw it all out right now if you want me to."

"Don't do that for me." This doesn't involve me. His past is not mine. His future isn't either.

"I want to. They're just reminders of a life I don't want anymore." His green eyes lift to meet mine and my resolve breaks like glass in the hands of someone careless. How can I so easily fall for what he's saying? Am I that much of a sucker for those thick lashes and soft eyes? The answer is yes because when he yanks the drawer from the cabinet and casually dumps it into his trash can like it's dinner scraps, I melt a little. He doesn't bother putting it back in place, just sets it on the marble counter. "I want you to tell me if I do anything that makes you uncomfortable, Lena. Fake or not, you deserve to be respected." His jaw stiffens. "After meeting Callum, I have a feeling that's not something you got from him."

I let out a little laugh. "I guess I'm lucky he cheated on me and dumped me then."

Decker doesn't match my lightness, but instead lets the profanities fly. "It took everything in me not to punch him yesterday."

I cross my arms, leaning into the counter beside him. "Yeah, no one could tell. You seemed super calm."

Now he smiles. "I don't like it when people disrespect you. And I hope he picked up on that."

"Oh, I think he did."

"Good." He eyes me as he lifts his toothbrush, adds a little extra toothpaste, and starts brushing again.

I hover beside him and the empty drawer. "So, how do you think the hard launch went?"

"Jason said he thought it went well," he says around his toothbrush. "What did your people say?"

I collapse a little. "My mom said my hair looked a little flat, and I haven't read all of Antonia's texts yet. Does it matter, though? Can't change anything now anyway."

He lowers himself over the sink and spits out his toothpaste, promptly following with mouthwash. We stand there in silence, and just as it stretches on a little too long, he spits his mouth rinse out too and turns to me. "If you could change anything about tonight, would you?"

I think for a short moment. "I mean, I guess maybe I'd step out of the way when Joss's face twisted like that." I shudder at the memory.

Decker laughs. "Yeah but if you had, you wouldn't be here right now."

"And?"

"And I like the way you look in my shirt. Way better than me." My heart pounds out of my chest as he leans closer. "I need to be reminded every once in a while that I can't always be the best-looking person in the room."

"Gotta keep you humble."

He gives me a lopsided smile.

Everything in me screams to lean in, to meet him halfway, to take advantage of his shameless flirting, but even after he's dumped the drawer in front of me—voluntarily—I know this is part of who he is. He's a flirt. If I'm going to be stuck with him, I might as well make it fun. I can't fight the truth much longer. Decker is sexy. The fact that he doesn't get more notoriety from the female fan base blows my mind. These women don't know what they're missing.

Finally, I tilt in too, letting my eyes feast as they roll from his green gaze, to his full lips, down to his cotton-covered torso. In one bold move, I place my hand on his chest. "Not everyone can look as good in a shirt as I do. Speaking of which, I think I prefer you without."

As cheesy as it is, I lay it on thick, winking before I turn and exit the bathroom. I walk to my side of the bed—

the one I assume is mine because the bedside table is void of much at all—and I sit. Decker emerges from the bathroom seconds later—shirtless—his eyes coasting over Joss to check that she's still asleep before he sinks next to me on the edge of the bed. My pulse climbs. What is he doing? I was joking. Kind of. Where is he trying to take this?

His lips brush my ear as he says, "I'll be on the couch if you need me."

And that's it.

He stands, taking a step away before I catch his arm and pull him back down. When we're face to face again, he's smirking.

"If she wakes up and sees we aren't in the same bed, she's going to think it's weird," I whisper.

"So? Who's she going to tell?"

"No one. I just think we need to make this as easy on ourselves as possible. If you're my boyfriend, I should sleep in your bed."

Decker's lips pull into a tight line as he salutes me and leans back, somersaulting to his side of the bed. I press a hand over my mouth to stifle my laughter. He switches off his bedside lamp, then scoots to the middle so I can hear him. "There's a charging pad on that table by the way. For your phone."

"I saw. Thanks."

I wait for him to return to his side of the bed, but he doesn't budge.

"Too bad you aren't staying for breakfast. I make a pretty mean omelet," he whispers.

"Is that so?"

"It is." He yawns. "I'll give you a rain check on it, though. For our next sleepover."

I laugh. "There won't be a next one."

"What if I throw in some bacon on the side?"

"Why are you always trying to feed me?"

"Because it's the one thing you let me do for you." He slides a hand under his pillow.

My heart skips as I tighten my grip on the comforter. Suddenly, I'm hyperaware of everything. The heady scent of his cologne trapped in the fabric of the sheets, how cute his tired voice is, how close he is to me.

He clears his throat. "So, rain check on omelets and bacon?"

I muster my typical snark, but even I can tell it lacks bite this time. "If I agree, will you let me sleep?"

"Yes."

"Omelets and bacon it is."

A silence spans between us before he finally speaks again. "Well, good night, Lennie-Pie."

"Gross. Don't call me that." I reach out, giving his bare chest a push, but even in the darkness, he stops the strike. My hand is locked in his for a long moment before I finally pull it away, tucking it under the cool side of my pillow. "Good night, Decker."

He doesn't roll away, but instead stays exactly where he is, so close that his heat radiates under the blanket and warms me too. As his breathing settles, so does mine, and soon the exhaustion overwhelms me until I can't fight it any longer. That seems to be the theme of the night.

CHAPTER TWENTY-TWO

LENA

DECKER WAS WRONG. My alarm doesn't wake him up when it pings at 5:00 a.m., but it does bring a groggy Joss popping up in no time flat.

"Who is it?" she asks in a sleepy haze.

I stifle a snicker as I inch away from Decker—who has shoved down the covers, leaving his perfect, suntanned physique on full display. It makes me wonder what he was up to all summer. Sure, there's a bit of a farmer's tan striping his biceps from practices, but his chest is smooth and taut, and I want to bury my face in it. The thought is startling, and I spring from the bed before I can do anything ridiculous. Joss rubs her eyes, black mascara streaking down her face. Quickly, I change back into my clothes from the day before, but I pull Decker's shirt over them and tuck it into my skirt, just in case we run into someone in the halls like last night. The early hour should negate that chance, but as we witnessed last night, the paparazzi are relentless. Princess watches as we tiptoe down the hall and out of the apartment. In no time, we're out of his building and in the private garage, standing in front of Gustav and our ride.

Gustav hands me a bag before he ducks into the front passenger seat, and I change yet again as we embark toward my fitting appointment.

Joss leans over an AC vent, letting the cold air blast her in the face. "Sorry about your shoes."

"I'll order new ones." I pull on a clean pair of boots as she grumbles something indecipherable. "Are you gonna be okay?"

"Maybe." She sighs. "You know, that's not exactly how I pictured my first sleepover at an NFL player's place."

"Oh? And what were you expecting?"

"For starters, I didn't think I'd be a third wheel." She leans back, pressing her fingers to her temples. "How did you find one that's so *nice?*"

"One of what?"

"I'm the one who's supposed to be falling apart here. Stay with me. *A pro athlete.* How did you find one that's so nice?"

"How many have you met? All of Decker's friends seem pretty nice. Cole was nice."

She grumbles again and pops up to face me. "Cole *is* nice. Maybe too nice. Don't know if I trust it. And I've met a ton of athletes at photo shoots. Kind of jerks. Dismissive, most of them."

"Well, Decker's different, I guess."

"You guess? I sure hope you've noticed he's different, otherwise you might as well dump him now so I can swoop in." The vehicle hits a bump, and Joss doubles over, stuffing her head between her knees. "I wish I was still passed out on his chaise."

I wish I were still tucked into his bed.

"Joss, can I get you something? Do you need meds?" I knock on the partition and stick a hand out to Gustav. "Ibuprofen, please."

He pops open the glovebox and pulls out a bottle of pills, passing them through before closing the barrier.

I hand them over, and Joss dry-swallows a couple. "Don't listen to me. Don't dump him. My personal life is in shambles right now, and—" She holds up a finger before I can ask her what's going on. "I don't want to talk about it yet. We're talking about you right now, and from what I remember, Decker was a million times better to you last night than anyone else I've seen during the entire duration of any of your previous relationships."

As much as I want to deny it, I can't.

"That's kinda sad, isn't it?"

She shakes her head and looks at me like I'm crazy. "Sad? No. It's about time you pull your head out of your perky little butt and take a look around at what a quality man is."

I bite back a smile. "Quality?"

She shrugs. "Better than the trash you usually lug around with you. You actually seemed happy with him. Like the whole night. I was also drunk half that time, but still."

My smile expands until it hurts my cheeks. It feels so good to hear that. She's right. The time I've spent with Decker has made me just that. Happy. And despite the chaos of the past few days, everything has been relatively easy. So easy that my brain is beginning to fill with delusion.

If my best friend believes it, why wouldn't others? Not only does she believe it, but she approves of it. Of him. It's been so long since I've heard those words from her, my mind swirls with figments of what could be. Me and Darlene watching Decker in the playoffs. Decker meeting me on the field after another win. The two of us posing for pictures as confetti rains down at the Super Bowl. Decker finally getting voted into the Pro Bowl and me watching— yet again—from the stands. Why couldn't this be our reality?

We could keep this going. For *real*.

A fear creeps in, coiling in my gut at the thought of how a solid relationship—the kind that lasts—may affect my work. Those types of romantic commitments need dedication and time. Is there room in my life for both a successful relationship and career? If there's one thing my string of broken hearts has taught me it's that it isn't possible. Yet, a sliver of delusional hope prevails, and the fantasy circles back to its source. I squeeze my eyes shut, remembering how Decker's lips felt against mine. How protective he always is any time the paps rear their sordid heads. How fun he is to be around. Joss is right, he's different, and I need to be honest with myself. Then it dawns on me, this isn't delusion. This is want. Despite my reservations, I want Decker.

I want to be with Decker Trace.

The question is, does he want to be with me, too?

★ ⋆

"You want me to take it lower?" I try not to distort my face as my seamstress tucks and pins the bust of my top. Breaths are few and far between, constricted by my costume. She wheels around me on her little leather-top stool, examining her handiwork thus far. A drawn on brow arches at the incessant buzzing of my phone. I want so badly to answer it.

"If it goes any lower, I might as well not be wearing one."

"I'm only doing what the design notes say, dear. Plus, with a figure like yours, if you want to accentuate what you have going on, this is the best way." Marguerite wrinkles her snub nose and pulls another pin from her lips, sinking it into the pink satin of my bustier.

My stomach growls. All I've had to eat are the puffs of artificial rose fragrance emitting from the plug-in nearby and the small talk with Marguerite I had to choke down. To say I'm tired of being here is an understatement. I want nothing more than to be finished with this fitting already. My mind's not present, it's somewhere back across town in a pillowy white bed next to a half-naked man that I let kiss me last night. Heat pulses from my cheeks down into my belly. I let Decker kiss me, and it wasn't bad. Quite the opposite of bad, actually. I sigh at the memory, at my predicament of being trapped here instead. Which only earns me a bigger sigh from Marguerite in return.

"I want to try adding a panel of another fabric down your side. Don't move. I'll be right back." Draping her measuring tape around her neck, she uses her short legs to repel off of the pedestal I'm stuck on. In a second flat, she's rolling across the slick floor and through her open office door.

Marguerite is kind of scary, and since she holds all the sharp pointy things during our meetings, I usually listen to her, but I can't keep my mind from wandering to my phone. My eyes lag across the bright room, trailing from the gold framed 360 degree mirror before me down and across the terrazzo floor. I rock on my heels, not wanting to disobey, but my phone beckons again. It's been buzzing for hours, it seems. Only God knows how long I've been trapped up here under Marguerite's fastidious stare. When she's out of sight, I cave. I step down, grab my phone, and check my messages. Joss has sent me a picture of herself burrowed into the satin sheets of her bed. Glad she made it home safe, though I know today—and maybe tomorrow—will be rough. Butterflies storm my belly when I see the next name. Decker. Despite the inkwell of hope that's opened in my chest, he doesn't mention anything about last night. Not the puke, not the whole sharing a bed thing, and definitely not that kiss production we put on for Maleko. Only a quick *good morning* populates my screen.

I check my clock. It's 7:30 a.m. He said he was sleeping in. Does he really consider this sleeping in? I commend him for that, but if I had a whole day free, I'd sleep until at least 9:00 a.m. I try to think of something cute to say back, but it never comes to me. Another text from Joss rolls in, asking for spoilers of my newest costume. She always gets the first glimpse.

I open my camera and take a few photos in the 360

mirror in front of me, both for her records and for mine. Then I lift my phone and emphasize "what I've got going on," as Marguerite so eloquently phrased it, tossing my head back and letting the low-V of my bustier take center stage. As the cherry on top, I bite my lower lip and snap the picture, snickering to myself as I examine the campy pose. Though my top is revealing, the pose doesn't fit it. There are loose threads and frayed edges sticking out from all sides and places Marguerite has marked up to change. I look ridiculous. Giggling, I choose one to send Joss, but Marguerite appears. I scramble to close out of my texts and drop my phone back into my bag. Just as swiftly as she'd returned, she's gone again, mumbling something about supplies she forgot. I unlock my phone once more, choose a photo, type a few quick words, and press send. Careful not to be jabbed with all the metal lodged in my outfit, I jog back to the pedestal.

Marguerite pops up moments later with fabric shears and her sewing kit, a trail of blue satin tossed over her shoulder. She gets to work, none the wiser that I'd moved across the room. She mumbles and pins, mumbles and pins, arching a brow every so often at the incessant buzzing of my phone.

"You ever turn that thing off?" she gripes.

"I do. When I'm not working," I reply coyly.

"And when is that?"

"Never."

Her lips push into a tight smile as she wheels around me, inspecting her alterations. One last pin drills in beside the boning in my chest, and then she backs away. "Very good. It'll be my favorite yet, I think."

"Are you adding the crystals I asked for?"

Her lips purse. "The note said this one is intended to be a bit more sleek than what you've worn in the past."

"Sleek?" I scoff. "It's candy pink. I look like I fell out of a pack of gum."

She lifts a reluctant shoulder. "Ultimately, it's your call."

I know she's right, but my whole life goal right now is supposed to be to get back on track, keep my record label happy, fly under the radar without removing myself from the spotlight entirely—which is truly a feat—and keep my career charging full steam ahead. It all feels impossible, but I know it isn't, not if I listen to the coaching from my team. The people my mother and I have so carefully chosen. Their salaries alone should reflect how good they are. I should listen to them. *Should.* But the more I do, the farther I feel from the girl who hired them in the first place. That Lena didn't know what she was getting into. That girl is in well over her head.

Marguerite leans in, whispering as though we aren't alone. "I'll see what I can do about your crystals. Now, go change. And don't screw up my pins."

"Or stab myself?"

"Yes. That too. Wouldn't want to get blood on such a fabulous piece."

I laugh as she retreats to her office and closes the door, giving me the privacy I don't always receive during these types of fittings. My phone continues to buzz, but I'm much too eager to pull my leggings and oversized t-shirt back on. Decker's shirt from last night, to be specific. The cotton was too worn and soft for me to give it up. I shimmy out of my costume, lay it across the tufted velvet couch nearby, and pull on my clothes. My bangs fall in my eyes, and I make a mental note to get them trimmed soon, but why wait for someone else to schedule it for me? I can book online right now. My phone buzzes in my palm, sending tingles through my hand, up my arm, and straight into my belly when I see the name blowing up my screen. Decker.

When I open our chat, I'm lost. And then I scroll up and see my cleavage. My stomach falls out of the bottoms of my size eight feet. In my hurry, I didn't check which chat I clicked on. Joss didn't get the photo I snapped. Decker did. It fills my screen, taunting me, taking our chat from barely there and G-rated to a whole new meaning of "barely there" and *at least* a rating of PG-13. Because I'm a masochist—apparently—I reread our texts, scrolling past my suggestive picture with burning cheeks.

ME

> Do you like?

DECKER

> I always like what I see when I look at you

> But speaking strictly as your boyfriend, I'd say I need to see this get up in person to give a thorough review

A blush spills across my face, radiating warmth through my chest. I don't know if I should be flattered or freaked out. Sure, he saw me in a towel last night, and yeah, we shared a kiss. A really hot kiss. But this feels so *personal*. Intentional. Even though it was an accident, I can't help but want to play along.

I take a deep breath, preparing a response, debating how far I should push it. I settle on something flirty but mild. If this ends in embarrassment, at least I know the new direction my team is taking my image and costumes is effective. Besides, if I truly do want Decker, I need to feel this out. Mustering all of my audacity, I let my fingers fly, and press send. It doesn't take long for him to respond.

ME

That could be arranged.

DECKER

Maleko rented out The Mule for his birthday tonight if you wanna join

ME

Is the bustier a requirement to attend?

DECKER

You can wear whatever you want as long as I get to see you again

Am I flirting with my fake boyfriend? As wrong as I want it to feel, as much as I still want to hate Decker for the way he acted when we met, I know he isn't a bad guy. In fact, he's a really good guy. Maybe Cole was right. Maybe this *is* endgame.

My throat tightens when I realize that I've never considered that with anyone else before. Not even Callum. Sure, I'd hoped we'd work out, but I never fantasized about something as menial as watching him from the stands. *Endgame.* It sounds so final, and I immediately regret thinking it at all. Endgame is for people in love, and I'm definitely not in love. In *like*, maybe, but in love? Absolutely not. My breaths become scarce, and I sit down and throw my head between my knees, counting and breathing.

Breathe in, 2, 3, 4. Out, 2, 3, 4. Get ahold of yourself, Lena! These are all just dumb words that mean nothing. You're flirting, not asking him to marry you. Calm yourself.

I suppose we're far past the flirt-texting milestone, considering the whole kissing thing last night, but that was staged. Me moving in on him was simply to cover both our butts. Plus, technically, he's the one who put his mouth on me first, right? My heart flutters at the memory. I don't know how I was expecting him to react, but a toe-curling kiss wasn't it.

"Are you okay?" Antonia's startled voice jolts me to my feet.

My mom stands behind her, poised per usual. "What are you doing?"

"Breathing exercises. Preparing for my session. Are we ready to go to that now? I didn't know you'd be joining me today." In fact, I'd hoped to have the studio to myself. There's a few things I wanted to practice that I know they'd have opinions on, and I don't want to hear them.

"We wanted to discuss the direction we're going with Decker. So far, everything we've implemented has worked out as planned," Antonia says calmly.

My mother's calm falters for a moment as the excitement fizzes out of her. "Have you seen the headlines this morning?"

I shake my head.

She nudges Antonia who pulls out her trusty tablet. *"Pop Queen's New King."* She scrolls again. *"Decker Trace:*

King of Lena Lux's Heart. The Player and the Pop Star: The Greatest Love Story of the Season."

"That all sounds a bit dramatic," I say.

"Say what you will, but it proves the strategy is already working," my mother says through a tight grin.

Antonia clears her throat, her tawny finger prodding her tablet. "We do want to give you both a little more time together in the spotlight; however, we don't want to drag this out too long. We want to finish on a high note."

"I hardly think a breakup is ever perceived as a 'high note,'" I say dryly.

Her eyes narrow behind her thick-framed glasses. "Let me rephrase that. We want to finish with a *bang*. In this case, I think it'd be best if you two end it the same way you started it."

"How we started?" I ask.

"Online. A breakup announcement at the pinnacle of your new relationship will completely flood all of the searches. I think we may be able to completely drown out any leftover rumblings about the whole music hall thing." Antonia taps across her screen. "We have yet to notify Jason, but at this point, Decker's gotten what he signed up for, so I think they'll both let us carry the rest of this out as we see fit."

"What he signed up for?" My brows crinkle. I feel so lost.

"His brand deal. Just between us, he was hoping for something with Vital Reign, and his call came in this week. They've reinstated his offer to be their first male spokesmodel."

"Oh. Right." I try not to sound completely clueless, but I'm not sure I'm fooling anyone.

She nods as my mother finally chimes in. "I think they were secretly hoping he'd bring you along for a photo shoot, but they'd never be able to pay enough to get you into their ads." She cackles and Antonia titters back.

I nod along like I'm not a little insulted he never mentioned this to me. Why didn't he tell me? Maybe I was misreading things, but I thought we were at least close enough to discuss our deal together. What else do fake boyfriends and girlfriends talk about when they aren't accidentally sending semi-nudes and pretend-kissing each other?

A tablet lands in my lap and I pick it up, staring at the screen. *Vista City Victory Gala: For the people who help our city win.* "I didn't think I was going this year. It's the weekend I'm supposed to be in Florida. To see Dad."

My mother clucks. "We can fly him here. It's important that you and Decker are seen together in public in a big way before calling it quits. We want everyone to fall in love with the idea of the two of you. Your posts online have done well so far, but we've skimped on the appearances aspect."

"I don't want dad to fly here. I want to go home. It's his birthday," I argue.

"Lena, did you not hear anything I said?" My mother's pert nose turns red. "We can fly him here if you insist on seeing him. Vista City is a much better birthday destination than that dilapidated town anyway. You and Decker will go to this event, you'll be happy and in love, and then soon after, you'll pull the plug on the whole thing."

"It really is brilliant. I couldn't have come up with it all on my own." Antonia beams at my mom. "Not only will everyone be blindsided that a happy couple is splitting—obviously amicably; we'll work out those details later—but it'll swamp the sports forums too. Everyone will be freaking out about whether or not it'll ruin the Kings' Super Bowl chances. That is, if the Kings make it to the playoffs and beyond, as projected."

Everything boils inside, coming to a head. I stand, too caught up in my mother changing my plans, forgetting about the tablet in my lap. Antonia snatches it right before it hits the ground. "I know you don't want to see Dad, Mom, but I do. I'm not letting you take this from me."

"We wouldn't have to do it this way if you hadn't screwed everything up, Lena." My mother steps forward, pointing a sharp nail in my direction. "When you stop being so determined to ruin your reputation, then we can talk. But you're doing this. I'll notify your father tonight. We'll have someone arrange his flights immediately."

I chew my lip, clamping down on any unsavory words that have cropped up. Without another word, I turn and leave, sending Gustav a text to let him know I'm ready to go to the studio.

"I wasn't finished," my mother tries, but I keep moving.

Distance is the only thing that can shut her up for now. I don't want to think about my ruined plans or losing Decker. I'm not sure what my mom and her sidekick's plans were, but I don't care. It's been too long since I've seen my dad, since I've been home.

I open Decker's chat, and though I'd like to ask him why he didn't tell me about Vital Reign, I know I've got secrets too. Ones he'll find out soon enough, like the fact that we now have a finite date for when this facade will come to an end. Without thinking, I text him something rambly about being stuck at the studio for the rest of the night. Which means no karaoke. Do I want to be trapped at the studio? No. But at least I can lock myself in a sound-proof box there. And right now, I don't want to hear anything but the music I've dedicated my entire life to. The only steady, unchanging thing, it seems.

CHAPTER TWENTY-THREE

DECKER

KARAOKE ISN'T AS entertaining tonight. Lena's never even come with me, yet somehow I feel her void. I want her here. This place probably isn't her scene, and I try to picture her gliding around tables and people, the tang of hops and old frying oil destroying her own sweet scent.

Leaning back against the rough brick wall of the bar, I angle my body so my phone screen isn't visible. A crick shoots up my spine as I maneuver awkwardly, but at least the position affords me some privacy from my unruly team-mates. Lena's photo move this morning did something to me, and I have to see it again. To remind myself that it's actually real. It was the unexpected wake-up call I didn't know I needed, both this morning and in the whole fake arrangement. The freezing shower I drowned myself in after hardly cooled me off. The towel last night was almost the death of me, but I couldn't even enjoy that with all her accusations and name-calling. *Perv.* I laugh to myself at the memory. She's the one sending suggestive pics, and I'm the perv? I laugh again because I know she'd slap me into the next state if I tried to make that argument.

"Texting Lena? Your face is a dead giveaway," Cole drawls.

I darken my screen and sit up like a preteen who's just been caught stealing their mom's lingerie magazines. Which, of course, never happened to me. Our quarterback, Ramiel, lifts his chin in a hello, and I nod to them both.

Ty pops up beside them, a beer in his hand. "Where's your girl?"

I narrow my eyes. "Why? You gonna tell her to her face that you've been fantasizing about how short her skirt is?"

Ty cocks his head back, widening his eyes at me. "Fantasize? I was making an observation."

"What if I said the same about your girlfriend?"

"I don't have a girlfriend," he says automatically.

"Oh, and I'm sure it's your mom you were gigglin' like a schoolgirl with on the phone a little bit ago." Cole snickers and elbows Ramiel in the ribs, who smiles timidly and rubs his side.

"We all heard you," I add.

For once, Ty is stunned into silence.

"I'm just kiddin', man," I finally say to cut the tension. Ty's not a bad guy, but I've found he has trouble with boundaries. Sometimes he needs to be put in his place, and talking about Lena is where I now draw the line. I haven't gotten over his locker room commentary yet. "I'm gonna go grab another drink. You guys want anything?"

To my relief, they all shake their heads, and I'm able to

make a break for it. I don't want another drink. I haven't had anything tonight. Our season just started. If we want a fighting chance to make it to the Super Bowl again, we need to stay in elite shape. As I survey the room, I think a lot of the guys are taking last year's Super Bowl win for granted. Yeah, they work hard at practice and on the field, but outside of that, some seem to quickly forget that this sport is a round-the-clock commitment. We aren't guaranteed anything. And as last year's winners, we've got a target on our back.

A microphone squeals, and I turn to face the stage. Maleko is taking his place behind the stand as music cues up. He finishes a glass of something dark and slams it down on the barstool beside him. Then he spots me.

"Deck! Deck! Come 'ere, man." He tries to wave me over, but I'm not in the mood to sing. His girlfriend sits front row, shaking her head. This is where he met her, and he still insists on spending almost every major event in his life here. That poor girl basically lives here because of him, on and off the clock.

"Trace! Duet!" Maleko insists, missing his intro for whatever classic rock song he's chosen this time.

I walk to the edge of the stage as my phone vibrates in my pocket. "Hey, man. I forgot Lena needed me to do something for her tonight. I'll catch you later. Call me if you need a ride, or I'll send Ives or whatever."

He points to his girlfriend, who is leaning over talking to some other girl. "She's driving tonight."

"Good. Happy birthday, and don't drink too much."

"Yeah, yeah. We're in season. Got it. You're the one who hosted a party last night though," he argues.

"Just cause alcohol is present doesn't mean you have to guzzle it like water."

"You're no fun!" he shouts, raising his mic to his mouth and finally mumbling his song to a start halfway through the chorus.

I duck into the bathroom before I leave and text Ives that I'm ready to be picked up. I didn't know if I'd drink, but just in case, I had him drop me off. I was too distracted by the thought of seeing Lena to do anything but stare at my phone like some lovesick loser. But that's an exaggeration. I'm not lovesick, because that would mean I'm in love, and as much as I crave Lena, I'm not in love with her. I can't be.

Then I open my newest text. The smile that cracks across my face would be embarrassing if I weren't the only one in here. That smile is immediately erased.

LENA

> Sorry. Tell Maleko happy birthday for me, I won't be able to do it myself. Too wrapped up at the studio =(

ME

> He's three sheets to the wind and screaming Free Bird on a stage. You sure you wanna miss this?

LENA

> As entertaining as that sounds, I'm so close to cracking this song I can feel it. Been stuck here for hours, haven't even stopped for food yet.

> Can I get a rain check on seeing you?

ME

> I think you have to if we're still trying to
> convince everyone we're falling in love

Immediately, I regret mentioning it at all. Why bring up the fact that none of this is real? Why remind her when things seem to have taken a step to the next, flirtier level?

LENA

> Which reminds me, we need to talk soon.
> Antonia gave me some news and I want
> to discuss in person.

My stomach drops. No guy ever wants to hear those fatal words, but it's even more cryptic with the added "in person" bit. All the mention of Antonia does is remind me that we're on borrowed time. Our clock is ticking, and soon, I won't have an excuse to be around Lena anymore. Our deal will be done. With my Vital Reign sponsorship officially on the table, it might as well be a done deal now. As great as it feels to meet that personal goal, it doesn't compare to being with Lena. Having her to myself. I think about life without her. Life before her. It was good, but bland. The sponsorship was what I'd been pining for, but now that's been replaced with a certain blue-eyed, brown haired girl. Dumping that drawer was as much for her as it was for me. I meant it when I said I was done with that stuff. I want what Nora and Ian have, and I want to see if I can build that with Lena. With time running out, I know exactly what I need to do.

★ ⋆

I call Lena three times before she answers. After our last run-in at the studio—regardless of how last night went—I'm not showing up unannounced. Sure, I feel a little overbearing, but this can't wait. Two brown paper bags are clenched in my fists. Niko reamed me tonight for lying to him last time I was in picking up lunch for Lena and me. I gave him another one about how I couldn't just expose my relationship "before we knew it was love." He seemed happy with that little insider answer, and I tipped him extra before I left with my order. Lies are okay if they're making people happy, right?

Ives sits in the car with his flashers on, waiting for me like he's my mom after school or something. I slide in, double-checking his GPS to make sure he has the address right. I don't speak to him the entire way there, my hands are too sweaty, my collar suddenly too tight, until we park and Lena throws the door open. She's like a breath of fresh air. And then I register her expression. She looks annoyed. Then her eyes fall to the bags in my hands.

"Niko's?" she asks.

I nod.

"Thank God. I don't even think I've eaten today."

"I know."

"What did I ever do to deserve a fake boyfriend like you?" Her hand slides up my arm, landing on my shoulder. It's such a small thing, but it feels so right. "Seriously. Thank you, Decker."

I want to reach out and grab it and never let go, but I have two greasy bags dangling from each of my fists, so that'll have to wait. "Gotta take care of my girl."

Her brows arch playfully, a little grin bending her

pink lips. Just when I think I've made a mistake, that maybe she'll correct me, she snatches up a bag and starts toward the studio. Paper crinkles as she digs in, grabbing a few fries and shoving them in her mouth. I follow her down the hall until we get to the studio door. Pressing her back against it before I can get it for her, she swings it open. It's then that I realize she's still wearing my shirt.

As cute as that sounds—and as she looks—the last thing I want tonight is to be reminded that this isn't real. That last night—the kiss, the sleepover, the show we put on for everyone else all night—wasn't real. Lena deserves more than a facade, more than someone using her for what she can do for them. Vital Reign ricochets around my mind. No doubt the deal with them will be sweet. Life-changing. It's exactly what I'd been waiting for, but using Lena to achieve it doesn't feel like much of an accomplishment. In fact, it makes me feel like crap. She's worth so much more, and I want her to know that.

Finally, I muster the gonads to say it out loud. "What did you do to deserve *me*? The real question is, what did I do to deserve *you*?"

I follow her into the dark room. She doesn't respond, ratcheting my pulse up a notch or two. She takes her time sauntering through the space, flipping on a lamp and saturating half the room in yellow light. No sound guy is here, no one is at the button board. We're alone. Lena sits in an armchair, splaying her food out on a small side table.

I sit opposite her, insecurity eating at me until I decide to try again. "If it weren't for you, Vital Reign wouldn't have ever looked my way again."

She takes a bite but doesn't look up at me. "How long have you known about that?"

"Maybe a few days."

She chews and swallows. Her eyes finally meet mine, and something in them looks hurt. "Why didn't you tell me last night?"

"I wasn't thinking about it."

She stares at me incredulously, her blue eyes lasering a hole into mine. "That was like the whole reason we're doing this thing, and you aren't thinking about it?"

"I was thinking about a few other things last night."

She doesn't break eye contact, and I feel my heart hammer in my chest at the fact that I did it. I mentioned last night. I've done harder things in my life, but mentioning our sleepover—something I very well could have misinterpreted the vibes of—is right up there with some of the most nerve-wracking things I've done.

When she doesn't glower at the memory, I forge on. "You kissed me."

She coughs, bringing a fist to her chest as she nearly chokes on her bite. She takes a few chugs from her bottled water then turns toward me again. "You kissed me first."

For a long moment, we stare at each other, no one saying a thing.

"I had to," I finally say.

"You didn't."

"I did. Maleko was watching. We needed to look convincing."

She crosses her arms and leans back, her brow arched in a challenge. "You dumped out that stupid junk drawer for me."

214

I hesitate. "I did."

"So it *was* for me?"

I nod.

"You said it wasn't. You said it was for you."

I lean forward, lowering my voice. "I lied."

She eyes me. "We've both gotten pretty good at that lately, huh?" Then she sighs. "Which reminds me. Antonia wants you to go to some gala with me that's coming up soon. It's for charity. She wants us to really play up the whole *we're falling in love* act."

"The Vista Victory one?"

She nods.

"I already got my invite."

Lena cocks her head.

"For my donations to the local animal shelter. I'm speaking at it."

"My big, tough softy." She smiles up at me, and I can't help but smile back.

"When is it again?"

"Next week." She toys with a loose thread on the arm of her chair. "And then we're supposed to break up online like two days later."

My stomach drops, my brow crumpling. "That doesn't make sense. Two days after?"

"Who knows? She might insist we do it the day after." She lifts a shoulder. "She says if no one sees it coming, they'll talk about it more—post about it more—and that we'll completely drown out any other noise about us online. And boom." She snaps her fingers in my face. "You got your brand deal, I got my name as clear as it's going to be online. That's it."

"That's it?"

She nods. "We both get what we want."

Finally, I take a bite of my sandwich, trying to process everything. Is this truly what she wants? To clear her name and let me go? Vital Reign partnering with me is nice, but it's not like I couldn't have found ways to secure something else with help from my manager. Fake dating Lena was a foolproof way to expedite the process, which has proven to be the case. This has been the trajectory of our entire agreement. It was always going to end, so why does it feel so wrong?

What if I want more?

The words are on the tip of my tongue when she stands and flips a switch on the wall. Lights turn on in the recording booth as she turns to me. "I wanted to ask your opinion on something new."

I pull myself from my stupor. Wanting more doesn't matter when someone else is involved. Lena's career will always take precedence. Travel for tours takes longer than my travel for away games. We'd never be able to sync up. I'd never be able to see her. What would be the point of trying?

I square my shoulders, running a hand through my hair. "My musical expertise? I thought you'd never ask."

She rolls her eyes and pops open the door to the room beyond the glass. Lena moves through the space, the sound of her steps drowned out by all the padding on the walls. Each footfall lands carefully over cords and around other obstacles until she reaches the far corner. A white guitar glitters up at her, and she swipes it off its stand, slinging it across her body. Seconds later, she's standing in front of me again.

She idles there, unmoving, until finally gesturing to the chairs beside us. "Are you going to sit down or continue to stand there awkwardly?"

"Awkwardly? Stoic, maybe. Awkward, never."

A laugh huffs from her perfect lips as she sits and begins to strum. "Whatever helps you sleep at night, I guess."

I'll miss her sassiness when we have to say goodbye. Her thick lashes fan over her cheeks as she watches her fingers pick and strum.

I sit. "You know, the last time I was here you called me a stalker."

"And last night I called you a perv. What about it?"

"Do you call all your boyfriends names?"

She looks up at me, her fingers stilling, her dark brow arching. "They're terms of endearment."

"They didn't feel that way."

"I'd apologize for hurting your ego, but I feel like that's impossible." She leans back unapologetically and begins strumming again.

"Lena Lukowski, you drive me crazy, you know that?"

She sucks in a deep breath, her bottom lip pulling into her mouth as she charges on into the song. Her voice softens. "Are you going to keep jabbering or are you going to let me sing?"

"By all means, sing."

And so she does.

Her voice is even more beautiful than I remember it being the first time we were here—the night she accused me of stalking her—and it far outweighs the unnecessary autotune that's applied to her vocals on all of her tracks. It's raw and real, soft with an edge. It's very Lena. If this is the kind of stuff her team has been suppressing, they're doing everyone a disservice.

The tune is different from her typical, not as poppy, and much better off without the bass they've been throwing on her songs lately. It's new—never been heard— and she chose to sing it for me. My heart ramps up, contrasting with the slow consistency of her beat. The passion in each strum of her guitar thrums through me, like a whisper to my soul. Her lips press together as she hums the final notes, her blue eyes locking with mine. Heat flares up my neck, and I have to remind myself to breathe. When she finishes, there's no "jabbering" left in me. I'm speechless.

"Well?" she prompts.

I clear my throat, giving the words a moment to materialize. "I'm not sure what kind of *expertise* you're looking for here."

"Was it good, Decker?"

"What do you mean 'was it good?'" I smirk, handing her a remark specifically catered to her brand of brashness. "I never thought I'd see the day that Lena Lux came to anyone—let alone me—for validation."

"I don't need validation." Her jaw clamps tighter with each syllable. "Was it good or not?"

I can't keep the frown from finding my face. "Of course it was good. Better than good."

She rolls her eyes. "You got your Vital Reign deal, no need to butter me up now. Be honest."

"I am being honest."

She's seething. Maybe my comment was too far, but I thought she'd find it playful or at least be able to handle it. After all, I've been slapped in the face with her words so many times I've lost count.

She stares at the strings of her guitar. "I don't need validation."

And then it hits me. Validation. How stupid have I been not to realize it or how deep my words would cut? Everything she's done thus far has been to appease her team, her ex, or her fans. She's always seeking approval from someone. And I can't blame her, sometimes it feels like the only option to keep a career afloat, but I hate that she feels like it's her only way to survive.

My hand finds her knee, her eyes locking in on it before slowly traveling up my arm to my face. In her gaze, I can finally see the insecurity I never realized she held. No smart-mouthed retort comes barreling from her lips to cover it up this time. Instead, they quiver until she breaks. Tears fill her eyes as she fights to hold them back.

"Come here," I say quietly. To my surprise, she doesn't refuse.

The guitar slips from her lap as she gently glides it onto the floor and rests it against the arm of the chair. Within seconds, she's in my arms, burying her face in my chest. Her cries are silent, but I can feel warm dampness seeping into the cotton of my shirt.

"It's just been a long day." Her excuse is muffled as she presses into my sternum. "I've been here too long."

"Did someone tell you that song wasn't good, Lena?"

She shrugs. "My manager didn't like it."

"Your mom?"

She shrugs again, her face anchoring deeper into my shirt. "She's usually right about that stuff, as much as I hate saying it out loud." She leans back, finally looking into my face, nose and eyes a little more swollen than moments ago. "She's the only reason I've been able to stay in the spotlight so long."

"What?" I almost laugh at how outrageous her claim is. Her mom is the reason she's famous? What have these people said to her to make her believe that? My blood boils as I consider the years of conditioning it took for her to believe something so illogical.

"I owe it to her—and to me—to at least listen to her. She always finds a way to save my butt. I screw up all the time. I disappoint fans. I embarrass myself. Say stupid things, make stupid choices." She sits back on her heels, rubbing a hand over her tear-streaked cheeks before throwing it in my direction. "Case and point. You wouldn't be here right now if it wasn't for this insane arrangement."

I miss the feel of her close to me, but I'm relieved the tears seem to have stopped. "Maybe not, but if you hadn't made those choices I wouldn't be here."

She arches a brow. "That's what I said."

"And I'm glad I am."

She pulls in a deep breath, her eyes tracing my face. "Me too."

CHAPTER TWENTY-FOUR

LENA

IN THE DIM LIGHT, Decker looks like something I'd stumble upon in some historic art gallery. He's beautiful. And the way he's looking at me... I have millions of adoring fans, a list of exes the entire world seems to be keeping track of, but no one has ever looked at me the way he is now. Decker's gaze is a tangle of tenderness and something else. My heart stutters for a moment. It's desire. He looks like he wants to kiss me. Again. And after last night, I want nothing more than to pull him to me and press my lips against his until I can't feel them anymore. Until I can't feel the uncertainty swirling inside me. Everything with my mom, Callum, my career, this horribly confusing arrangement with Decker... I want to push it all aside and go numb.

Before I do something I'll regret, I hoist myself back into my chair and pull my guitar onto my lap. Music is my escape. It's the closest thing I can get to a distraction, to mute the world around me. The sets for my shows may be carefully curated to appease the thousands who come to watch me, but outside of that stage, I get to choose what I play. Music can exist as both a chore and an escape. Some of the most worthwhile things in life seem to be that way.

I pluck a couple of notes, reminding myself that if I kiss Decker right now, that's it. I can't go back from that. I'll be putty in his strong hands, his to toy with however he pleases. For a brief moment, I let myself meet his gentle eyes. As much as I want to believe that Decker wouldn't hurt me, that the adoration he's gazing at me with now is real, I can't deny his past. Bouncing from girl to girl used to be his norm, and there's no doubt that at least a handful of those women thought they could be the one. And he broke their hearts anyway. Why would he treat me any differently? Something inside hisses that he won't, despite his displays lately. It's painful to consider. What's even more painful is the thought of my sweet Decker being the type of guy who hurts someone and moves on like it's nothing. Worse than that, I can't quiet the tiny part of me whispering that my judgment in men is wrong yet again.

My sweet Decker.

Ugh. Who talks like that? Not me.

I strum my guitar a little louder, drowning out the fact that as much as I wish I wasn't...

I think I'm falling for Decker Trace. Like *really* falling.

Which only complicates things further. If there's anything I've learned about myself over this year's disasters, it's that I don't know how to find balance. I overwork myself. I throw myself too far into relationships and get hurt because of it. However, if there's one thing I now know for certain, it's that with a little strategy, my career can be saved even when my relationships can't. And so my career must continue to come first. I've worked too hard to build what I have to throw it away for someone who could just as easily toss me aside. I didn't spend a decade busting my butt to be someone's fling. I've missed out on school dances, birthdays, and holidays, and smiled all the way through it when I felt like falling apart. I'm stronger—more successful—because of it. The thought hits me in the gut like a sucker punch. This whole year, I've been playing with fire, letting myself take this job for granted when I've sacrificed so much to be here. I won't do it anymore.

I dip my head, my fingers bounding over the strings, strumming faster. The tune is something I've been working on for a while. My intention was for it to mimic the pounding of my heart when falling in love, but I now realize that was silly. Because from my experience with Decker, sometimes falling is slower, sweeter, calmer. And mostly unexpected. Playing it now feels contrived. When I look up, Decker isn't watching me play, he's staring into my eyes.

He wets his lips, and I watch them as they part. "You're glad I'm here?"

My heart pounds, finally keeping up with the harsh rhythm of this dumb song as I play louder. "What?"

Slowly, he reaches out like I'm some wild dog that might nip and runs his hand down my arm, stilling my playing. "You said you're glad I'm here."

My teeth find my bottom lip, and I chew it as I watch his mouth curve into that megawatt smile of his. For a split second, I waver, a million questions bursting through my brain. What would it feel like to kiss him alone in this room, without an audience, on our own accord? What if all the times I thought we could work, I was right? What if Decker was the end of "Sad Girl Lena?" What if I could have my career and Decker too?

"I did say that," I admit, dropping my guitar to the floor again.

"You also said your mom is the reason you're famous."

"That's not really what I said—"

Decker snorts.

My guard flies up at the sound. "What?"

His voice is soft when he finally speaks. "I want you to listen to me." His eyes search my face before he continues. "Everyone fell in love with *you*, not your mom or your team or whatever. You don't owe anyone anything—not even the fans. You've worked hard for what you have. Don't let anyone else take credit for that."

I press my lips into a tight line, willing them not to bend at his words.

"Never for a second think that your ideas, your songs, shouldn't be heard. Your opinions matter just as much— *more*—than any of theirs. With them or without them, everything you've accomplished is *yours*." He veers across the small table between us, resting his elbow on it. He wants to be closer to me, and I'd be lying if I said I didn't want the same thing. "Forget everyone else. Just be you, Lena. That's more than enough."

The sentiment feels like blasphemy. Forsake my fans? My team? But the lightness that replaces my question is answer enough, and I know he's said exactly what I've been needing to hear.

For a split second, I give in and lean, soaking in what

could be one of the last times I see him besides the gala. Our arms touch, and I let my hand give into the urge, lacing my fingers through his amid the crumpled napkins and now-cold deli food atop the table. Blood whooshes in my ears as he stares at our interlocked hands.

I suck in a deep breath, holding it for a moment before letting it gush from my mouth in one rushed explosion. "I worry people only love me for what they can get from me. What I can offer them."

He shakes his head, pinning me with a steadiness in his eyes I didn't know I craved. "Lena, you're easy to fall in love with. Trust me on that one."

I lean closer from where I sit, wanting to fall to the floor again and launch myself back into his arms. I want to feel his heart beating in my ear as the rhythm of his breathing soothes me. I want to bury my face into his shirt so I can smell nothing but that comforting scent of *him*. My mouth is desperate for his, but still, despite the things he's said, I fear that if I kiss him now, I may ruin everything we've worked for so far. What if this fake relationship blows up in my face, too? So I resist, bringing his warm hand to my lips and gently pressing them against his knuckles. His free hand finds my cheek, and he cups it there, holding me together for a shadow of a moment.

My eyes sting, and all I can do is think about how desperately I want to reciprocate his sentiment, but I've been here before. In my last relationship. Callum always knew what to say to talk me down, to get what he wanted. Because words are words. As sweet as they may be, they're empty until proven otherwise. But there's one thing Decker and I can both agree on. I've worked too hard. I can't let my heart keep pulling me back into my judgment patterns that take me—and my relationships—nowhere. Falling too fast, too soon, is part of the problem. It isn't romantic. It's reckless.

"I think I should go home," I whisper, releasing him. "I need to rest."

Decker hesitates, his other hand falling from my face. "I'll give you a ride."

I squeeze my eyes shut, shaking my head. "Gustav is waiting around back with a driver."

He won't argue, but I know he doesn't want to go. I wonder if he wants what I do, to tangle up on these chairs together and never leave.

Decker's eyes are sad little green pools as he nods. "I'll talk to you tomorrow?" It's not a statement. It's a question.

"We'll make plans for the gala. Maybe squeeze in one last public appearance before it."

"If that's what you want," he says.

I smooth my trembling lips into what I hope looks like a smile. "It is."

His jaw tics as he stands and shows himself out without another word.

CHAPTER TWENTY-FIVE

DECKER

IVES IS WAITING down the block when I emerge from the studio. The walk isn't long, but it's lonely. I run a hand through my hair, prying loose the pomade I'd used to perfect it earlier. I'd hoped maybe Lena would be the one undoing it, but nothing ever seems to go the way I hope.

My ride kicks on as I approach, and I attempt to smile at Ives as I jerk open the back door. A couple of teenage boys pass by, yelling something about football, and I nod back. I think one even snaps a picture, but I'm too wrapped up in the fact that Lena had nothing to say to me. I told her she was easy to fall in love with, and she had nothing to say. I wish she would have at least denied me, told me I was outkicking my coverage, anything. The way she looked at me, touched me, the way her lips brushed my hand... There's no way she feels nothing. Something's there—we both know it—even if she won't say it out loud. So why didn't I come straight out and tell her?

Lena Lukowski, I've fallen in love with you.

It's the sappiest thing I've ever not said.

More confused than ever, I sink into the leather seat and pull out my phone. Lena's name is at the top of my inbox, and though I wish I could text her right now, I wish even more that I were still with her. Maleko's name is next, some drunk gibberish asking where I went, followed by an uneventful group chat with Mom and Ian.

Fake dating someone is incredibly isolating. No one else is in on it, so when you fall hard for the other half of your faux relationship, there's no one to talk to when you need it most. Except someone else does know. He's the reason I'm in this situation. I open my call logs and scroll until I find his name. Jason Lancaster. Sucking in a deep breath, I click it.

He answers in three rings. "Decker, what is it?"

"Well, hi to you too, Jason."

"You never call me first. What's wrong?" he presses.

"Nothing is wrong. I just wanted to touch base about wrapping up this relationship with Lena. She mentioned something about another public appearance this week and then the gala. Wasn't sure if you knew details about either." I put the call on speaker and tilt my head back against the seat.

"Antonia's been taking the reins on most of that. I'll have to revisit the contract."

I clear my throat, already concocting a plan. I can't force Lena to tell me she loves me, but I can show her how much I love her. She deserves the best. If this is my last shot to prove it, I want to make it count. I don't want to tell her goodbye, and I'll do everything it takes to make her want to stay.

"I want to make it feel special. Really make people take notice so the shock is that much greater when we call it quits, you know?" I don't even like saying it out loud, but it's my reality. "I want us to finish on a high note, as they say."

"They do say that. Not usually about breakups, but who am I to judge." He chuckles. "What did you have in mind?"

For a moment, I wonder if I'm overstepping by asking him for favors. He's not my personal assistant, but as my manager, he's the only one as invested in this as I am. "Can you find out what color Lena's dress is for the gala?"

"Why can't you ask her?"

Because it might be awkward, given how we parted ways tonight. And also the last thing I want to do is remind her one more time that we're almost over. Almost.

"Just find out, please."

He snorts. "That's it?"

"And I need the number of the best florist you know. And some balloons."

"Balloons?"

A few moments and a little explanation later, I hang up on a confused but compliant Jason.

I want our last evening together to be special. My chest pinches as my street comes into view ahead. I knew someday we'd end, but I never expected to not want it to. I could never have predicted I'd fall in love with her. Sadness slithers in that a night which could be so memorable is going to be completely overshadowed by what I now accept is simply a business deadline.

I fall in love, and Lena still sees a deadline.

A bitter laugh escapes me when I think about how desperately I wanted to kiss her tonight. Embarrassment streaks through the pain. I was thinking about being alone with her, and she was thinking about dumping me. And it's all happening the night that I meet her dad? Admittedly, that's still something that makes me nervous, but what puts me even more on edge is the fact that I'll be meeting him... and then dumping his daughter.

As Ives pulls into my garage and I shuffle out into the dark night, I decide to take the stairs. There's no time for the gym tonight, and the only thing that helps me process my thoughts is moving. And I have a lot to think about.

CHAPTER TWENTY-SIX

LENA

"ARE you sure this doesn't look ridiculous?" Dad adjusts his velvet jacket, tugging at the lapels. The deep rosewood shade of it perfectly mimics the details of my mother's ball gown. I can't remember the last time I saw him dressed in anything but a linen shirt.

My mom rolls her eyes. "It doesn't, Roger. It's great with your complexion, and it matches your new glasses."

It's the closest thing to a compliment I've heard her give him in years. She sashays down the long hall of my house, leaving me alone with my dad.

He straightens his collar again, gazing out the wall of windows overlooking the dusky coastline before turning to me. "Please tell me she isn't just trying to shut me up."

I smile, more than glad he's here, even if we aren't spending his birthday lowkey, at home, and in Florida like we'd originally planned. "You're the most handsome birthday boy I've ever seen."

"Ha! Boy." He arches a graying brow from under the

frame of his round glasses. "You and your flattery. That's why I miss you when you're gone."

I roll my eyes. "I learned from the best."

He smiles at himself in the mirror before reaching back out for the bubbly my mother poured him an hour ago. No doubt it has lost its chill.

"I'm glad you're here, Dad."

He sips and smiles. "Me too, Lena-Love."

My mother clomps through the room, shoving in her chandelier earrings and dismissing the staff that helped us dress and get ready tonight. Antonia flits around behind her, wearing a wide-legged plum pant suit that beautifully complements her bronze complexion and fits her personality. She's all about function and practicality.

"Oh! When do I get to meet this boyfriend?" My dad drains his glass and sets it down as one of our assistants scoops it up and replaces it with another.

My stomach drops. It's not the usual I-get-to-see-Decker drop that typically slams into me. It's harsher, edged with dread, and it takes me a few moments to find an answer. My dad is meeting Decker on the last night I get to spend with him. The last night before our breakup.

"Tonight. He's going to meet us there." I lean into the marble mantel, cleaning up a nonexistent eyeliner smudge in the gold-framed mirror above it.

"Actually, there's been a change of plans." My mom emerges from the shadows like some fairytale villain. "His manager called and said Decker has arranged a private ride for the two of you, and the more times you two are seen mooning over each other, the better. Especially since our attempts to schedule a date earlier this week fell through."

"I thought I was riding with Dad," I argue.

"He's coming with me. You're going with Decker," she says with her typical finality.

I square my shoulders. "But I don't—"

"It's fine. I will be with you the whole night. And the whole weekend. Heck, maybe even the whole month if you'll have me." My dad takes the fresh glass of champagne from our assistant before wrapping an arm around me. "You spend time with him. It's not often you get a fancy date night. You work too much. Enjoy your evening."

"It's still work," I say, rolling my eyes as I take his flute of golden bubbles and down it. It feels wrong to call a charity event work, but if my mom planned it, in my eyes, it's a chore.

He pats me on the back. "It's only work if you think it is."

My mom claps her hands, breaking up our conversation. "Well, Jason said Decker should be here any minute. Do you have everything?"

"Everything?" I ask, as I watch people float about the room. By way of answer, someone brings my shoes and gold clutch. One even tries to put my shoes on for me before I step back, thanking them and sending them on their way. I plop on the couch to pull them on myself.

"Your dress will crease," my mom sneers.

Rolling my eyes, I continue lacing the fat satin ribbons up around my ankles. They're a dip dyed lilac that darkens into a deep fuschia to match my dress. Kings blue nails gleam up at me from the open toes, and I wiggle them, enjoying the freedom. I love wearing boots, but nothing beats a fresh pedicure and air on my skin.

Decker's car arrives before I have time to do more than finish a quick glass of champagne and grab my bag. It's my second drink of the night, and due to some unforeseen but exciting additions to my upcoming work schedule—which involved a few chaotic last-minute video meetings—I haven't eaten much since before lunch. The liquid buzzes through my veins, tingling down my arms and warming my chest as I kiss my dad on the cheek, take a deep breath, and head out the door. My stomach flip flops as I think about telling Decker my recent work developments. I know he'll be just as excited as I am.

Gustav meets me outside, ushering me to the circular drive. In the dim light of the waning day, I spot Decker looking more handsome than ever, if that's possible. His tux is sharp: a classic black with clean lines that accentuate his broad shoulders, his hair pushed back and less tousled than normal. My eyes trail up his chest, over his black bow tie and Adam's apple, and land on his fresh-shaven jaw. A warm sensation pools in my belly at the sight of him. Although I love his laidback look, seeing him like this nearly knocks me over.

Decker truly is a work of art.

He smiles as I approach, his eyes never leaving me. A jittery feeling surges inside, and suddenly, I'm more than a little grateful I guzzled those glasses. He swings open the door like he's my chauffeur or something, leaning into the backseat and popping back out with an armful of candy-colored flowers. The bouquet spills over with bright pinks and yellows and faded purples, feminine and bursting with life. Though I've never told him what type I prefer, what-ever assortment is in this bouquet is my new favorite.

"I got you these. Antonia texted Jason to tell him you're wearing pink. So I just kinda went crazy with it." His eyes crinkle as he passes them to me. "You don't have to keep them, it's not like you can take them in with you, but they reminded me of you."

I press my face into their petals, taking in the sweet scent. The champagne rears its head in a coy question. "Why's that?"

"Because they're vibrant and beautiful." A grin spans his handsome face as he takes my hand and helps me to the front of the SUV. He must notice my confusion because a smirk quickly takes its place. "Just wait."

When we round the vehicle, I see two plastic boxes sitting on the hood. Decker takes my bouquet and passes it to Gustav, then reaches for the little boxes.

"What's that?" I crane my neck as he pries one open, and I immediately know what it is. "You bought me a corsage?"

"I did." He gently lifts my arm into position, stretching the elastic band before sliding the bundle of blooms onto my wrist. It's like a miniature version of the bouquet that Gustav looks so out of place holding right now. Decker's smile pushes into his cheeks, and I'm afraid his face might crack. Then I realize I'm smiling too. Maybe even harder. Handing me the other box, he makes a show of brandishing his lapel. "Your turn."

In my hands is a matching boutonniere. I pop open the case, pulling it out and panicking when I remember I have to *pin* this on him. "Do you really trust me to pin this? Especially after all the times you've annoyed me this week?"

I mean for it to be playful, but his smile wavers. "Good thing I got a magnetic one then, huh?"

I smile brightly, hoping his will return too. Within seconds, his pink cluster of flowers is securely attached via magnet to his silky lapel. When I turn back toward the vehicle, ready to climb in, he catches my arm.

"One more thing." Carefully, he spins me around and positions my body in front of him so my back is pressed flat against him. Sliding his hands down my arms, his fingers find mine, and my heart pounds as they lace together. His head dips so his lips graze my ear. "Smile for the camera."

I tilt my head, more than confused, and then there's a flash. Ives darts around in front of us as Decker uses me for a prop, just like we did all those weeks ago in my living room as we prepared to tell the world about us.

"What's going on?" I ask.

"Oh, sorry. Right. You've never been to one." He clears his throat. "Happy prom!"

A shocked laugh bursts from my throat. "Happy prom?"

"Okay, that's probably not something people say, but you told me you never went to prom, so I brought you—" He grabs my hand, thanks Ives, and yanks me to the back door before throwing it open. "A prom!"

A purple balloon floats out like he planned it that way, and I watch as it disappears into the evening sky. He helps me climb into the back of the vehicle, which has been completely engulfed by streamers and an assortment of balloons.

"What do you think?" he asks.

"I think..." I try to find the words, but I'm nearly speechless. "I don't know what to say. I wasn't expecting..."

His smile falters as I lose the ability to articulate a response. I'm not even sure what I'm thinking.

"I know it's not actually prom, but I wanted our last night to be memorable. And I wanted to thank you for putting up with me." He tweaks his lips into a crooked little smile that's so adorable I want to leap across the seat.

A snarky remark pops to the front of my mind, but I tuck it away. After this stunt, the least I can do is drop the sarcasm and offer him something sincere. I try to keep it as professional as possible. "This means a lot, Decker. It's so... thoughtful. I've had a lot of fun with you over the past couple of months. And I'm glad out of everyone Antonia could have set me up with that she picked you."

He smiles and fidgets with a balloon that's drifted into his lap. I've been to a lot of awards shows, galas, and red carpet events, but this time it's different. It really does feel like I'm going to prom, which is pretty magical considering I had other priorities as a teen. However, I can't regret that. I got what I wanted. The fame, the fans. The sacrifice got me to where I am at this very moment. Prom may be about seven years too late, but hey, at least it's happening. And it's all because of Decker.

Gustav climbs into a different vehicle parked behind us, and soon we're all on our way. The inside of our ride is set up kind of like a limousine. There's various seating so we can face each other or sit next to one another, even though the back of it isn't quite as large as a typical limo. I'm not sure what I would have done if he'd picked me up in one. It would have been incredibly cheesy. A bouquet bigger than my head is cheesy enough, but just the right amount. Though a limousine definitely has big prom energy, I'm glad he opted for something more modest. This is a charity event after all.

"Are you excited to meet my dad?" I ask, eyeing the bottle of champagne sticking out of a built-in ice chest. There's certainly no shortage of bubbly on an event night.

"More nervous than excited, if I'm being honest."

I'm much more charmed by that than I expected. "Nervous?"

"It's always nerve-wracking to meet your girlfriend's dad."

My cheeks pink at his admission.

He follows my sightline, reaching for the glasses secured in velvet near the bottle. "Drink?"

"Trying to curb those nerves?"

"I figured we should at least toast to the closing of our... agreement," he says.

"You always make it sound so awkward. Agreement, arrangement, partnership. We aren't done yet. You might as well keep calling it a relationship until it's over."

"In what? Like..." He wiggles his arm, a thick gold watch sliding out from under his jacket. "Four hours?"

Is that all we have left? I raise my glass and smile despite the fresh sadness that's cropped up. "Cheers to finishing strong."

He raises his too, his green eyes somber as he drains his drink.

My phone rings and I apologize to him before I answer it. Typically, I would let my mom go to voicemail, but after our meeting today and the rapid developments, I know keeping her docile tonight means I need to answer. If not for my sake, for my dad's. He's the one who will be trapped with her all night.

Decker kicks at a balloon, staring out the tinted window impassively, his empty flute dangling from his fingers. I hang up the phone and wait for him to continue the conversation.

"That was my mom," I finally say when I can't take the silence anymore.

"How is she?" he asks flatly, pouring another glass.

"She's good. She was talking to me about the big news I have."

He pauses mid-pour. "Big news?"

I take a deep breath. "At least one of us has been confirmed to be playing at the Super Bowl."

I try to smile through the nerves. My mom wasn't excited when I immediately agreed to play the Super Bowl —there's more money elsewhere she says, and of course, she's right, but it's been on my bucket list since I was little. When the opportunity finally arose, I couldn't resist.

At first, I'm not sure how he's going to react. He sits there, pensive, and then a smile sprawls across his full lips and he raises his free hand for a high five. "That's awesome! Congrats! I thought they already booked the entertainment months ago."

"They did, but since Kota Sky's recent arrest and all that chaos, he'll be a little tied up to say the least. They dropped him and called me. My tour doesn't start until summer next year, so it worked out. It'll be a good place to test one of the re-recordings I've been stuck on lately."

"I thought you didn't want to re-record everything."

I shrug. "I've already redone half the album, feels like a waste if I don't go through with the rest. Plus, like I told you, listening to my team hasn't failed me yet."

He shakes his head, staring into his glass.

"What? It's the least I can do since my mom is already outraged I jumped on the chance to perform at the Super Bowl before confirming it with her."

"That seems to be a theme, you rebel."

I reach out, striking his knee with a quick flick. He winces playfully, but the judgment doesn't leave his eyes. My insecurity builds. I know he thinks I'm too dependent on them. "Obviously, it works, you neanderthal. You got your brand deal, and I got asked to perform at a major event. It's like everyone totally forgot about my little mishap with Callum."

"Callum." He sneers. "What a joke."

"You really don't like him, do you?"

"I like him enough not to break his knees."

I can't help but laugh, dissipating some of the tension. "Oh, is that what you were going to do to him the day he picked up his crap?"

"I thought it'd be easier than cleaning blood out of the rug."

I grimace, but honestly, I'm flattered he'd stand up for me like that. Even if it does feel a little too aggressive.

Silence falls between us as I stare out the dark window. Lights flash by, but I can hardly make out any detail against the night sky.

Decker shifts in his seat. "So, the two of us are playing at the Super Bowl."

I roll my eyes. "If you make it."

"Again? I think we will."

"You're a bit cocky."

"Always," he says.

"Well, I guess you have a reason to be now."

"Now?"

"According to Antonia and my mom, your popularity has skyrocketed." I wait for him to respond, but he doesn't flinch. "Did you know your jersey is currently the most purchased in the entire NFL?"

"I did."

"Weren't gonna tell me?" I ask, my words clipped.

"I figured it didn't have anything to do with us."

Us. As much as I love to hear him say it, it has everything to do with us. Our plan. It's all working, and as grateful as I am for that, it stings a little to know that my name is being capitalized on. Which is silly. That's the entire reason we're together, for what we can get from each other, and I wish that weren't the case.

"Should have you sitting pretty for The Pro Bowl at least." I lean back, staring at the diamonds in my bracelet.

"I'm not sure I care about that anymore."

"That sucks. Wasted a lot of time with lil' ol' me then," I joke, giving him my cheesiest grin.

"I'd never consider any time spent with you a waste." His voice lowers. "I'd trade The Pro Bowl for you any day."

My face flushes as he draws his eyes up to meet my stare. As much as I want to ask what he cares about now and hear him say it, that answer was enough. A flutter of wings shimmies through my belly at the thought of him making any kind of sacrifice for me. I clear my throat and ask for another half pour.

"Plus, I don't know if you know this, but if—*when*—we make it to the Super Bowl, they won't let me go to the Pro Bowl. They'll send someone else in my place. Can't risk getting hurt before the big game." Decker shrugs as he tops off my glass. "It's probably stupid I want to go so bad. It's not like it really means anything—not compared to the Super Bowl, at least."

"It's not stupid if you care about it," I say.

Decker smiles and my heart stirs.

We chat and drain our drinks as the driver flies down the last few blocks of our excursion. Months ago, I never would have thought we'd be here. A pleasant conversation with Decker Trace—one that doesn't make me roll my eyes the whole time? Never. But now, it's something I'll miss.

Decker downs the last of his bubbly before shoving the flute back into its velvet encasement, and within seconds, he's across the SUV, sitting beside me. His jacket brushes my bare arm, and suddenly I wish we were back in his room—with that jacket in the closet and his shirt missing again. His comforting scent fills my lungs, and I want nothing more than to sneak back in his bathroom and read his cologne label one more time so I'll know what it is he smells like after he's gone. After tonight.

"You look stunning, by the way. I meant to say that sooner." He nudges me with his shoulder, and I turn to face him.

"Had to have a few glasses before you could muster a compliment for your girlfriend?"

"You are pretty intimidating."

"I am not."

"You held a grudge against me for like ever because I

ate gummy worms that I didn't know were supposed to be yours."

"Only because you ruined my post-show tradition."

He pauses. "Post-show tradition?"

I nod. "It's something my dad started. That was the first time in ten years I didn't get a single sour worm after a performance."

"I didn't know I was interrupting a tradition." He grimaces, then his face softens, his green eyes wistful. "I'd be pretty mad too if someone interfered with something my dad started."

I hate when that sadness creeps in, and I reach out, gently placing a hand on his knee. His eyes meet my fingers first before finding my face. Something in my chest dances as his smile resumes, and I have to look away.

"Regardless of tradition, didn't Darlene teach you it's rude to be the one who empties the candy bowl?" I jab playfully, hoping to recover the once buoyant mood. Whipping my head to face him, I wobble and realize I've had a couple glasses too many. The first priority at the gala is to find a snack. And some water. If this is our last time together, I can't risk forgetting it because I drowned myself in champagne again. I've never heard Decker speak publicly. I want to remember his speech, this night, *him*.

He lifts a dismissive shoulder. "That's subjective."

"Well, you subjected me to a whole lot of rudeness and not a whole lot of gummy worms."

"I made up for it later at least." His hand slides across the seat to clasp mine and my heart nearly stops.

"Fine. I guess I can overlook your bad manners after the whole candy shop stunt."

He brings my hand to his face, his lips brushing over it in a whisper of a touch as he says, "So we're closing the book on the gummy worm-fueled hatred?"

I can't pull my eyes away as he drags kisses across the top of each knuckle. "Slammed shut." My heart pounds as I open my palm and press it against his cheek. Finally, I pour out something I've held in since I met him. "Have I ever told you how handsome you are?"

He shakes his head, his eyes locked on mine.

"You are, Decker. You're handsome and sweet and part of me wishes this whole thing were—"

The car brakes, jolting my words to a halt. I look out the window. Of course, we're already at the gala. Before I can finish my sentence, our door is being thrown open. Decker gives me one last lingering look, and then he's gripping my hand, guiding me down the shortest red carpet known to man. Tonight is not as much about who the guests are as it is about the charities and how much attention these guests can bring to them. It feels incredibly intimate for a red carpet event, and that's fine by me.

We pose side by side, smiling and laughing—genuinely laughing—for the cameras. He kisses the top of my head for one picture, and our audience erupts. The next thing I know, he's lowering his face to mine, his green eyes searching for approval before I answer him with a chaste kiss on the lips. This does nothing but make my pulse and the decibels in the vicinity climb as photographers shout our names, asking for more angles of the "lovebirds." My racing heart is enough to keep me moving. I grab his hand and lead him inside the old theater, wanting to keep him all for myself, but knowing I can't.

The venue is one of my favorite Vista City landmarks. It's breathtaking. Art deco designs and lush rugs surround us. Hand-painted walls and ceilings guide us further into the impressive space. I smile and wave as we rush through the crowd, Decker still trailing behind, a dreamy grin pasted across his lips as his eyes dart from our surroundings to me. It's been so long since we discussed it, I almost forgot that the whole reason he's here with me now is because I burned up part of his retirement investment. The one that was supposed to fund his purpose: giving care and finding homes for the creatures he's most passionate about. It makes my chest ache to think that not only did I damage a tiny piece of history that night at the music hall, but a piece that Decker wanted for his own. I'd buy him a million places just like Gable's if it would make him happy. I'd even buy him a place for his shelter if he'd let me.

Before I can stop myself, I'm whirling to face him in a flurry of pink satin and pressing my lips to his again in a quick peck. I turn back around, carting him toward the ballroom where the event will be held, but I only make it three steps before he's yanking me back and spinning me to face him. Our eyes lock before his head dips and he drops a quick kiss right back on my lips. A crooked smile is pasted across his mouth when he pulls away.

My pulse accelerates as I pivot back toward our destination. "We need to find our table. Don't want you to miss your speech."

If I look back now and meet his eyes again, I'm afraid I won't be able to control myself. So, I blaze a path through the tables, not sparing a single glance over my shoulder.

Decker marches along behind me until I realize I probably look like a child lugging her doll around. Dropping his hand, I slow up, join him at his side, and loop my arm through his.

I spot our table. My mother stands, followed by my dad as we approach. Decker draws in a deep breath as he closes in on them. It's cute that he's nervous.

"Decker, this is my dad, Roger." I unhook our arms and he steps forward, exchanging a firm handshake with my dad. "And you've met my mother, of course."

"Of course. You two look great." Decker beams.

"I could say the same to you two," Dad chimes in. "And I'll be honest with ya, Deck—" I die a little at the nickname. "I haven't seen Lena-Love glow like this in... I don't know—maybe ever." He lowers his voice. "Her job can be pretty demanding."

Endearing is not typically a word I use to describe my father, but I always find it cute that he continues to refer to my hectic career as a "job," like it's any other nine-to-five. To be honest, these days I wish my schedule were as predictable as a 9:00 a.m. start and a 5:00 p.m. finish. But I know how fortunate I am to have a job some only dream of. I'm also fortunate that to my father I'm still his little Lena-Love. I'm not the girl on the stage, I'm not a paycheck, I'm simply his daughter. I smile at him, knowing he means well, but also hating that my faux-glow is fooling even him.

Decker and my dad chat it up while I stuff my face with hors d'oeuvres in an attempt to absorb some of the champagne. Bonus: If I keep my mouth full, I don't have to answer any probing questions or engage in any Super Bowl talk with my mother. A waiter in a white button-up and black bowtie drops off a salad, and I pick at it as my mother engages in a conversation with some other local philanthropist. Antonia is happily chatting with some local politicians across the room, and Gustav has stationed himself near the door, but even he seems distracted.

As much as I want to catch up with my dad, I don't want to interrupt his conversation with Decker. Both of them are fully engaged, smiling and laughing, only breaking when Dad needs a sip of his scotch. Decker sneaks me a wink and warmth spreads across my exposed decollete. I dip my head, digging into my salad and wondering if anyone else notices the flush. The two of them continue on and the butterflies in my belly multiply tenfold as Decker politely excuses himself when someone on stage summons him to the podium. He leans down and pecks my cheek, drawing it out a little longer than necessary before climbing the handful of steps toward the microphone. When the applause stops, he flashes that million-dollar smile and starts in about his passion for The Vista City Rescue Society.

I'm completely enamored with him, along with everyone else in the room. His passion for these animals is palpable, and I find myself wishing I were something he talked about that dearly. Which is kind of weird—to want to be spoken about in the same way as an animal rescue. But I know he loves it, and deep down, though I know it could never work between us—because of our careers and the timing and the fact that it's too soon for me to seriously consider dating for real and about a thousand other reasons —I kind of wish he could love me too. And then his eyes flash to where I sit. My breath catches in my throat at the sudden shift in the room as everyone turns my way. Decker hones in on me, his full lips parting into a smile that would make anyone weak. Everyone falls away as he wraps up his speech.

"And I want to acknowledge you, Lena. If anyone deserves an award for their devotion to helping others, it's you. Our time together has changed me—my life—for the better in unimaginable ways, and I have you to thank for that." His eyes lock with mine a split second longer before dragging back across the crowd, leaving me melting in my seat as a collective *awww* sounds throughout the ballroom. Though he's moved on to address everyone else, I can't take my eyes off him.

A tapping sound pulls my attention. I turn to find my mom reaching across the table, a fork poised between her fingers as she raps it against the floral centerpiece between us.

I yank the fork from her, and she smiles gleefully, her voice a loud whisper. "Did you tell him to include you in the speech?"

I shake my head, trying to keep the annoyance from shadowing my features.

Her eyes light up. "Brilliant move on his part. People will eat that up."

I try to reciprocate her smile, but I know why she's glowing. Because the fact that he mentioned me will only fuel the rumors after our impending breakup. Deep down, I know that Decker didn't do it for that purpose, but the doubt still slithers in. What if he did? What if his words were just another way to ensure he's set once we go our separate ways?

He gives his final thank you for the award and lopes back to our table, sliding into his seat next to me and giving my hand a light squeeze. When he smiles at me, any uncertainty drifts away. Decker wouldn't do that to me. He can be strategic, but he's not manipulative. We may be headed for a breakup, but it isn't tonight. We still have time. The butterflies in my belly kick up speed, turning into something far more aggressive than those irritating little bugs I've gotten so used to over the past couple of months.

Decker sits beside me, none the wiser, as my parents congratulate him on a speech well done. My mother slathers on how *wonderful* it is that he mentioned her beloved daughter in his acknowledgments. Decker's smile doesn't falter, his words remain polite, but there's an emptiness in his eyes as he responds. He's already tired of her, and he's hardly even been around her since we began our arrangement. Finally, Dad has the good sense to cut her off, thanking Decker for his dedication to the charity as he totes my mom off to chat with some table across the room.

A smile is cemented on my face as passersby shake Decker's hand, patting him on the back, thanking him for being a "voice for the voiceless." Of all the men I've dated —real or fake—none have been referred to as anything even remotely similar to that. It makes him sound like some kind of vigilante superhero. He's humble as he accepts each compliment, and dare I say, he sounds *modest*. Decker Trace, the guy whose ego and attempted humor gets under my skin, is actually modest. And *charming*. Both of these I've experienced, but watching him now, I know for sure that I didn't imagine it.

An older man with an impressive handlebar mustache

shakes Decker's hand, gives him a jolly pat on the back, and disappears back to his table as the next speaker is announced and emerges from the crowd. Decker leans back, nodding to others as they compliment him from their tables and whisper about his job well done.

Finally, he turns my way and catches me staring, his mouth quirking into an irresistible grin meant just for me. I can't take it any longer. I seize the opportunity. Tired of sharing him, I grab Decker's hand and my clutch. Before I lose my nerve, we zigzag between the tables, to the edge of the room, and through the closest exit.

"Where are you taking me?" he asks as we maneuver through the shadowy wings of the stage.

Though it's been a while since I've performed here, I still remember the route. "I thought we could use some fresh air. Follow me."

"It doesn't seem like I have much of a choice."

A minute later, we're in the dark dressing room tucked behind the stage. Since these are strictly reserved for performances, they're empty tonight. The space is totally blacked out, save for the red emergency lights casting a dull scarlet glow that reflects off the expansive vanity and rounded bulbs lining the long mirrored wall. It's a little eerie, and I grip Decker's hand tighter as I fumble through the space looking for the lightswitch. I find it and flip it. A vampiric hiss spouts from Decker before his hand comes down over the switch again, killing the overhead lights.

"You have to warn a guy. I think you burned my retinas, and the air is *not* fresher here." He coughs dramatically.

"Baby."

"I think you mean *babe*."

I toss my clutch onto the countertop. "Can't wait to finally hear the end of that."

As soon as the words fly from my mouth, I regret them. If there's anything I've come to realize lately, it's that as much as I hate the whole nickname exchange, it hasn't been as stomach-churning with Decker on the other end of it.

"What else can't you wait for?" Decker asks, his voice lowering. I can't interpret what he means in the dark. I'm not close enough to see the quirk of a brow, and it's too dim to pick up on a glint in his eye. Did he mean that *suggestively*? Or is that only my wishful—lustful—thinking?

Suddenly, the red light morphs into something more sexy than eerie, and I take advantage of it. I step closer, so close that I can smell the remnants of mint and champagne lingering on his mouth. He moves in too and my chest brushes his torso.

At the touch, I lose my gall, and turn to face one of the mirror-lined walls instead. "For starters, I can't wait to have my time back to myself again."

"You mean, to give your time back to your team?"

"To not have a tagalong anymore," I continue on.

He moves swiftly, and soon he's behind me. "You'll miss me."

"I won't." Not even I'm buying my comebacks. I step away until I almost crash into the vanity counter bordering the room. "You're too cocky. It makes you sound delusional, you know that?"

"Getting what you want always takes a healthy dose of delusion. You of all people should know that."

"I forgot how irritating you can be."

"You like it." He moves closer, backing me against the counter until I have nowhere to go.

In the red light, I can see the perfect outline of his face. His high cheekbones, his sloping nose, the curve of his lips. His hands come down on either side, pinning me in place until fighting this is the last thing I could ever want.

He hesitates, the silhouette of his throat bobbing in the dim light. "Tell me, am I delusional for wanting you?"

I long to tell him no, that he's not, because I think I want him too. I think I more than want him. I think I want to love him, but I'm realistic, and because I know we have no future, I don't say a single thing.

Instead, I throw my hands around his neck, lifting to my toes to feel his mouth against mine. He meets my lips with the same urgency, satisfying the longing that's cropped up inside while simultaneously leaving me craving more. I'm insatiable as I greedily press my body against his, my fingers tangling in his hair. Rough stubble rakes against my skin as velvety lips devour mine, the stinging sweetness a delicious contrast. His breath hitches when we come up for air, his forehead dipping to press against mine. In a second flat, his fingers are trailing down to grip my hips, lifting me to sit on the counter at my back. And then his mouth finds mine again, his hands coasting down my spine until they're flattening into the surface on either side of my thighs. I nip at his bottom lip as things heat up again, eliciting a low growl that lets me know he's just as into this as I am.

My phone buzzes, emitting an obnoxious blue light from my open purse until it finally fades, but Decker isn't deterred. He slows the kiss, deepening it as his fingers come up to cradle my face. His hands are strong and steady, and every bit as sweet as his mouth. My phone vibrates again, this time aggressively enough to wiggle its way from my bag. Decker stills as both of us come up for air, and I can't help but to glance at my screen. Of course my mother would be calling me right now.

"Ignore it." Decker's voice is husky. His mouth captures mine again as goosebumps prick up my arms.

I tilt my head back, breaking our kiss and staring at the red emergency light overhead. "Decker," I manage to say as I catch my breath.

He doesn't stop. He stays close, his nose grazing my cheek as he trails kisses along my jaw, sending me gasping for breath when he finds the sensitive spot on my neck that drives me wild. I giggle as my hand flies to cover it. Gently, he pries my fingers away.

I bite my lip as he lands on the spot again, but the incessant buzzing starts up once more, and I can't help but to grab my phone. "Sorry, I just... I just want to make sure everything's okay since we didn't tell anyone we were leaving."

"Oh, right. Forgot to ask your mom's permission to leave the table."

I shoot him a glare I know he can't see. "In case you forgot, this is technically a work function. My manager is allowed to be in the know."

"Sorry, didn't realize we're on the clock."

"Of course we are. A deal's a deal. And right now, no one can see us." I hold up my phone in his face. "At least someone is still thinking straight."

"Who? Your mom?" He laughs. "You can tell yourself that, Lena, but I think we both know that excuse isn't valid."

"It's not an excuse."

"Just admit your mom still pulls all the strings—well, her and Antonia—and despite all the crap you said about doing this on your own terms, you still aren't. You're letting them yank you around like some demented puppet masters."

His words have teeth, gnawing at me more than any of the other dumb things he's ever said.

I suck in a deep breath, an attempt to steady my pulse that's now soaring for an entirely different reason. "Maybe we should move this to somewhere more public. Since we're *on the clock.*"

"I didn't know you were into that sort of thing."

I roll my eyes. "My life already lacks enough privacy as it is. Case and point, our deal. If we're finishing strong tonight, I figured we'd go out with a bang."

He chuckles.

I groan. "Not literally. I just thought you'd want to make sure you were seen with me one last time."

He sucks in a ragged breath, leaning back to peer down at me in the crimson light. "Lena, if I never shared you with anyone again, I'd die a happy man."

My stomach clenches. "That sounds a little dramatic."

"It's the only way I know how to say it."

"Try again." I poke him in the chest in an attempt to keep things light. Blood whooshes through my ears as I buy time from the words I can already sense forming on his lips.

"Lena, I'm falling in love with you."

My mouth goes dry. I don't know whether I should kiss him or laugh. Is he serious? Of all the love confessions I've ever been on the receiving end of, this is the one I want to believe the most. And I do. Because it's Decker. Because I've never felt anything but comforted and cared for while with him. The notion of him loving me is both exhilarating and terrifying.

Like clockwork, a phone begins to buzz, but this time it isn't coming from my clutch.

Decker backs away, reaches into his pocket, and pulls out his phone. "How did your mom get my number?"

A lump builds in my throat. I want to be angry with her for interrupting us yet again, for calling him when she has no business doing so, but my weakness wins over, and I click to answer. "Hello?"

Decker backs away as my mother launches into some kind of scolding that I only partially hear because I can't take my eyes off of Decker and the way he slumps in the dark.

"Really, Lena?" he whispers.

I pull the phone from my ear, pressing the mute button as I do. "I'm sorry. Too much hinges on tonight for me to ignore her calls."

Decker shakes his head, ducking out the door without another word.

CHAPTER TWENTY-SEVEN

DECKER

"DECKER, WAIT." Lena's dress rustles as she rushes to catch up with me in the dark wings of the stage. "Wait!"

My heart beats double time as I hesitate, expecting to hear her confess that she's finally come to her senses and told her mom to screw off, but all she says is, "Here's your phone."

I take it from her, and once again start on my path to anywhere but here.

"Why are you so mad?" she asks, jogging to catch up.

"That wasn't exactly the reaction I was hoping for," I say as I trail ahead of her numbly, still trying to process the last five minutes.

Her sharp brows crinkle. "You're angry because I'm keeping up my end of the bargain and making sure we're seen together publicly—like it states in our contract?"

I stop under an exit sign dangling overhead. "I kissed you. I told you I love you, and all you could think about was work and your mom. Do you understand how messed up that is?"

"I just feel like the whole kiss thing was great practice, but we need to get that stuff on camera or it doesn't count." She shifts uncomfortably. "I'm only looking out for our best interest."

"Are you? Do you hear yourself?" My laugh startles even me as it tears from my throat, my feet rooting in place. "Lena, even you don't sound convinced."

She stops for a moment, her piercing blue eyes hardening as they lock on me. "Tonight is our last night to sell this illusion, Decker. You can't tell me you're in love with me right now."

My face collapses in confusion. "Why not, Lena? I meant it. I love you."

"It's understandable there's a little bit of attraction between us. We've spent so much time together, but that doesn't mean it's love. We just got a little carried away and—"

"You're the one that hauled me into a random dark room, Lena. What's your game?"

She bites her soft lip, and the memory of her taste floods my senses. "I'm not playing any games. Maybe I just thought we should get it out of our systems."

"I don't want you out of my system, Lena." It sounded better in my head than it does strung along the tension thickening the air. Clearing my throat, I lower my voice and close the divide, wanting nothing more than to remind her of the electricity that coursed between us until now. "If that's what you thought, then why can't we just carry on like we were back in that room—"

"Stick to the plan, Decker."

"Why? What's the point? You can't tell me you don't feel anything for me, Lena. I'm not buying any of your excuses."

She inhales deeply, and for a moment, I think she might admit that I'm not the only one feeling this undeniable desire.

"Plans change," I add softly, praying to convince her it's true, but she only doubles down with a shake of her pretty head.

"Our deal is over. We're over," she says firmly, that unbearable fake smile sliding too easily onto her lips. "Let's just act like the whole dark room kiss thing never happened, okay? It was the champagne and the adrenaline from not seeing each other after tonight and—"

"I don't want to break up," I blurt.

She tosses a dark curl over her shoulder and steps closer. I melt into her palm as she swipes something from around my mouth and wipes it on her thigh. Her lipstick. "Let's just go freshen up and we'll talk about this after, okay?"

She grabs my arm, but I pull free, straightening my jacket as I follow behind. She keeps moving down the empty hall until we're far from backstage, and sconces are lighting our path instead of those dang emergency lights.

"There's no way you don't feel this too," I say as confidently as possible.

She spares a glance over her shoulder. Hope builds as her scowl softens, and I slow my pace, desperate for her to meet me in the middle.

Instead of stopping, she faces forward, doubling down. "There's that cocky oaf I know. I knew the charming, modest guy from the podium wouldn't stick around long."

I can't help but roll my eyes as I hoof it to catch up. "Come on, we both know you don't mean that."

Something gentler stirs in her gaze, and then it ices over. "Anyone can give time and money, Decker. Don't think you're special because you got to talk about it behind a microphone. I know your type."

"Stop pushing me away."

"I'm not." She picks up speed as though she can lose me, but her legs are too short and her heels too high.

"It's like you're addicted to being miserable."

"I don't have time for this."

"You don't always have to settle for being the sad girl." It's a desperate attempt for her to say something—anything —that I can work with, but the wounded breath she draws in signals that I've taken it too far.

"You really are intolerable." Her eyes turn colder than I thought possible. A tired sigh seeps from her lips. "Let's just finish out tonight and announce online we're going our separate ways tomorrow after the first articles about the event are posted."

"I forgot how calculated this all is."

She presses on like I never spoke. "I've already made the post and saved it to my drafts. I can make one for you too and text it over tomorrow morning."

Her announcement bites into me, gnashing at my heart, my disbelief stunning me into silence. She premade our breakup announcement. The confession is like squeezing lemon into the papercut her insult created. How did we get here from what we shared mere minutes ago?

I want to regret what I said, I know pulling the sad card is a low blow, but it's hard when she sounds so callous. I know she isn't the sad girl everyone gossips about, I just don't know if she realizes it. She's vibrant and sassy and lovable and everything I never knew I needed, and I wish she could finally see that. I arch my brow in a playful challenge she doesn't take.

"Why are you doing this?" I hate how pathetic I sound. "What happened to making your own decisions?"

She steps closer. "I am, Decker. I'm being realistic, and realistically, we can't work. Between our schedules, our differences, and... and everything else. It's not real. This isn't real." Her eyes narrow, and I swear I see her lips wobble. "We both did our part. We aren't obligated to stay together. It's done."

My jaw hangs open, all air and words leaving me.

Her blue eyes scan my face before she turns away. "Wait here. Let me check my makeup, and when I get back we can finish out the contract." She turns and disappears, her heels echoing on the ancient tile floor.

For a moment, I obey. I stand with my hands in my pockets, waiting for her, too dumbstruck to move. And then I feel foolish. Sure, maybe she only wants to be my business partner, but I did my time. We both got what we wanted, so why drag this out? I was stupid to think that picking her up and bringing flowers for some fabricated prom was enough to win her over. That's the bare minimum, the lowest bar. Lena deserves so much more. The fact I convinced myself that my gesture, along with my love confession, would be enough to keep her around was asinine. Maybe she's right. Maybe I am delusional. I pace for a moment, weighing my options, but humiliation wins out. What's done is done. She said it herself.

We're over.

CHAPTER TWENTY-EIGHT

LENA

LEANING OVER THE SINK, I take a deep breath to steady my nerves. Berry-colored gloss feathers from my lips, and I do my best to clean up the edges of my pout with a shaking finger. I don't know what I expected when I dragged Decker backstage, but it wasn't that. Sure, his attraction was obvious, and yeah, I've fantasized a few times about him confessing his love, but I never imagined he would. And then he did, and I did what I always do. I put my head down. I stuck to my agenda. I didn't tell him that all I think about when I go to bed at night is how I wish he was next to me, or the fact that I've pinpointed the exact color of green his eyes are on the Pantone chart. Or that if he kissed me one more time tonight, I may have been willing to throw away everything we've worked so hard to salvage. But I chose to keep us on track and stuck to the stupid contract.

Opening my clutch, I pull out my compact and begin powdering the bare places around my mouth and nose that no doubt are now smudged across Decker's handsome face. My phone buzzes once, needling under my skin as I tuck my makeup away. No matter how annoying my team can be, Decker's wrong. Following through is the right choice. He may not understand, but I'm doing us both a favor. Celebrity relationships always have a messy ending. If we tried to keep this going, I'd ruin his career like I did his retirement dreams.

Footsteps click across the tile behind me, and I duck my head, pretending to be enamored with scrubbing my hands. When I surface from the bathroom, Decker isn't there. Instead, in his place stands Callum.

"What are you doing here?" I ask, all my frustrations filtering into those few words. If anyone deserves it, it's him.

He looks around like I could be talking to anyone else in the empty hall. The desolation this long hall provides is exactly why I opt for these bathrooms any time I visit. Callum tilts his head at me like a confused puppy. "It's a charity event."

"Exactly."

He tips his head back in a condescending laugh. "Hey, come on. I'm not that bad. I donate to charities, too."

I can't help but to roll my eyes. "Name one."

"If we're being specific, I'm here tonight because I gave to the children's hospital, but to name another, I donated to the Cover Lena's Screw Up Fund as well."

"You what?"

"The fire." He sighs, pushing his hands into his pockets as he steps forward. "Look, I know we may not have ended things on the best terms. And I know that maybe we weren't compatible, and because of that, I wasn't always the best boyfriend. Now that I'm in a relationship that works, I can see that."

"In a relationship with the girl you cheated on me with?"

He lifts a hand like there's nothing he can do about it, which now, I guess there isn't. "Regardless, I told everyone it was an electrical fire. Faulty wiring in that fossil of a building that went crazy when it mingled with the alcohol of my aromatherapy sprays."

"Your sprays are alcohol free."

"They don't know that. Everyone just accepted that answer. The only person who asked any questions was the manager, and I gave him a hefty sum and a threat to drop it. Neither you nor I need this following us around. Especially with my first international tour in the works."

"So you did it to protect yourself, not me."

"We both benefited."

My jaw tightens. The tour that he and I put into motion before our breakup. The one that I pulled strings to get arranged. It doesn't seem fair that someone who once broke my heart is still benefiting from what I'm able to offer. Looking at him now, I'm much less disgusted than I thought I'd be seeing him again. And then it hits me. I feel nothing for this man. As much as I want to be angry with him, as much as he deserves it, only a strange gratitude remains in its place. I'm grateful he closed this chapter for me because I was so enamored with him, I never would have. I'm grateful that his awfulness and my outburst pushed me to get involved with Decker. Despite not realizing it until now, Decker was what I needed. I've never been treated, protected, or listened to the way I was with Decker. Most of all, staring into Callum's blue eyes now, I wish they were the warm green of the ones I peered into all night until mere minutes ago. The ones I thought I'd find waiting for me here.

I've made a horrible mistake.

"Thank you, Callum. Truly. Thanks."

He gives me a tight smile and a nod as a pretty blonde girl—the one I once hated without ever meeting—latches onto his arm. Her smile flounders when she sees me, and I try my best to look pleasant through the trepidation growing inside. In the end, Callum Porter saved my reputation just as much as Decker did. I never thought that would be the case. Callum found love. Somehow, after everything, he still thinks he's worthy of good things, so why don't I deserve them too?

I turn and retreat down the hall, wobbling on my heels in the thick carpet as I track toward the ballroom. I have to find Decker. His phone rings as I call him once, twice, three times, but there's no answer. My mother's alarmed eyes greet me when I arrive at our table breathless.

She checks around us to see if anyone else is gawking. "Decker already gave us his goodbyes, dear."

"He said he had an urgent business matter to tend to at home." Dad's brow furrows with concern. "Lena, is everything okay?"

I collapse into my chair, not caring who's watching, as my head falls into my hands against the tabletop.

Decker is gone.

★ ←

Decker hasn't returned my calls in three weeks. He didn't respond when I sent him the pre-made post I texted over the morning after the charity gala, and when I searched for his account to check if he uploaded it, I couldn't find him. He deactivated his socials. I open my phone and shamelessly click on my top search, Decker's name. Only a little gray circle pops up. Decker still doesn't exist online outside of the articles about his team's wins over the past few weeks.

I miss that deli he took me to. I miss Princess. I miss him.

I get out my notebook, jotting down some lyrics, ones I'd been too afraid to write when we'd been together. Words pour from my mind, filter through my heart, and scrawl out through my hand as I do what I do best. I write my stupid sad girl lyrics.

Since our breakup, more than half the gossip about me online has been speculating that this breakup will lead to my best album yet. Regardless of how amicable we tried to make it sound, not everyone is buying that we both went our own happy ways. In particular, they say there's no way I would have let him go. Even strangers can see what I tried to deny. I'm exactly who the internet has been rumbling about nonstop since forever. The sad girl who is only inspired by her sad little love life.

And this time, they aren't wrong.

As pathetic as it is, I want to run across town, knock on his door, and throw myself into his arms, but a deal is a deal. This was strictly business, and as always, I treated it as such. Decker wanted more. We could have been more. Tears blur the ink on the page, and I slam the book shut, pressing the heels of my hands into my eye sockets so hard I see streaks of lightning behind my eyelids. My stomach growls. Did I forget to eat again? I pull out my phone to make an order, but quickly hang up and text Gustav to get the car ready. As bizarre as it is, if I can't have Decker, at least I can have his favorite sandwich. If sitting in that dilapidated parking lot while someone runs in to grab my sandwich makes me feel like I still have a piece of Decker, I'm willing to give it a try. No matter how completely pathetic it is.

CHAPTER TWENTY-NINE

DECKER

EVERY TIME LENA CALLS, the knife digs in a little deeper. It's been a month and a half, and from time to time she still hits me up. She never leaves a voicemail, and I never answer. I want to, but I can't. My worst fear is that one day they'll stop, which I know will happen eventually. That day will probably be soon. The thought of it almost hurts more than her rejection when I bared my heart to her.

"Head in the game, Trace! Quit playin' with your dinghy. It's not what'll get ya to playoffs." Coach's mustache twitches as he adjusts his cap. Even from here, I can see his eyes narrowing.

I run a towel over my sweaty hair before dropping it on the bench and sprinting back toward the field. Practice has been rough this week, my knee has been aching, a stark reminder of last year's injury. But Coach is right. I should be focusing on the playoffs. It's just the distraction I need right now anyway.

When did the playoffs become the distraction?

Maybe I should take a page from Lena's book. I worked too hard for this to let her be the end of my career. Even if I've been gunnin' for retirement, I'm going out on my terms. She's the distraction now, though I never got to thank her for the popularity boost and the major hike in Pro Bowl votes. The results come in next week, but if the trending hashtags are any indication, I might actually make it on the roster this year. It's not like it's a real game. It's basically flag football, but it looks fun and was an unofficial goal of mine. And now it could be a reality. Barring that we don't make it to the Super Bowl, of course—and odds are looking pretty good for the Kings on that front. Even if I have to miss the Pro Bowl, I can't help but wonder what Lena would say to me if I had the chance to share my excitement with her face to face. Probably something sarcastic or sassy that makes me want to shut her mouth with mine.

Get ahold of yourself, Decker. She's gone. She doesn't want you. She's only calling you to torture herself like she does with every single relationship she's ever been in. You aren't special.

As I plow the sled down the field, my mind does what it absolutely shouldn't. It wanders. My head is anywhere but here today. Thank God it's a practice and not a game. I think about her eyes, her smile, the feel of her against me, about how the internet completely melted down when we broke up. I have to be honest, it was pretty validating to see how upset everyone was. I thought we were a perfect match, too. Of course, I went off socials after our disastrous night, so any updates I received were from Maleko. Even

Ty looked like he felt sorry for me, and that's the last guy I ever expected to show me any sympathy. Poor Princess has been extra affectionate lately, and half the time that old girl just wants to sleep. She's lost valuable nap time lolling in my lap and monitoring my well-being. Ian's always joked she's the only girl who could ever love me, and I'm starting to believe he's right.

When practice is over, I bolt to my car. I'm covered in grass stains and sweat, but my driver's seat will recover. I'll shower at home. Locker room chaos is the last thing I need, especially since it's off the charts today due to the holiday. New Year's Eve. Most of the guys are behaving since we have too much riding on us at this point in the season. We're so close to making it to the Super Bowl again. Plus, Princess hates the fireworks everyone will no doubt be lighting off. She'll need my support. And a Benadryl. I've been with the guys all day. I want to be home. I want to be alone.

I drive in silence the entire trip to my condo. Princess greets me when I walk through the door, and I stop long enough to rub her velvety ears before heading to shower. Leftovers from the fridge will have to do for tonight. This evening is all about minimal effort.

I settle in on the couch next to an overjoyed Princess. For the first time since this morning, I check my phone. Lena texted me. I don't open it. I can't.

Part of me is relieved she's still trying to get ahold of me, but she and I are at different places in our lives. She's at the height of her career, while mine is finally starting to die down. I have my brand deal with Vital Reign, a few modeling opportunities outside of that, and some voice-over work Jason's been begging me to take. After football season is over, it's odd jobs from here on out. I can finally retire. My body gets to rest. I get to set my schedule and choose my own work. Gable's demise could be one of the best things to happen to me.

My stint with Lena proved to be successful, and because of it, my dog shelter could actually be a reality. With what I have lined up now, once football is over, I can start planning. Find a location and volunteers. Invest in it to get it onto its feet while we work on registering it as a legitimate nonprofit. It'll all be up to me. It's surreal. I won't be at the beck and call of an entire team, something I know Lena is unwilling to give up. Her work posse dictates her life, and I've come to accept that. Though it's none of my business anymore.

I turn on the TV and dig into my three-day-old Chinese takeout. The chicken is drier than it should be, but still good. Turning to the channel where the ball drop will be televised, I see her. Lena Lux in the cutest, fuzziest earmuffs and brightest red lips I've ever seen. Her gold dress shimmers as she giggles and exchanges clever quips with the emcees while they discuss her midnight performance. From all I can see through the screen, she's doing fine. That's enough to get the TV turned off for the rest of the night. I toss a cheese rangoon to Princess, and she swallows it whole. Can't wait to kiss that slobbery mug when the clock strikes twelve. I shove another pitiful piece of chicken in my mouth and stare at the blackened screen. Tonight is shaping up to be the most uneventful New Year's Eve I've ever had.

Eventually, my boredom and curiosity win out, and

finally, I open her text from this morning. I suck in a deep breath and read.

LENA

Hope you're well. Wanted to let you know I'm taking your advice on that new song. Think I'll test it out tonight during the ball drop if you wanna see. Maybe you can give me some of those pointers you're so good at.

If I'd opened this text earlier, I wouldn't have flipped on the TV and endured that ball drop jumpscare as I attempted to find some semblance of New Year's normalcy. Watching Lena smiling and interacting in a live interview is almost too much to bear. It's so much different than seeing her in the snapshots we took that I still haven't deleted.

My phone buzzes over and over, my heart leaping a little at the thought that maybe it's her.

Of course it isn't. She isn't stalking me, just trying to keep in touch.

The first text is from Maleko, the second is from my brother, and the third is a call from my mom. I don't answer any of them. Instead, I shut off my phone, roll onto my side, and close my eyes, hoping 8:00 p.m. isn't too early for bed.

CHAPTER THIRTY

LENA

A CLOUD of cloying hairspray fills my lungs as I sputter into a coughing fit.

"Oopsie, sorry, sweets." My mother hasn't called me "sweets" in ages. She prattles on with Antonia like she didn't asphyxiate me, too chipper for my liking, considering she protested until last week about my Super Bowl gig. I think the shift has something to do with the fact that I'm nominated for five Grammys this year, and next week we'll find out which ones I'll be taking home. Nothing like focusing on the next awards show to distract you from your current woes.

Mom's ring-studded hand smoothes my bangs, just like she always did when I was a little girl. She's the last person I would normally want behind the vanity with me, but with what I have planned for my halftime performance, I'm sucking up as much as I can now. The humidity in Florida has never been kind to the natural wave of my hair

—any attempted style needs the ten pounds of hairspray she insists upon—so I'll let her have this win.

For a moment, I'm back in our prefab home in Lake County, Florida, sitting on a creaky stool as my mom yanks and pulls my hair into pigtails. I shudder. I always hated that time with her. I had no idea the Super Bowl is what would finally bring me back to my home state, but I'm grateful it did. My stomach flips. It also brought Decker here. It's been weeks since I last texted him, but knowing he's in the same stadium tonight has me wondering if I should reach out. Part of me hopes he's planned something big, that he's been waiting for tonight to finally forgive me, but it feels silly to hold on to that. Decker is busy. He's got an entire game to play. He isn't thinking about me.

The Orlando Pit Vipers vs. the Vista City Kings is estimated to be a close one, but I have faith in the Kings. I grew up in a Pit Viper family, but after my time with Decker, my loyalty lies with him. If I don't see him tonight, I worry this is it. My schedule before the tour this summer is chock full, and if today isn't the day we reconcile, I fear it will never happen. Maybe I need to let him go. I had him. He was mine, and like always, I was too caught up in everything else to see what was right in front of me: Decker Trace, falling in love with me when I didn't deserve it. I squeeze my eyes shut, remembering the last time I saw him. How somber his eyes were, how cold I was. Why did I do that to him? He's right. I pushed him away. For what? A career I barely recognize anymore?

Someone dressed in all black with an earpiece and a crackling radio darts into the room, signaling to me that it's time.

"Do you remember the new choreography?" my mother asks.

I nod.

"Don't forget the last two eight counts of *So Demure* have changed. Do you want to mark it?"

My eyes flicker to Antonia, who clears her throat and steps forward with her tablet. "Blythe, will you please take a look at tomorrow's itinerary? I wasn't sure when we should try to squeeze in lunch."

My mom's eyes linger on me a second longer before she reluctantly takes the tablet from Antonia.

I give myself one last look in the vanity, checking to ensure the clips of my volumizing extensions are fully blended before smoothing out the pink-mirrored fringe of my skirt. Moments later, I'm being hauled through a wide concrete tunnel below the stadium stands in a golf cart. When our wheels hit the astroturf, my pre-show nerves kick in.

A stage is set up in the center of the field that connects to the stadium by its own tented tunnel, completely concealing any crew or performers for my show as we maneuver to the mainstage. Shrouded by the massive cream colored canvas, I'm guided toward backstage, assisted out of the cart, and handed my favorite guitar. The guitar Decker watched me cry into that night in the studio. I push the memory from my mind as I step into yet another tent center stage—this one gauzier, sparklier, and a fraction of the size of the tunnel tent—exactly as we'd rehearsed days ago.

The cheers pick up as the announcer comes over the speaker, finally stating my name. Everyone loses it. Vipers vs.

Kings, who? It's something I'll never get tired of, despite how draining it can be. My band is already on stage. They begin the intro to *Not Goin' Nowhere* from my first studio album. I strum my first chord, a second, and a third, and then the curtain drops, spilling silky swathes of fabric in a circle around me. It pools, leaving me in a glittering ring of pale pink chiffon. It's a play on my first album cover. It was a simple picture, one snapped during a photo shoot of me peeking between a rack of assorted prom dresses. I was so young.

During each tiny break between songs, I can't help but peer off to the side, to the tunnel I know Decker and his team disappeared through. I didn't text him, didn't tell him to meet me, but he knows I'm performing. I'm not sure why I think he'll suddenly materialize. This is the Super Bowl, not some high school football game. He has a lot riding on this, and the game is tied. Deep down, I know the last thing he'll be looking for is a distraction. The last thing he'll probably ever look for is me.

I plow through my set, switching out guitars, costume pieces, and bedazzled microphones along the way. When it comes to the last song, I make a surprise announcement. This one will be acoustic. I thank my band and dismiss them, only asking for the piano bench before they leave. They exchange confused looks as they step away from their instruments and funnel offstage. A couple of my dancers carry the bench to the end of the runway, planting it directly behind me. I sit and pull in a deep breath. Even if Decker isn't listening, I need to do this as much for myself as I do for him. If it weren't for him, I wouldn't have had the self-respect to honor my abilities. My artistry.

I close my eyes, strumming the opening chord to *Pretty Hard to Find,* my first single. The one I played the night I met Decker backstage at *Late Night with Lanza.* Except this time, I'm playing it the way I originally wrote it as a lovesick teenager in the quiet of her modest bedroom, only a few towns over from the massive stage I sit on now. I perform it the way I've always intended for it to be presented. Soft, acoustic, lovingly. No heavy beat, no breakneck tempo. Just me, my guitar, and the song I wrote about a love that I thought I'd never experience in my lifetime. One that seemed, well, pretty hard to find. Until I met Decker.

When it's over, I stand to a stunned-silent crowd. My pulse picks up, my palms sweating as I consider that maybe this was a mistake. I quickly discard that notion. This is my music. I can't be what everyone wants me to be. If there's one thing Decker taught me, it's that I can be loved and accepted for who I am. It isn't always about appeasing the masses. It isn't about meeting others' expectations. I just need to be me. Lena Lukowski. Musician. Singer. An imperfect person who is still deserving of love and good things.

The moment I'm certain my career is over, the crowd finally explodes in whoops and cheers, and relief snuffs out the doubt. I hate that I'm still so swayed by what everyone thinks, but it's hard not to be when you're standing alone in front of an audience. A smile breaks across my face as I take a quick bow and jog offstage, my eye on Decker's team tunnel the entire way. I don't know what I expect to see. Decker is done with me. He isn't going to be there. As I climb into the golf cart, I pop my head out of the tent one last time. Decker still isn't there.

It's time I let him go.

CHAPTER THIRTY-ONE

LENA

THE KINGS WON the Super Bowl. Per usual, a week later they had the celebratory parade. I was grateful to be traveling out of town for the Grammys when the streets of Vista City clogged for both of those events. The last thing I needed was Vista City's newly voted #1 *Most Eligible Bachelor*—yes, he clenched that title this year too—being marched around town and thrown in my face. I get it. I was the one who made the mistake, and it's something I'll have to live with until... Well, I don't know yet. The heartache is different this time around. Deeper. More desolate. Not even the buzz of three fresh Grammys can soothe the ache.

As much as I wanted to, I didn't text or call Decker to congratulate him. I didn't tell him I was going to be in town again this week, a mere two weeks after the Super Bowl performance I never saw him at. It was wishful thinking. I refuse to call it delusion. Still, it's embarrassing to think I truly thought he might leave the locker room for me.

As though his absence didn't sting enough, the tongue-lashing I got from my mom for going "off script" during my halftime show was pretty painful, but it felt good to finally tell her I'd be changing a few things about the direction my career was heading. Beginning with taking control of my sets again, starting as soon as my tour commences. It was a little belated, but it was a victory nonetheless. Decker was right. I let my mom and everyone else pull the strings for far too long. They drove me to a point that I was willing to sacrifice my needs, my wants—even Decker—for what they thought would sell. Realizing how much my clouded judgment hurt Decker was the breaking point.

Antonia and her tablet kept to themselves in the corner, but I could see her bite back a smile as I laid out a brief outline of my demands to my stunned mother. Which my mom quickly accepted when I reminded her the ten-year contract I signed with my record label at the dawn of my career would be ending soon and I would have full control to do whatever I want. Even recording and releasing independently. I wish I would have set up a camera to have her confounded blabbering on record forever. Of course, I was bluffing. My label has been good to me, and honestly, they probably listen to me better than my own mother does. Thank God she let me talk some sense into her because I'm not ready to part ways with my record label quite yet.

Joss gasps across the room. I'm grateful that she followed me back to Vista after our photoshoot this time. I need the distraction. I need my best friend.

"What?" I ask.

She shakes her head, her lips pressing into a line so hard they pale.

"What just happened?"

"Please don't assassinate me."

I arch a brow.

Sheepishly, she turns her phone screen toward me as though I can see it from where I stand across my open-concept kitchen. "Decker's back on social media."

My heart leaps into my throat. "And?"

"And people are flooding his most recent post with comments."

"So?" I open the fridge, ducking my head inside and sucking in the cold air. It does nothing to force my heart back into its rightful place between my ribs.

"So everyone is going nuts. They're saying he's being cryptic."

I slam the fridge shut, wanting to tell her to shut it too, but I can't. I need to know more. "Cryptic about what?"

"You."

That's when my heart slams into my guts, splattering them everywhere. There's no way. He never returned my calls. Never texted me. As much as I wanted to hang onto hope that maybe there was still a chance, I was tired of torturing myself. So I let it go. I let him go.

Well, until this moment, I'd thought I let it go.

When I don't say anything, she clears her throat and continues on, her tone too steady. "He posted your lyrics, Lena."

It takes a few seconds before I remember to breathe. "It could be a coincidence. It's not like my stuff is original. Half my words themselves are cryptic." I try to laugh but she rolls her eyes.

"Stop, Lena. When you're in love with someone, you

don't let it go that easily. Even if they hurt you. You cling to it no matter how pathetic it is."

"Thanks."

She rolls her eyes harder this time. "I'm not talking about you, necessarily. I'm speaking from experience here, okay? And if there's one thing I know, it's that there's no way Decker moved on from you that easily."

"It's been months, Joss."

"So? I just think it's worth exploring. I think you need to try one more time."

I pull an already-opened bottle of rosé from the fridge and two coffee mugs from a cabinet and fill them with the cold liquid. "What song is it?"

"Pretty Hard to Find."

I throw back the mug and almost drain it.

She clears her throat, answering the unspoken question poised between us. "More specifically: *Through the dark nights, I still search for the sun. In my deepest dreams, I still hope you're the one."*

Suddenly, I feel hot and cold and like I may combust all at once.

"Dang, Decker! Lay it all out there, why don't you?" Joss huffs out a giggle. "If that doesn't convince you, I don't know what will."

Steadying my voice, I challenge her. "If he's back on social media, why didn't he reach out? Why didn't he tag me?"

"Tag you? You already embarrassed him once, Lena. Do you honestly think he'd let you do that again? On the internet of all places? I know you think your half-baked halftime stunt was gonna grab his attention, but be real."

"Rude."

"I'm just saying. I'm with the Lena Lovers on this one. You two were something special. Anyone could see it."

"You and the Lovers are just obsessed with romanticizing things that aren't actually there."

Her lips press into a tight line. "Fine. You can let him go—if that's what you want. Do it. Drop him, and I'll never bring him up again. But if you think for one second you might regret it. This is your chance. Find him. Go to him. Lay your heart out on the line and see what happens."

"That sounds..."

"Scary?"

"A little."

"He did it for you, it's only right you return the favor." She laughs and finally stands from the couch, grabbing her mug from my hand. "I mean, look at the timing. You just so happen to be in town and he's posting your song lyrics? I don't want to read too much into it but—"

"You are."

She widens her eyes. "BUT this is a sign. We have to find him."

"And how do we do that?"

She pulls her phone out and scrolls. "1314 Sunny Cove Drive."

"Stalk much?" I gulp my wine, hoping it settles my nerves. Am I really about to do this?

"The Malted Mule." She looks up from her screen, her face brightening. "It's Thursday. Karaoke night."

I arch a brow. "And how do you know that?"

"I may have been invited."

"By?"

"Does it matter?" She smiles coyly.

"Kind of. Yeah."

"Cole. He heard I was in town. It's no big deal."

"Mhmm." I sip from my mug. "No big deal at all."

Another text rolls onto her screen, and she darkens it immediately. "He's been a good friend."

"And he's also friends with Decker."

She nods. "And I have a hunch Decks is gonna be there. So you better change out of those stained sweatpants because we're going to a karaoke party."

Thirty minutes and a wardrobe change later, Joss is yanking me out the door and into the driveway. Due to the wine, I thought maybe a driver would be in order for the night. Gustav sits up front with him as I twist the hem of my lavender shirt, wondering if I chose the right shade of blue jeans. Reclining into my seat, I try to breathe through the rising anxiety. I won't be drinking any more tonight—I don't want any excuses for what I'm about to do—but I wish I had a little liquid courage surging through my veins outside of the meager pink wine I consumed over an hour ago.

"Are you ready?" Joss asks, throwing open our door in the alleyway behind The Malted Mule.

I nod, staring at the brick facade. I've been ready for months. The words have circulated through my mind on repeat since the day I realized I'd lost my chance with him. I need to get this off my chest and out of my head before it eats me alive. Sirens blare in the distance, setting me even more on edge. Despite Joss's insistence that we make a plan, I didn't want to think about it. Speak about it. At least not out loud. Not yet. If I vomited all over the back of that car, I wouldn't have been surprised. No stage nerves have ever rivaled this. Groveling with Decker to take me back. No matter how much Joss insisted that it's not groveling, that it's destiny, it sure feels like groveling to me. But if I don't lay it all out there now, I may never get a chance, and I could lose him forever.

We pass a dumpster that reeks of decaying ketchup and stale beer, and I have to swallow the sour ball that rises in my throat. Once inside, the ketchup scent subsides, but the beer stays. Deep whoops and cheers come from up front as some male voice chirps along to a Madonna song that's at least an octave too high for him. Joss's shoulder bumps mine as we slide along the back wall, her face in her phone the entire time. She's texting someone again. Cole, presumably. Gustav surveys the room from a full head higher than us, signaling that he'll stay parked in the back corner.

The place is packed. Normally, I prefer it that way because my night could go one of two ways: I fly under the radar—though that's nearly impossible these days—finding it easier to keep my anonymity in the throngs or one person asks for a picture and then everyone decides it's personal meet and greet night, and I have to leave early. To save myself from embarrassment, I should probably be hoping for the latter, but as I spot Decker leaning against the bar across the room, I'm hoping the crowd is able to hide me until the time is right.

His hair is different. Shorter. He's shaved it off since their win and subsequent public appearances. My heart picks up pace in my chest. It feels good to see him, even if it is from a distance. Decker smiles and laughs, throwing an arm around the big guy next to him. Maleko. I've missed him, too. A little brunette butts up beside Decker, and my heart sinks when he smiles down at her, squeezing her to his side for a quick hug. For a moment, I scan for the nearest exit. This was a dumb plan. Why did I think he hadn't moved on? Why did I believe Joss's speculations? The brunette grins at something he says, laughing as she scoots around him and presses into Maleko. He tilts down as she pushes to her toes and plants a lingering kiss to his lips. Bitter envy leaves my veins as relief pumps through me. Of course. That's Maleko's girlfriend.

Madonna-Man finishes his song to enthusiastic applause and the music dies down. A mic crackles on, and the DJ announces it's time for a brief intermission. I seize my chance. Joss and I part ways as I dart for the DJ booth, digging into my pocket and keeping my head down as I navigate through the crowd. A couple of whispers and gasps break through the chatter, but I don't look up. Usually, I love meeting fans, but tonight I have one goal.

Decker. That's it. He's the goal.

Pulling a few bills from my pocket, I slide them across to the DJ who freezes with his water bottle halfway to his mouth.

"This probably seems weird, but can I request my own song? And can I jump the line? I'm kind of on a tight schedule."

He counts the money, his eyes wide. "Miss Lux, you can do whatever you want."

I didn't expect him to say otherwise, but I'm still relieved. Before I can fully process what I'm doing, he's cutting the intermission short, and I'm mounting the stage.

Gasps echo through the room followed by a couple of screams and phones being thrust into the air. I take a deep breath. If there's one thing I've learned, it's that even if this ends in a monstrous disaster, trying to fix it with a publicity stunt isn't the answer. Whatever happens happens, but I'll fix it myself this time. The boards squeak beneath my feet as I adjust the mic stand. The stage is more of a makeshift platform, but it props me high enough to see Decker and Maleko still hovering near the bar, lost in conversation.

I nod to the DJ, and he starts the track. The tinny karaoke instrumentals of the original recording of *Pretty Hard to Find* seep into the room through the speakers. I keep my eyes on Decker who stiffens as the music starts, his shoulders losing the nonchalance they held seconds ago. Maleko turns around first, a broad smile lighting up his tan face. I fill my lungs, squeezing my eyes shut as I send up a quick prayer that this is enough to at least get Decker to talk to me.

The first few words come out soft and subdued and rife with nerves. As my voice floods the room, I open my eyes. Decker is now facing me. Staring up at me. *Smiling* at me. Adrenaline takes over as I power through the song, my eyes never leaving his. Seeing him smile at me is like chugging a big glass of water after singing until all the moisture has left my mouth. Refreshing. Nourishing. *Needed.*

When I hit the bridge, Decker begins making his way toward me, navigating through the packed bodies like we're two magnets destined to reconnect. And we are. Well, at least that's how I feel. I hope he does too.

He stops when he reaches the front row, standing beneath me, gazing up at me with that adoration I never deserved but he always gave me anyway. In one sizable step, he places a foot on the apron of the rickety stage. With a smirk, he pushes up to my level so we're face to face as the song transitions into the instrumental break. There are whistles as he steps closer, my heart thudding in my chest harder than the bass from the amp nearby.

"Hi," he shouts over the music.

"Hi." Suddenly, I've completely forgotten a single thing I wanted to say to him. He's talking to me. That's more than I expected.

"I heard you were in town."

"I heard you were posting my song lyrics."

He shrugs. "It's a good song."

"Did you have to Google them?"

He shakes his head. "I've known them since your first album."

I arch a brow, ready to dispute because there's no way that's true, but then again, Decker has been nothing but honest with me from the jump.

The instrumental portion ends, and it's time to sing again. Before I can utter a word, Decker pulls the microphone from the stand and starts in on the last couple of verses. Honestly, he's not a bad singer. I would have never guessed.

I bite back a smile, completely elated to be in such close proximity to him again and excited by the fact that, despite loving this man, I still have so much to learn about him. And I want to. I want to know every tiny detail of Decker Trace. The good, the bad, the downright embarrassing. His mom's story of him puking on the sidelines pops into my head, and as disgusted as I should be by it, nothing can scare me away now. Stories of his past only add to his irresistible layers.

Watching Decker sing, I laugh in shock of this entire situation. The fake relationship, the fact that he's here now, that I don't think he hates me like I believed he would. Joss stands halfway through the crowd next to some big dude I can't quite make out. I assume it's Cole. She gives me an over-the-top thumbs up and her cheesiest smile. I cheese right back.

When the song ends, everyone goes nuts. Decker and I link together like we're in some Broadway show, lifting our clasped hands above our heads and dipping down into a deep bow. My fingers tingle at his touch, and my body goes berserk when he helps me down off the stage and leads me out the back door. We park by the deplorable dumpster, and I couldn't care less. The ketchup and stale beer stench is quickly replaced with the smell of Decker. I breathe it in, not knowing how long I'll have the opportunity, how long he'll stay. I don't know if this is the last time I'll see him, but even if our last moments together are in this wretched alley, I'm just glad to have them at all. We press our backs against the cool brick wall beside the exit out of the glow of The Malted Mule's security lights.

"You're a pretty good singer, you know," I say, turning to face him.

"You're not so bad yourself."

I nudge him with a fist, and he rubs his shoulder where I prodded him. It feels natural, and fear immediately strikes through me that this is all too good to be true. How can he act so normal after how I denied him?

I suck in a deep breath. Time to rip off the proverbial bandage. "I miss you. And I'm sorry."

He stares at me for a few moments, his green eyes thawing into something soft and loving I'm not sure I've earned. "I missed you too, Lena. So much."

It's the confirmation I need to plow through what I have to say. "I'm sorry I acted like I didn't care. I do care. A lot. Sometimes it's so much it scares me." My gaze drops to my feet at the admission. "I know this started as something fake to salvage my career, but, Decker..." I chew my bottom lip as I finally let my eyes meet his again. "None of that matters as much as you do. You're the realest thing I've ever known and the only thing I care about fixing is us."

"*Us?*" It's like he's trying the word on for size.

I chew my lip again, nodding as I wait for him to process everything.

His eyes widen. "You want to be an 'us' for *real?*"

"I've never wanted anything more, Decker. I love you."

He steps forward, sighing heavily as he pulls me into his arms, kissing the top of my head as I melt into him. "You have no idea how long I've been waiting for you to say that."

"Let me guess. Three months?" I look up at him, my chin pressing into his sternum as I do.

He shakes his head.

I take a step back, my face contorting. "The gala was three months ago."

"And I've been waiting longer."

At that, I can't resist another moment. I launch to my toes, my lips finally meeting his. It feels like home, like something I never knew I was searching for but now that

I've found it, I never want to let it go. I never want to let *him* go.

His hands unwrap from around me, trailing up to my jaw and cupping my face. His kiss lightens as he pulls away, his long lashes still fanning across his cheeks as he starts to smile. When his eyes open, he examines my face like he's memorizing it.

"Lena, I'd relive the gala a hundred more times if it means this is the outcome." He smiles, broad and sincere. "Yeah, it sucked, but we both got the time away we needed and we still found each other. You wouldn't be my Lena if you didn't bring me back down to earth in that unapologetic way only you can."

"Someone's gotta do it," I grin.

He presses a kiss to my temple, and I savor the feel of his soft lips on my skin. "And I'm glad it's you. It'll always be you."

EPILOGUE
SIX MONTHS LATER

DECKER

LENA SMIRKS, the new pink streaks in her dark hair flopping wildly as she throws her head back and freezes center stage. An ear-splitting roar emits from the crowd when she steps out of her ending pose, blowing kisses and waving before darting off stage into the exposed wings flanking either side of it and straight into my arms. We're on the last leg of her tour on this side of the ocean. In a few days we'll be heading overseas to meet her international fans.

After officially retiring from my football career following the Kings Super Bowl win this year, I never thought I'd be the boyfriend getting hauled around from place to place and waiting in the wings. Given all those years of trying to keep out of the limelight outside of football and interviews, being a backstage boyfriend sounds right up my alley. However, I gave up any hope of privacy when I gave Lena my heart.

She leaps into my arms, crushing herself against my body. Her smile is infectious as I spin her in a little circle before she plants a swift kiss on my lips. Another berserk response from the crowd, and I look over to see us both on the big screens positioned around the arena, the rest of the cameras surrounding the stage all swinging to face us. Case and point, this exact moment. Goodbye, low profile, hello, Lena Lukowski.

"Ready?" she asks loud enough so I can hear her over the roar.

Ready? I've been waiting all night to finally be alone with her. I nod, and we both turn one more time to wave to her faithful fans. Lacing her fingers through mine, she tows me to her dressing room, promptly propping herself onto her vanity counter and pulling me in by my shirt collar.

"Well, hello," I say, stepping closer so I'm positioned between her knees. The beaded fringe of her skirt rattles against the counter as she makes room for me.

"Hello yourself," she says softly, her nose grazing mine.

She loops her arms around my neck, frowning as I break free and take a step back. I reach for the thermos of water I always make sure is filled for her when she comes offstage.

"Drink. We're not having a repeat of last time. Your charley horse scared Princess out of her mind," I say.

"I didn't know she was so skittish," she giggles, "or that I was so dehydrated."

"I think anyone would be skittish with someone collapsing and screaming like that out of the blue. Dramatic much?"

She rolls her eyes, but takes a long swig, caps the bottle, then pulls me back in. "You better kiss me before my mom barges in on us again."

I brush a piece of hair from her face, it's always a little wild—and a little sweaty—after her three-hour shows. "Say no more."

I brace the back of her neck, tilting her head up to meet my mouth as her fingers dig into my shoulder blades. Even after six months of being officially—*really*—together, this never gets old.

Like she was waiting for this exact moment, there's a knock, and her mother's nasally voice penetrates through the closed door. "Your flight back to Vista is in two hours." She shoves open the door, marching in like we aren't partially tangled on a makeup vanity. "Your tickets are printed, bags are packed and loaded, and Gustav is waiting with your ride."

Antonia appears behind her. "Vital Reign reached out about squeezing in a couple's shoot while you're in Vista. I've been in touch with Jason."

Blythe clucks like an offended chicken. "I thought we agreed she wasn't going to be partnering with them."

"She won't be, it's a one-off shoot with Decker since he's the partner." Antonia doesn't look up from her screen.

Her mom's eyes dart from Antonia to the two of us. "I thought—"

"I proposed the idea a while ago, but I didn't think they'd take me up on it," Lena says.

Blythe frowns. "Of course they'd take you up on it. You're the only marketing they'll ever need."

"I don't think that's true." Lena scowls at her mom before turning toward me. "Do you think there's time for that? We have a tour at that prospective shelter location, and we have to visit your family. I don't know if—"

"We'll make it work." I smooth her hair.

"Are you sure? I don't want you to have to cut the tour short. You've been waiting for this for years."

I cup her cheeks in my hands, grateful I can do it without her pulling away. Never in my lifetime did I ever think she'd let me, but now she's mine. "I'm sure."

She smiles up at me and gives Antonia the go-ahead to schedule it. Her mother lingers awkwardly when Antonia leaves. Lena's hands slip up my arms until she's pulling my fingers from her cheeks and lacing them into hers. "We'll be ready soon, Mom."

Blythe waffles in the doorway a minute longer before huffing out the door and closing it behind her. Lena lifts my knuckles to her lips, kissing each one with feather-soft pressure. I'll never understand how something so delicate can send me over the edge.

I lean down and kiss her on the forehead before pulling her off the counter and into my arms. Lena kicks and squeals as I carry her to the door. "Come on, we have a flight to catch and a niece to meet."

LENA

"Please don't make her call me Aunt Lena." I try to hide my smile as I sit back into the worn tweed couch.

"Why not?" Decker asks, gazing down at his baby niece's sweet face.

"I'm not her aunt just because you're her uncle."

He lifts a brow, his eyes finding mine for a split second before falling back on baby Charlotte Darlene, named after his mother, naturally. "Not yet, at least."

I nudge his shoulder like I always do when he makes a dumb joke, but by the way things have been going lately, I don't think it is. I would be perfectly happy with Decker as my husband, and if he thinks he can put up with me until death do us part, I won't turn him away.

"Let me see that baby!" Darlene's face is beaming with that new-grandma glow.

Reluctantly, Decker hands her over. It's cute how much I can tell he doesn't want to. He's been dying to finally meet her for months but refused to leave my side on tour. This break lined up perfectly, though, because Ian is in the off season, and he and Nora were able to fly in to meet us before we jet off again. It's been hard for Decker to be so far from his family, and maybe even more difficult for him to be away from Princess. The good thing is, my tour stretch overseas is short, and when we get back to the states, we're ending it in Vista City. And then we intend to stay here—together—in my Vista residence with a yard for Princess while we get everything in line for his nonprofit.

I'll actually be taking a break for the first time ever. Nowadays, I'm focusing on finding the balance I've been missing all these years, but that's not even the best part. I get to watch Decker make his dream of the special needs shelter come true, and I'll be by his side the entire way.

Decker throws an arm over my shoulder, and I lean into him, soaking in the warmth of his mom's house. It's cozy, like one big invitation asking you to nestle up and never leave. The smattering of mismatched frames all over the place, encapsulating my favorite little green-eyed guy, makes it even more homey. Above the mantle, beside a basket stuffed with spicy cinnamon potpourri, is a photo of his entire family, his father included.

I nod toward the frame. "You look like him, you know."

He follows my sightline until it lands on the picture. "Everyone says I look like my mom."

"You have her eyes, but you have his bone structure." I lean back so I can get a better view of his face. There's a sheen to his eyes, and I almost feel bad for bringing up his late father.

"He'd be so proud of Charlotte," he finally says.

"And you." I poke him in his massive bicep, and he turns to peer down at me. "He'd be honored you're naming the shelter after him. The James Trace Silver Paws Sanctuary. It has a nice ring to it."

"Are you sure the name isn't too long?"

She shakes her head. "I think he'd love it."

"He'd love *you*." A faint smile crosses his lips before he leans down and kisses the tip of my nose. "How could he not?"

I grin back at him, eating up every bit of the cheesiness he casts my way.

"Food's here!" Ian announces as he erupts through the front door, hauling in an armful of brown paper bags.

Brown paper bags that have now been upgraded with a logo.

Nora helps him unload the freshly delivered food from Niko's Deli, placing each paper-wrapped sandwich on a plate and sliding them down the laminate counter. The tang of vinegar and French fries makes my mouth water.

"Niko got new bags!" I squeal, turning to Decker.

He kisses the top of my head and grabs a plate. "He fixed the taped window, too. Must have had some extra cash to burn thanks to *someone*."

"No thanks to anyone. He did this all by himself, and it's well deserved."

"Yeah, and I'm sure your social media post about his deli had nothing to do with it."

I shrug. "People needed to know what they were missing."

"I told you. You're a philanthropist through and through."

I can't help my smile, but I roll my eyes just so he knows how annoying it is when he thinks he's right. Something wet and snorty pushes into my leg, and I look down to see an antsy Princess.

"Looks like someone's gotta potty," I tell Decker as I pat her head.

"Come on, girls," he says to us both.

Princess and I follow him out into his mom's backyard, clicking the door shut behind us. Princess darts off to do her business as I admire the new patio furniture and freshly painted fence Darlene finally caved and let the boys gift her. And then Decker's pulling me out of view of the sliding glass door, sinking a lingering kiss onto my lips.

"I can't get enough of you," he whispers against my ear, sending goosebumps across my skin as I lean back against the vinyl siding of the house.

Gazing into his face, into his fervent green eyes, I wonder if this honeymoon phase will last forever, if we'll always be so wrapped up in one another. My heart hammers in my chest as I consider what kind of future he could give me. One full of bad jokes, endless kisses, and genuine love.

Decker's fingers graze my cheek, pushing my too-long bangs out of my eyes and to the side. "What?"

I shake my head. "Nothing. I just..."

I shrug, unable to articulate what I want to say. If I had my notepad, my guitar, maybe then it would come bursting out in something catchy and melodious and worth remembering, but my words fail me now. And then it hits me. It's something so simple—so foreign for so long—no wonder I couldn't place my finger on it.

"For starters, I love you, Decker Trace." I drop a kiss on the only place I can reach without him leaning over, the base of his throat.

He closes his eyes at the touch of my lips, reopening them when I pull away. "I love you, too."

"And I'm just genuinely happy, that's all."

Decker leans down, pressing his forehead to mine. "Call the press. Sad girl Lena Lux is no more."

I swat his chest, but even my feigned annoyance can't

hide my smile. He grins back, his arms wrapping around my waist as I tilt my head up. "Yeah, what is my next album supposed to be about now that I'm in a stable, loving relationship?"

"Don't pretend like that's a bad thing."

"I think we both know I'm not very good at pretending." I lift to my toes, wiping away his smirk with a quick kiss. "Not when it comes to you."

Thank you for reading *The Player and the Pop Star*!

If you enjoyed this book, I hope you'll consider writing a small review. Doing so really helps out indie authors like me!

Thank you so much,
Cait Elise

ACKNOWLEDGMENTS

Let's just start off by acknowledging the fact that I actually finished and published a book. (I can still hardly believe it!) I couldn't have accomplished this feat alone, and I have a few shining *stars* of my own to thank. Now for the mushy stuff.

First, thank You, God, for the life you've written for me. You're the ultimate author and creator, and I'm in awe of Your goodness every day.

Brandon, without you, none of this would be possible. If I wrote out every single thing I'm thankful for about you and the way you've contributed to not only my author journey but my life, these acknowledgments would turn into their own novel. I love you. You're a blessing and proof that happily ever afters do exist.

To my daughters, you inspire me every day. Thanks for the laughter and for keeping me on my toes. I love you endlessly.

Whitney Amazeen, when I signed up to be your beta reader, I didn't know I would find such a wonderful cheerleader, critique partner, formatter, and friend. You've so generously been there every step of the way, and your enthusiasm for this story and these characters has kept me going. Thank you for being you, and thank you to Michael and the kids for letting me borrow you so frequently. (And thanks, Michael, for the IT help!)

Mom and Dad, thank you for always encouraging me and allowing me to indulge in each creative whim that came my way. Thank you for always being supportive, never making me feel silly for doing the unconventional thing, and for loving my family and me so well. I'm proud to be your daughter.

Rachel Fikes, thank you for being the best critique partner, beta reader, and friend a girl could ask for. You've been there since day one, providing encouragement and honest critiques. Though I highly value your feedback, I value your friendship more. You're a real one.

Coriahjennix (Jenn, Nix, and Moriah)... Thanks for the group chat that keeps on giving. Not only are you lovely ladies some of the most talented writers I know, but you're also amazing, praying friends, and I'll always be grateful for you three.

Jenn, thanks for reading this little baby story when it was just a "fun thing" I wrote in my free time. You read the first 8,000 words when it was no more than something that was destined to die in my drafts folder. Thanks for lending me your eyes and your unfiltered honesty.

Nix, your contagious light and encouragement is enough to make anyone believe they can do the impossible. Thanks for sharing both of those with me.

Moriah, your suggestions are always crucial to the development of my stories, and this book was no different. You have the best ideas, and I'm grateful for your willingness to share them with me. Thanks for letting me pick your brain.

A massive thank you to my beta readers, Rachel, Moriah, and Whitney, as well as Alexia and Lyzz. This story wouldn't be what it has become without your time, energy, and feedback.

To my ARC readers... It blows my mind how many people wanted to help get this book on its feet. Your excitement for Lena and Decker's story has been fuel for me to stay on track. I hope you know how important you are to the publishing process and that your early reviews make all the difference. Thank you.

Pixie Perkins, without you, I might not have a book blurb. Thank you for helping me write the perfect one, and thank you for being a sounding board for my cover design ideas.

Sonia, my cover artist. You've brought my favorite football player and pop star to life. You're so incredibly talented, and I'm just so stinkin' happy with the cover artwork. It's beautiful, and you're wonderful. Thank you. (Find her on Instagram @ArtBySoniaGX)

A big thank you to my typographer, Journey in Hue, for working with me until the cover typography fit my vision. Your talent and patience is unmatched. (Find her on Instagram @JourneyInHue.Co)

To my editors at Prose Perfect Editing, thank you for helping to clean up my story both grammatically and developmentally. You've made this process seamless, and I can't wait to work with you again in the future. (Find them on Instagram @ProsePerfectEditing)

Linda, thanks for being the best book buddy and neighbor. God knew what He was doing when He dropped us next door to you. It's a joy to call you friend.

To the Instagram writing community, thank you. There are far too many people to name, but please know your friendship means the world to me. I attribute my growth as a writer to you.

To my friends and family who have checked in on my writing at any point in time over the years... Thanks for caring and acknowledging my art, even when I had nothing to show for it.

And last, but certainly not least, thank YOU, reader. Thanks for taking a chance on my story, and I hope you loved it as much as I loved dreaming it up for you.

ABOUT THE AUTHOR

Cait Elise believes in romanticizing the mundane and emphasizing the silver linings. She writes honest char-  acters and swoony scenes, but most of all, she loves creating healthy relationships with addictive banter. Cait's living her happily ever after at a former azalea nursery in The Sunshine State with her husband, babies, and four furry rescue critters.

Connect with Cait on Instagram @thecaitelise and subscribe to her newsletter to never miss her fun bookish updates!

Made in the USA
Middletown, DE
30 June 2025

77473024R00187